I0563162

Salvation

by

Katja Desjarlais

The Haunt Vault, Book Eight

Cover Art by *Diana Carlile*

The Wild Rose Press, Inc.
PO Box 708
Adams Basin, NY 14410-0708
Visit us at www.thewildrosepress.com

Publishing History
First Edition, 2025
Trade Paperback ISBN 978-1-5092-5984-7
Digital ISBN 978-1-5092-5985-4

The Haunt Vault, Book Eight
Published in the United States of America

Dedication

For Momma and Not The Momma

Chapter One

"On your knees, dog," Khthonios snarled as the wooden heel of her sandal kicked against Boy's spine and forced him down into the sand along the banks of the Red Sea.

He kept his eyes on the dark expanse ahead, zeroing in on the faint light in the distance while his creator grasped his long hair and yanked his head back, pushing his collar's spikes deeper into his throat.

"Sit," she commanded, nudging his knees apart with her foot. Her blackened irises were ovaled in anger, her delicate features hard under the starlight. Releasing his hair, she gripped his chin and dug her sharpened nails into his skin until he felt his blood drip along his jaw. "Do you see the town?" she purred, the sudden softness of her voice causing his shoulder muscles to tense up and knot. "You may join me there when the flame of the last candle is out. Not a moment sooner."

She stepped back, straightened, and smoothed the linen of her dress. "You've forgotten your place and your position at my heel. Perhaps a night listening to the death knells of the humans you chose to place above me will serve as a reminder of where you belong."

His fangs lengthened involuntarily and she backhanded him, splitting his lip before turning her back to him and walking away.

1

This disobedience must be eradicated before the mutt believes himself worthy.

Khthonios's unspoken words rang in his ears long after she disappeared along the dark horizon. The first screams of the townspeople carried on the faint winds and he memorized every cry, every shriek. One heartbeat after another was snuffed out and the town's illumination grew dimmer until all that remained were a handful of flickers on the eastern border. The last flame died as the first glimmer of dawn breached the desert sky and he ran, the searing rays of the sun blinding him as he reached the silent town. Crawling on his hands and knees, he dragged his burning body into the home of the final candle where Khthonios stood, waiting to save him.

****

The clatter of pebbles along the rock formation to the south drew Boy's attention and he crouched in preparation, ready to attack. Stumbling over the jagged Nevada desert terrain, his prey made its location known without hesitation, its internal beacon driving its movements.

Armed with a simple blade, Boy listened for others before descending from his perch. The creature grunted and continued its approach, undeterred by the stench of death radiating up from the desert sand. The blood of the others was masked only by the dust that kicked up during the daylight hours, the fine layer resetting the battleground night after night.

Honed by hours of careful whetting, his knife slid cleanly through the throat of the Deviant and Boy was back at the base of the mountain he called home before the body thumped to the ground.

Three hundred eighty-two.

His kill count was rising steadily, yet nowhere near enough to make a dent in the hordes of undead moving across the land. Scooping up handfuls of stones, he filled the pockets of his worn cargo pants and scaled the steep slope, quickening his pace when he heard the telltale hum of Nichol Kaius's drone in the distance. He emptied the contents of his pockets along the narrow ridge outside the small cave and ducked inside to avoid being seen by the intrusive flying orb.

It was difficult to remain undetected in the larger space where his meagre supplies were stored. Nichol's continued electronic presence in the region meant he was forced deeper into the cave system more often than not, shimmying on his back over the smooth rock until he was fully protected from the drone's tiny red dot he knew recorded everything.

The waves of Deviants had continued unabated for three months now. His creator's mindless army hunted instinctively for her blood, following its call deep into the desert lands of Nevada where he lay in wait, his veins pulsing with Khthonios's venom and his mind swarming with the insanity of her bastardized vampire turnings.

Each Deviant he ended cut another thread to his creator, quieted the din in his head by another howl. Marked on the walls of his resting place, he tracked their elimination one by one, their jagged teeth and gnarled fingers reduced to a simple line in the rock.

The scurry of a scorpion caught his attention and he covered his face with his arms, his broad shoulders and long limbs wedged tight.

The Kaius hauntmates had yet to give up on their

search for him and the nightly presence of their drones was almost reassuring.

But he didn't want to be found.

Not yet.

His body was a lodestar for the Deviants. His dead creator's blood mixed with his own in his veins and screamed for them to join him, to heel to his command. He wanted no other to stand between him and the mindless killers scaling the mountains to reach him, drawn to the poison and depravity Khthonios carried in her very being.

They were his and his alone to destroy.

Destroy, or embrace.

Chapter Two

Creeping along the browned brush, Boy stalked the lone cow grazing on the outskirts of the small ranch, the lights of the farmhouse having gone dark an hour ago. A light gust of warm air danced across his foot and he frowned as he glanced down at his worn combat boots and wiggled his exposed toe.

Centuries spent barefoot at Khthonios's side had made him vigilant about his shoes once he was no longer tethered to her spiteful edicts. His first pair of leathered soles lasted close to a century. Taken off a plagued corpse and meticulously cleaned, he'd worn them only during his longest journeys, wrapping them in a silken scarf and strapping them to his back when not in use.

He'd mourned the night they succumbed to the salt of the Mediterranean Sea.

He ran his finger along the shredded leather of his boot, resigning himself to the fact he would need to acquire new footwear soon. The slowdown in Deviant activity in the region was temporary, the steady volume increase in his head indicating another wave was making its way toward him at a strong pace.

The cow snorted and chuffed and he resumed his hunt, inching closer until he could graze the coarse hairs of the animal's hindquarters with his fingertips.

Deviant blood was toxic, nauseating for a species

that didn't become ill. Animal blood was a mediocre substitute for human, but in the middle of nowhere, it was that or continue to fight on his weakening energy reserve.

He rose from his position with a fluidity unappreciated by the cow and his fangs breached the tough hide without notice. Although he didn't breathe, had no need to inhale, the thick scent of the animal managed to coat his tongue and ruin his first meal in weeks. Unsatisfied, he slipped back into the bushes and crawled toward the narrow road slicing through the barren terrain.

Tuning into the closest of the howls polluting his mind, he veered east and followed the crumbling highway for a good eight miles. The stars in the clear sky lit up the rocks and mountains, stealing away his favorite part of the hunt when he easily spotted three bobbling shadows lurching along the road. Resigned to a night without the thrill of the chase, without stealth and cunning, he gripped his blade and strode toward them.

Khthonios's voice hushed beneath the wails and his hand went to his neck to brush away the phantom pains that always accompanied her reminders he was nothing more than a disobedient mongrel. He scrunched his exposed toes and tried to ignore the sensation of fine desert dust gathering in his broken boot where tiny pieces of gritty sand were worming through into his sock.

With the distraction of his damaged footwear lingering in every step, he almost missed the faint murmur growing louder in his head, holding its own against the howls until it overtook them.

Look at these stumblin' fools, falling all over themselves. Over here, dummies. Yeah, that's it. Right here.

It took him a moment to process the woman's heavy southern accent, his split-second hesitation long enough for a gunshot to ring out in the wilderness.

Then another.

And another.

Ew, ew, ew. Those nasty guts better wash out. Gross.

He broke into a run, skidding to a stop when a short blonde woman stepped out from behind a pile of smooth boulders. The barrel of her rifle was aimed at his face and the scent of magnolias filled the air. She was dressed in ripped blue jeans and a bright pink blouse which scooped low across her chest and drew his eye before he looked away, ashamed.

"You're gonna want to stay right there, buddy," she called over to him as she adjusted the position of the weapon against her shoulder. "Say something so I know you ain't one of these zombie things."

Raising his hands, he shook his head and prepared himself to take a shot.

Guy doesn't move like those things, all jerkin' and twistin' around.

She cocked her head and her grip relaxed a fraction. "You don't move like them. But I'll feel a lot better if I hear you talk, mister."

Shaking his head again, he took a step backward to show her he wasn't a threat.

"What? You don't talk? You one of them people who can't or something?"

Tracking the stillness of her trigger finger, he

nodded.

She took a few steps his way and lowered her rifle, her hold on it indicating she was ready to take aim again in a heartbeat. "Well, you're probably gonna want to go get back to your car and get out of the valley. Night ain't safe around here."

Shouldn't be walking around out here like that without a gun. Poor guy's gonna end up as dinner for one of those nasty creatures.

Backing up, she kept her body turned toward him. "Not a good idea to be walking trails alone in the dark. The place has been crawling with those zombie things for months and they'll kill you faster than a hot knife slidin' through butter."

He lowered his hands slowly and bowed his head in acknowledgement of the warning as she sidestepped along the boulders, leaving nothing but her mess of a ponytail visible. Listening to the sound of an engine revving up, he held position until she rode into view on a small motorbike. She spun her rear tire out along the sand and kicked up a cloud of dust as she zipped up beside him just out of his reach.

Zombie food is what this poor guy is gonna be. I'll probably see his picture on the news by next week.

"You good?" she asked, pulling a black and pink helmet on and fastening it under her chin. "Phones don't work so well out here, so if you're in any trouble, better tell me now so I can send help. Otherwise you're in for a long walk to the closest town and I don't particularly want to be seeing your face on some missing persons list by Monday."

He motioned a little farther up the road and gave her a thumbs-up, something he'd often seen his hauntmates do. The movement seemed to appease her and she smiled, driving off with a wave.

"Take care," she hollered over her shoulder, her thoughts growing quieter the farther she went until all he could pick up was the low rumble of a Deviant eighteen miles away.

Pausing to listen for one of Nichol's drones, he doubled back toward his mountain cave, filled his pockets with stones, ascended the steep incline, and nestled back into the safety of his shelter. He eased his boots off and examined the rip in the leather, the faint starlight more than enough to see the cracks along the toes. Running his fingers over the rough, dry edges, he tipped them over and shook out the sand before putting them back on and contemplating whether revealing his location to Nichol would be worth a new pair.

****

Lexie Grace circled around the gate to her grandmother's ranch and came to a stop so her headlight illuminated the road and pasture.

"I bet that damn fool's on foot," she muttered to herself, doing a quick count of the nearby cattle as her beam passed over them.

There hadn't been a single vehicle on the highway, nothing abandoned on the vast plateau of the valley. Even before she'd come across the tall guy with the long blond hair, she hadn't seen any signs of humanity save for the few miles of rickety fence running along the outskirts of the narrow pass through the eastern hills.

Reaching into her saddlebag, she double-checked her magazine count, closed it, and patted the rifle lying flat against her back before she eased back onto the highway.

Her heart was still pounding from her kills, the adrenaline in her veins ensuring she remained alert to the nocturnal movements of the desert. The rev of the motorbike's engine stole her sense of hearing from her on the drive, leaving her with only her headlight to detect danger.

Slowing as she approached the lifeless bodies of the three creatures, she wound along their mangled limbs and continued on for another ten miles before she came to a stop and scanned the terrain.

"Hey there," she called into the darkness, pulling her rifle out of its holster. "Mister? Are you still out here?"

She turned off her engine to listen, wrinkling her nose when she was met with silence.

"Right. Y'all don't talk," she grumbled. Exhaling and straightening her leather jacket, she hollered out as loud as she dared in a place crawling with zombies. "I can give you a ride or something. Maybe get you to a phone before the whole area goes offline?"

The stillness stretched out as far as she could see and she shook her head as she started her engine up and turned toward the ranch. "Okay." She looked around a final time. "Well, good luck, I guess. Hope you don't die."

Chapter Three

Boy slunk along the side of the barn, stopping long enough to scrape his boot over a clump of weeds to remove some of the fresh Deviant blood from the cracked leather. Lifting the wooden level, he tugged the barn door open, slipped inside, and began his hunt.

While new shoes were a luxury he was grateful to have, he didn't mind old ones with sturdy soles and softened leather that molded almost instantly to his feet. Searching the shelves lining the walls, he picked up a pair of weathered gloves and tugged one halfway on before abandoning them to continue his perusal. Rows of dusty tools, empty gas cans, and teetering piles of wooden blocks were crammed in from one side to the next and each item he touched jostled the precarious balance of the others.

He knelt down to examine the bottom shelves, so focused on not toppling a lopsided stack of horseshoes that he was caught off-guard by a familiar Southern twang crashing over the waves of Deviant howls in his head.

Damn easy access. Knew I should've bought an automatic lock when I had the chance.

The thrum of her heartbeat thumped in his ears and he became acutely aware of how close the woman managed to get to the barn without his detection. With a quick glance around the disorganized space, he slipped behind a riding lawnmower and tucked himself tight against a ladder as the door swung open and the barrel of her rifle jutted in.

"Anyone here?" she called into the darkness while remaining outside the confines of the doorframe. "Speak now or get a bullet in the teeth."

Motionless, he watched her as she yanked a flashlight from her back pocket and turned it on. The beam passed over the cluttered shelves and rows of garden tools leaning against the back wall before skimming the mower. He braced himself for a scream, relieved when the yellow glow passed over without outing him.

Come out, come out, wherever you are.

Her thoughts sung in his mind and he did his best to blend her voice into those of the Deviants while he stayed tuned into the sound of her movements.

Emboldened by her initial assessment, she nudged a bucket of dirt in front of the door to keep it open and stepped into the barn. She lowered her gun and scanned the room slowly again. The regular beam of the flashlight passed over his hiding spot two more times. Apparently satisfied, she hefted the bucket aside and pushed the door closed.

He stayed still and waited for the beam to drop and lock him in, only to be met with the soft click of a rifle cocking. Her heartbeat remained close, the clear night sky allowing the stars to cast her shadow through the wooden barn slats. The minutes ticked by and he zeroed in on her internal dialogue, allowing it to overtake the din in his head.

Lavender's blue, dilly dilly. Lavender's green. When I am king, dilly dilly, You shall be queen...

Frowning, he rose to his feet slowly, keeping his gaze on the break in the lines of starlight striping the worn floorboards. She continued to sing in her mind, the key of the song shifting up and down every few lines while she held position outside the barn. Moving with the stealth of a stalking lion, he crept to the door and paused.

Bianca Schumann used to sing in her head, too. Long before she was the mate of his hauntmate Jagger, she would scamper through the halls of the Kaius haunt. Beautiful arias from operas he'd never seen or heard would reach from her mind to his while she folded laundry and brewed tea.

Lifting his hand to the door, he made a fist.

With another large wave of Deviants approaching from the east, any human in the vicinity was at risk of being slaughtered by the creatures crawling along the mountain passes. How this woman survived this long, he didn't know. Two hordes had passed this way in the last few months. Their collective hunger had screamed into his mind night after night until the last of them lay dead at his feet, waiting for the rays of the sun to burn them to ash.

A single woman with a rifle wouldn't stand a chance if they scented her fresh blood.

He flattened his palm on the door and scoured the peaks of the barn for another exit. His eyes settled on a framed plywood square nestled between the trusses above him. He crept over to the lawnmower, listening above the noise in his head to the quiet shifting of the woman's feet in the grass outside as he eased the ladder from its place and leaned it against the wall. He climbed to the top rung, aimed for the plywood, and drove his hand through it. He ripped the jagged pieces away and hoisted himself onto the roof toward freedom while the doors were flung open and a shot was fired below him into the empty barn.

****

Lexie Grace's heart pounded in her chest as she stood beneath the hole in the barn's roof. Thick chunks of splintered wood scattered across the floor and an old ladder leaned against the wall, still wobbling on the uneven boards. She steadied her rifle as she listened for movement across the roof, hearing nothing but her own ragged breathing.

She'd been so certain a human was hiding in there. The zombies she encountered over the past few months were noisy and sloppy in their movements, lumbering forward with a singular focus toward the mountain range to the east. Whoever was in that barn was stealthy, the only hints of their presence an unlocked door and the muddied shoe treads along the brittle weeds alongside the old building.

With dozens of kills under her belt, she figured she knew friend from foe by now and could spot the enemy a mile away from their graceless movements and unintelligible grunts.

But no human could have busted apart plywood an inch thick in a single hit.

Turning her flashlight on, she put it between her teeth and adjusted the position of the ladder, climbing up to get a look at the dark stains on the jagged edges of the broken roof.

Whoever—or whatever—had escaped was injured in the process. She plucked a few torn threads and held them in front of the light to examine the dark green fibers. Wrinkling her nose at the blood, she crawled back down and braced her gun against her shoulder as she crept out of the barn and scanned the roof and field for signs of life.

Determining she was once again alone in the darkness, she jogged to her door and fumbled the key in the deadbolt before she made it inside and locked the door tight.

One by one, she checked the windows and doors. She'd outfitted each with a crude security barrier shortly after the first of the zombies attacked. Thick wood boards swung on industrial strength hinges and locked with heavy duty bolt latches she found among her deceased granddaddy's stash in the barn. During the day, the windows could be open to provide light and warmth, but at night, they sealed the little home up tight against the hordes moving across the land.

She filled a glass of water and set it on her bedside table before crawling under the covers and slipping her rifle under the bed.

Two years in the barren wasteland her grandparents called home and she was tired. Her grandma was first to pass, the cancer which brought Lexie Grace to her side progressing too fast to be contained. Granddaddy held on with his broken heart weakening his body until three months ago. He went to sleep and never woke. Now she was twenty-nine years old and alone, defending the only home she had in a place she still didn't understand.

She despised the dryness in the still air and loathed the waves of dust the sharp winds carried. The insects were small but fast, almost invisible against the hues of browns and grays and the fine sand coating everything from her skin to her meals. Even the blue of the daytime sky was tinged by the beige of the land.

Only the blanket of night was familiar to her. Every star above shone brilliant and clear, the constellations popping against the black heavens. Back in the Tennessee Smoky Mountains, she had spent hours gazing up at the stars, enthralled by the faint twinkling she could make out if she looked at them long and hard enough. Foster homes came and went, but the night sky remained the same.

And now those stars came with zombies and their ragged teeth and gnarled fingers, the stench of their filth reaching her from fifty feet away.

Listening for a break in the silence outside, she lay back on her pillow and stared at the ceiling, knowing she wouldn't sleep until dawn broke and spread its repellent beams of light across the desert for another day.

****

Boy sat on the cliff outside his cave and examined the tears in his cargos under the moonlight. The shredded skin along his hips was already healed and dried blood flaked as he ran his fingers over the torn fabric of his pants.

It was an unnecessary risk, hunting for shoes so close to his home base. He'd fought barefoot before. He could do it again.

He unlaced his boots and set them aside, turning the toes away so he wouldn't be reminded of their defects.

The hum of Nichol's drone drew closer and he stood, stretching one last time before crawling into the smaller cave and pulling his broken shoes along with him. Shimmying across the stone, he placed them deep into his sleeping area where they would be safe and in reach should he need them.

Dawn's arrival was imminent, a mere thirty-seven minutes away. He tuned into the movements outside, reaching past the Deviants in his head, past the echoes of the Tenders still tethered to him through unwilling bloodshares, and past the whispers of Khthonios trying to slither to the forefront of his mind.

Nichol's drone was a good two miles away now. The gentle padding of a mammal on the sand below was steady, the small beast likely making the trek back to its burrow after a night of hunting. He could pinpoint the location of a snake moving along the rocks and he zeroed in on the sound of the fluid movements until it went quiet and the rising sun sent a slight tremor through his bones.

Closing his eyes, he retreated back from the outside world and deeper into his head where Khthonios still lived.

****

The sunset tossed an orange glow across the grassy knolls and the shadows of the lush trees lay long and dark against the emerald-green grass. He knelt silently in the dying light and waited for his mistress to emerge from the forested region where she slept, his heartbeat quickening when the last of the rays disappeared.

Moments later, she appeared, her long onyx hair neatly plaited down her back. Her black eyes and ruby lips were striking against her pale skin, making her appear as ethereal and dangerous as she was. She held the hem of her dress off the ground, her sandaled feet tiny and delicate while she glided to him and nodded in acknowledgement when he bowed his head. He lifted his blade to her in open palms, flinching when she slashed it across his fingertips before placing it in her satchel for safekeeping until dawn.

"Come," she said, dropping a gold coin as she passed him without another glance. "I'm hungry."

Picking up his payment for another day spent guarding her while she rested, he added it to the rest in his heavy sack, the coins clinking until he wrapped them tight against his hip.

The nights she rose hungry were the ones he dreaded most. Years at her heel had done nothing to harden him to his mistress's feedings. The sight and smell of the blood she spilled churned his stomach and tightened his throat every time, and the screams of her victims stayed with him long into the morning hours.

He remained behind her as they reached the road, not daring to overtake her until she gestured for him to take the lead.

Khthonios had no appetite for the blood of the old or the sickly. She turned her nose away from the destitute. Her tastes ran rich, and she preferred her meals to be plump with milk and meats, their bellies as full as their purses.

The dirt road was smooth under his feet, well worn by travelers and merchants passing through. Rough and calloused, the soles of his feet felt only the largest of stones, ones he could avoid when the stars and moon were high in a cloudless sky.

"Hold," Khthonios murmured. She stopped and turned, her black eyes narrowing as she scanned his form. He stilled while she approached him and cupped his chin in her hand, tilting his head to the side before

she released his face. "Strip."

Without hesitation, he untied the fraying rope around his hips, removed his wool tunic, and extended his arms to the side for assessment.

Her hands were cold against his warm skin as her fingers pressed along his ribs and down to his hips. When she stepped back, he turned around and braced for the icy hands as they felt along the bones of his spine.

"You've been neglecting your physical needs," she stated, continuing along the road without another glance at him. "Tonight, we will remedy this."

He tugged his tunic over his head and followed her as he slung the thinning rope around his hips and cinched it tight. "My apologies, mistress. I become distracted by my responsibilities and forget my hunger."

Straying from the beaten path, she led him across a field toward a large hut in the distance. "By neglecting yourself, you neglect my wishes and reduce your worth. We shall both dine this evening. And let this be the last time I am forced to address your carelessness, boy."

He inched his hands up to his neck and grazed his fingers along his throat where the phantom pains were centered.

Khthonios had lured him from his northern settlement when he was nothing more than a brash youth, her promises of riches and golden coins drawing him to her side while his clan huddled together in the darkness, timid and hungry.

As winters came and went, his purse grew heavier and heavier until he had little choice but to bury his treasures along the unending roads his mistress traveled. And with each changing season, Khthonios would appraise him. She noted his height, pressed her palms against his shoulder blades, and wrapped her hands around his forearms. He would stand motionless while he was sized up as one might an ox for purchase, thorough in her assessment of his health and his strength.

At first, he feared she would sell him, perhaps trade him to work the soil of the fields they passed night after night, far from the land he'd known.

Seven winters into his service to Khthonios, he wished she had.

Chapter Four

Lexie Grace slung her rifle off of her shoulder as her motorbike skidded to a stop and kicked up a cloud of dust into the air. She patted the loaded clips secured to her belt, lined up her first shot, and squeezed the trigger.

The first creature stumbled back and fell, knocking two others off their feet. She glanced back to ensure none of them were sneaking up behind her, centered the largest of the three in her scope, and tossed her shot wide when a familiar blond jumped into the fray.

"Whoa!" she exclaimed, dodging a dismembered head as it flew in her direction. "Where did you come from?"

The guy acknowledged her with little more than a brief look before continuing his swath of destruction, leaving decapitated zombie bodies to litter the sand in his wake.

Keeping a tight grip on her gun, she jogged out wide to pick off the stragglers on the outskirts of the horde encircling the man.

The noises coming off the mob were horrific, a mixture of grunts and howls punctuated by the sound of bones crunching and flesh hitting the earth with a thud. They flocked to the blond man with a singular focus, a handful jostling past her from behind and sending her heart into her throat.

"There's gotta be a hundred of these bastards," she whispered as she approached the teeming mass step by step.

She kept her hits a dozen yards off the blond's location. She was a good shot, but she wasn't a perfect shot. And that guy was killing off six to every one she took out.

Catching him in her crossfire would be detrimental to her goal of survival.

The stench of unwashed bodies teared her eyes as she moved in, the dead now outnumbering the living. The blond guy was a machine, razing the horde with his bare hands while her rifle did little more than peck at the weakest. No longer able to safely shoot into the crowd, she moved to higher ground, crawling atop a large boulder and using her advantage to call out to the lone fighter.

"Biter on your right," she hollered over the chaos, exhaling when he yanked the creature to its feet before removing its head from its shoulders with his bare hands. "Big one behind you."

The minutes passed like hours until the blond was the final one standing amid a sea of motionless limbs and red-stained sand. In the stillness, she watched him navigate through the piles of flesh. His movements were almost serpentine in their fluidity while he skulked around the perimeter of his kill zone.

The darkness of night kept his features hidden from her and she strained to track him when he extended his patrol to the farthest bodies lying in the sand. One by one, he removed the heads from her own kills, tossing the bodies aside as though they weighed little more than an empty jug of milk. He stalked the desert with the gait of a predator. His head tilted with every faint sound carried on the light wind and lifted periodically as though scenting the air.

"I'm going to hazard a guess y'all aren't lost," she stated when he slowed to a stop a hundred yards away. "So what are you then? A hunter? Bounty hunter? Trophy hunter? Did the military send you in? Or are you just a guy with a lot of pent-up rage?"

His shoulders hunched a fraction and he angled his face from her.

Tapping on the remaining bullet clips on her hip, she scanned the darkness. "Whatever reason you're out here, I'm pretty damn glad you are. I doubt I would've been able to hold off this many. There must be a hundred and twenty of those suckers ready to ash up in the sun." Met with silence from the mute man, she shrugged and made a slow circle on the rock, scouring the pile of corpses for movement. "It was like a shark feeding frenzy in the center there. I mean, y'all were just destroying those things like a Great White, all growling and shaking them down and tossing them away." Miming one of the few kills she witnessed from beginning to end, she snarled and threw an invisible body over her shoulder. "Like that."

The guy was watching her, keeping a cautious distance.

"Come on up," she called out, using the butt of her rifle to tap the broad flat surface of the boulder. "There's a three-hundred-sixty view from here. And at your height, you could probably see Canada."

He took a small step toward her but stopped as though second-guessing. He glanced down at his foot and gave it a small shake.

"It's kind of nice, having someone else out here trying to keep these zombie things at bay," she continued on, following his gaze when he looked over to the hills in the west. "My granddaddy refused to leave when they started arriving because he didn't want to abandon his animals or house. Now he's gone and I can't bring myself to abandon the old place either." Tracking him as he moved closer, she inched to the middle of the stone to give him room to climb up. "So where are you staying? There isn't anything around here for miles. I didn't see a vehicle. Or do you have an off-roader? That bike of mine is great on the pavement, but it can't handle the sand at all without spinning out."

He hoisted himself onto the boulder and stood, keeping his eyes averted and head slightly bowed as he scuffed his foot a few times. His biceps and forearms were caked in blood and sand and a dozen deep bite marks marred his skin. Even in the dim starlight, she could see dust and damp streaks on his black shirt. The fabric was torn along the neckline and framed the series of claw marks across his throat.

He towered over her by a good seven inches, even with the hunch of his back as he shoved his hands into his pockets and stared ahead. His honey-blond hair reached his shoulders, straight locks tangled and streaked with blood. The cargo pants he wore looked military-grade and worn, a large tear across his left thigh exposing a deep gash that appeared to be healing already.

Exhaling, she hooked her rifle over her arm and mimicked his pose. "So, you're a vampire, hey?"

Although he didn't respond, the muscles under his shirt tensed.

"It's okay. I'm not a Purifier or anything. Those Species Purifiers are wingnuts." Looking eastward, she kept him in her peripheral. "Were you left behind during the Exodus into Denver? That was absolutely wild, the way those Kaius vamps coordinated everything. But so sad, all those deaths. I watched the memorial on TV and basically cried from the minute it started until two days after." Wincing at her own insensitivity, she glanced over at him. "I'm sorry. You probably knew some of them."

He gave a slow nod.

"It sucks to lose people you care about," she continued, filling the silence. "My granddaddy passed away a few months ago. Died of a broken heart, I think. He held on for me, but once Grandma Minda died, he didn't have his reason to wake up anymore."

Something caught his attention to the north and she watched as he cocked his head and assessed the threat before returning his gaze to the west.

"You've heard the rumors about the blockades and SOS protocols, right?" she pressed. "People around here are saying the government is taking control of the area, putting up roadblocks and guard houses and everything. Now, I don't know much about the law so I don't think they can actually do it to those of us who own places out here, but if it's true, someone like you who isn't from around here might end up in some trouble. Last update I saw online said anyone caught trying to breach the perimeter after the army moves in is gonna be shot on sight as long as those zombies keep coming."

****

Boy waited until the talkative woman hopped off

of the rock before he followed suit, doing his best to keep his gaze off her heart-shaped ass and the tight fit of her pink tank top which matched the ribbon wrapped around her hair.

"So where are y'all staying?" she asked as she checked the barrel of her rifle and swung it over her shoulder. "You don't have to tell me if it makes you uncomfortable or anything. I read on the Internet that vamps are pretty secretive about that kind of thing but I know there's none of those fancy vampire hotels around here so I'm just making sure you have a place to hide when the sun comes up."

He side-eyed her, only mildly surprised when she kept talking.

"Those zombies are attracted to blood, so you're gonna want to wash up, but you probably know that already. You can use the hose out back by the barn if you like. The water's cold but it's clean and I can stand guard so you aren't feeling exposed or anything."

She walked to her bike and straddled it while she fastened her helmet. "You're more than welcome to hop on, but I don't make any promises about my balance with a guy your size riding bitch." She patted the small space behind her and grinned. "You coming?"

He shook his head and let his hair fall into his eyes before he backed up and shoved his bloody hands into his pockets.

Poor thing is probably scared to death, all alone out here. I sure hope he has somewhere safe to go.

Her thoughts flittered into his head and he frowned.

With a sigh, she started the engine and revved it a few times. "Well, I know you know where I live. If you have any problems or change your mind on that cold shower, you come on by and knock, okay? No need to go sneaking into my old barn if you're looking for a place to hide."

He watched her double back down the road toward her home while she sang a song in her head that Mikhail Kaius often used to practice his air-guitar.

Even in her thoughts she was loud. But it wasn't terrible. Her singing overtook the noise in his head and he latched on to it while he counted bodies. Each one represented another mindless scream gone silent, another Deviant who was tied to him through the tainted blood running in his veins eliminated.

The humming became quieter and quieter until it disappeared completely, leaving him alone with the howls and whispers. He checked the position of the moon and looked toward his cave on the western edge of the valley while he stretched his senses for any hint of solo Deviants roaming closer. Finding none, he wiggled his toes in the ill-fitting boots he took from the barn the night before and paced the sand, poking at the odd headless body and tracking a scorpion coming closer to investigate.

Loneliness was not something he knew or understood. He'd experienced centuries of forced isolation followed by several more of solitude, but he had no emotion associated with those times. His lifetimes with Khthonios taught him to stay silent and still, to remain in the shadows and the darkness where the voices in his head were faceless and nameless. Loneliness had no place in an existence where whispers and screams were his constant companions, companions he couldn't escape or reveal.

But every so often he would encounter a voice

which stood out above those of his hauntmates. Sometimes it was the Tenders he was tethered to monitor over the decades, women trained to live and serve in vampire society. Every so often it was a stranger nearby with a unique voice. And always, he heard Khthonios's ever-present reminders he was nothing more than a useless dog.

Bianca Schumann was one who stood out. Audra Verdi was another. Both women spoke sweetly to him and thought kindly of him. They defended him passionately when he was nearby and advocated for him rabidly when he wasn't.

And he found he liked it.

He liked being greeted by smiles instead of bared fangs. Warm eyes were infinitely preferable to cold stares. Gentle voices were far more pleasant than snarled warnings and barked orders. Bianca and Audra didn't see him like the others in the haunt did. They didn't treat him like a servant or a mercenary or a threat and their hands were as soft as their words when they moved his hair out of his eyes or patted his arm in reassurance.

Before Bianca and Audra, he viewed kindness as a weapon, wielded to ensure his compliance and his obedience. And while he couldn't help but be wary of their intentions, their thoughts were never anything but pure.

Unlike those of his creator.

****

The setting sun brought with it a familiar sense of dread and he took a deep breath to slow his racing heartbeat. The heavy shackles around his ankles rattled as he rose from his bed and he clasped his hands behind his back to await his mistress's arrival.

His body sensed her before she entered the room. His skin crawled with a peculiar mixture of anticipation, expectation, and fear. Candlelight illuminated her beauty as she stepped into his line of sight, her ebony hair shining and her white skin as flawless as it was all those years ago when she'd first enticed him from his home.

Her nail skimmed along his bare back, across his chest, and down to his thickening cock as she walked a slow circle around him. "Finally," she murmured, her black eyes narrowed and intense. "A perfect specimen."

He swallowed against the combination of disgust and desire he felt every time she touched him. His mind screamed in protest but his mouth stayed silent. Khthonios was not one to entertain protests or complaints, and he had neither the inclination nor the fortitude to withstand another punishment under her hand and fangs.

A cool tongue flicked along his throat as she wrapped her small hand around his length, her delicate grip and tiny stature belying the immense strength contained in her small frame.

He was not fooled.

Ten summers past his fifteenth when he'd been lured to her side and he was no longer blinded by useless gold or promises of riches and freedom. Her hand was as quick to give him release as it was to mark his skin. Her lips sparked his lust while they spoke lies against his. Her teeth brought him pleasure and pain he both detested and craved.

He was bound to this demon until she determined

him no longer fit to grace her presence and she owned every piece of him, from his body to his mind to his soul. His blood was hers to taste, his scent hers to track, his life hers to control or take.

"Not a single marking or scar remains," she mused aloud as she slipped her gown from her shoulders and allowed it to fall to the floor. "A flawless human body." Her voice was as soft as her touch as she traced his lips and looked up at him with onyx eyes burning with desire. "When you are worthy, I will make you a god. But tonight, I will make you mine."

****

Walking east along the empty road, he filtered through the chaos in his head and located the nearest Deviants, quickly determining them to be two nights away at best.

A familiar sound infiltrated his mind. He cocked his head and allowed the off-tune song to drown out his creator's words spoken five thousand years ago, words which lived deep in his core alongside her caged soul.

Unlike Bianca, this woman was not a good singer in her mind. Her tempo was unsteady and he wasn't certain she was using the correct lyrics, but he was drawn to it all the same.

Instinct kept him monitoring his surroundings as he approached the farmhouse where a single sliver of light escaped through a crack in the wood slats fortifying the windows. The sweet scent of magnolias drifted on the faint breeze and he stilled near the perimeter of the home to listen as her internal song went quiet and he heard the electric charge of a television turning on.

He liked television. The Kaius haunt had several hooked up to perfectly balanced sound systems and he was fascinated by the fact he could watch actors speak and act onscreen without hearing their thoughts. So few of his interactions were as quiet as those he had when his hauntmates were gone and he was free to enjoy a movie of his choice.

The woman was watching a show she found funny and he inched closer to the thin gap in the board. Her laughter was even louder than her speech, a sound which would draw the attention of Deviants for miles if any were in the vicinity.

Deciding it wouldn't be right to leave her without security while she relaxed in her home, he scanned the yard, spotted his way up, and silently scrambled up the trellis to the roof where he stood guard until the protection of dawn arrived.

Chapter Five

Lexie Grace crossed her arms and faced the military down on her front porch. "I'm not going anywhere."

The only man not dressed in camouflage stepped forward and smoothed his hands down his black suit jacket. "I understand your hesitancy, ma'am, but as of this morning, you're the last person left residing in the restricted zone. Most of your neighbors fled with the first and second waves and those who remained have accepted our assistance to temporarily resettle them until the danger passes."

"That's mighty sweet of you," she drawled as she crossed her arms and leaned against her door frame. "But I'm gonna be just fine."

"With all due respect, ma'am—"

"First of all," she interrupted, "Calling me 'ma'am' is the wrong way to go about getting my cooperation. I am not my mother." One of the men behind him snickered and she rose on her toes to give a friendly wave. "Second, I am more than prepared to protect myself and my property as I've been doing since those things first started coming over the mountains. And third, unless you have an arrest warrant, I'm not stepping foot out of my house." Softening her harsh tone with a smile, she tucked a lock of hair behind her ear. "But I do thank you and the American government for being so concerned about my welfare."

The man in the suit frowned and gave a curt nod as he pulled a card from his breast pocket and handed it to her. "Do you have a functioning landline on the premises? A generator?"

"Both, yes."

He took a step back and clasped his hands behind his back. "We cannot guarantee the continued function of satellites or power in the region for the duration of this situation but should you change your mind prior to the quarantining of the region in four days, this is my direct line."

Slipping the card under her bra strap, she moved to close the door. "Thank you. Now if you'll excuse me, I have cattle to tend before nightfall."

The man's hand shot out and held her door ajar. "You're aware you won't have access to supplies once the roads are shut down."

"It's a good thing I stocked up during that lull in the action two weeks ago, isn't it?"

Forcing the door closed, she secured the locks she usually reserved for sunset and rushed to the living room where she could witness the retreat of her uninvited guests through one of the peepholes she'd drilled into the plywood blocking the windows.

Five military vehicles drove off in formation, leaving nothing but settling dust in their wake once they disappeared over the ridge. She breathed a sigh of relief, slumped onto her sofa, and picked up her cooling cup of coffee.

It wasn't like she hadn't noticed the roads were quieter than normal lately or that the dappled lights from distant neighbors she usually saw on the horizon at dusk were no longer visible. And she knew plenty of folks hauled tail out of there after the first wave decimated those who weren't armed, prepared, or downright lucky, but she hadn't considered the fact she'd be the lone holdout.

Looking around at the dated decor, she trailed her fingers along the sofa's fuzzy, scratchy upholstery.

This old home had saved her in so many ways. Her grandparents gave her a safety and security she'd never known. They provided her a glimpse of what true love looked like up to the morning she woke to find her granddaddy lifeless in his bed. Here, she'd been needed and wanted without judgement.

And free.

She wasn't a bad person. She was a good one who made poor choices in crappy situations and Tennessee was littered with her lousy decisions. The day she aged out of the foster system was bittersweet. She escaped one cage only to fly into another. Her teen years were spent in a group home where she learned how to use her looks and her voice to survive. Her string of big boyfriends provided one level of security outside the house; being the loudest in the room helped her inside. While most of the others who came and went from the home were either sullen and quiet or angry and aggressive, she found it served her well to be too much. She talked too loud, too long, and too often. She was too stubborn and too eager. Her makeup was too bright, her clothes too colorful. She was too much for anyone to handle for long, but she was also too seen in those homes to become a statistic.

But the group home wasn't the real world. Meals may have been cheap and meager there, but they were consistent. The power was always on. The water heater always heated eventually.

The day she walked out of the group home was the day her years of reckless decisions caught up with her. She had no job, no education, no skills, and no guidance. What she did have was a big boyfriend with an apartment, empty promises on his lips, and a clunker of a car. He opened his door for her and she jumped at the chance, leaving one year later with a couple of new bruises, a part-time job, and a tiny fistful of cash.

After three days of couch-surfing on a coworker's couch, he became her next big boyfriend full of sweet, meaningless vows and broken promises.

And then she met the next.

And the next.

Up to the point when her grandmother found her and reached out on social media, her life was a revolving door of low-paying jobs, low-rent apartments, and low-brow men.

Swallowing the last of her cold coffee, she stood and went into the kitchen to rinse her cup.

Her grandparents gave her a fresh start out here. A reset of sorts. And for that, she was eternally grateful. She could push past the loneliness and isolation if it meant she was warm and secure and safe in a home built from the ground up by two people who loved each other in a way she'd only ever read about in the books she bought for a quarter apiece at yard sales. This farm represented the first contentment she'd known and she would be damned if some half-dead zombie from Arizona was going to be the reason she walked away from it.

****

The plump brunette lay naked and eager on the bed, her body and scent teasing Boy with promises to sate the hungers clawing at him night and day. His new fangs lay long over his bottom lip, slicing it as he fought against the overwhelming need to bury himself inside her and drain her of the rich blood pumping through her veins.

"Do you not like what you see?" the woman purred, sliding her hand down the length of her body to the juncture between her thighs. "Or do you prefer to watch?"

Boy remained motionless and silent, the heavy shackles around his ankles keeping him anchored in place while the woman pleasured herself, unconcerned his gaze was fixed on the gold coins sitting atop her purse instead of on her writhing form.

"Does she not appeal?" Khthonios whispered behind him.

Her fingers grazing down his bare spine before she knelt to undo his bindings. "Do you not desire a sample? A taste?"

He had no trust in his voice nor his words. This new hunger she'd awoken in him when she changed him into a blood-drinker was like nothing he'd ever known. It consumed his every thought, raging and howling to be unleashed. He could hear the heartbeats of the humans in the town a night's walk away, could sense the fluttering pulses of the woodland animals in the trees. His fangs ached to sink into a vein—any vein—to slake his obsessive thirst, but his creator gave him no more freedom to feed than she did for him to leave.

For twelve cycles of the moon, Khthonios had kept

him tethered and bound. She fed him from her vein when she was pleased with him and left him rabid and starving when she was not. He craved her blood as he once craved water and she wielded it against him. The pleasure of her vein was both a gift and a torture. Every drop was earned through his obedience, his reverence, and his body. She enslaved him with her blood and her power, and her whispers reminded him always he belonged to her and her alone.

She approached the bed with a smile and dropped two more coins onto the brunette's purse before crawling on to the bed beside her and skimming her nails across the woman's breasts.

"Have you enough control?" Khthonios taunted. "Or have I chosen poorly?"

He knew this was nothing more than a game to her, a way to test his loyalty and submission to her desires above all else. His body thrummed with want. Every muscle was poised to attack. But Khthonios wanted him to give in to his weaknesses. Her thoughts told him she was desperate for him to disobey. Eager. She wanted to mete out his punishment, to remind him of his place.

Tiny wounds opened under his mistress's touch and the woman cried out, her body trembling as she came.

The scent of sex and blood slammed his senses and his precarious control snapped. Unbound, he lunged for the woman only to be met by the jagged ridges of Khthonios's gold rings slicing across his cheekbone as she struck him.

Neither the pain of a broken bone nor the sensation of his blood dripping down his face detracted from his need to hunt, to satisfy the dueling appetites warring inside him. He snarled and lurched once more for the meal now draped across his mistress's lap and was silenced only when his creator brought him down mid-air and slammed him against the floor.

"You are weak and unworthy of the gift I've given you," she hissed into his ear as one hand tightened around his throat and the other around his cock. "Tonight, I break your will. Tomorrow, I build you into the god you are meant to be."

****

Fighting the urge to bat Nichol's drone out of the air, Boy remained motionless deep inside the mouth of the cave until the faint electric hum disappeared along with the single dim illumination emitted from the drone's underbelly.

With Khthonios's voice still echoing in his thoughts, he stepped into the night and stretched his arms overhead as he wiggled his toes in his boots and wrinkled his nose at the uncomfortable fit.

They weren't the worst he'd worn, but they were nothing like the boots Nichol ordered on his computer. Those ones fit like they were handcrafted for his feet and his feet alone. Going from custom quality to boots he stole from a barn was not the worst of his troubles, but it was one he could use to anchor himself while Khthonios's blood rose from his core and swirled in his veins.

Focusing on the slight pinch of his heel, he crawled down the mountainside, hopped the final fifteen feet, and enjoyed the size of the dust cloud his landing produced.

There was a familiar stillness to the night and he scanned the desert terrain, knowing a handful of Deviants were close from both the volume of their howls in his head and the silence of the nocturnal animals hunkering nearby.

Deciding to meet them head-on, he made the trek from the western mountain range to the vast plains to the south. His creator's blood called the misturned vampires to him, beckoning them to seek him out and kneel before him.

But he had no need for an army, no desire to rule. Unlike Khthonios who sought to become a goddess among mortals, he wanted nothing more than to return to his life of quiet anonymity. And perhaps some new Italian leather boots with those sturdy reinforced toes.

He had no use for a mindless hive prepared to do battle on his whim, but his blood said differently. Khthonios's desires pulsed in his body and mind night and day, whispering promises of idolatry, power, and retribution. She lived inside him now, and he felt her presence as it waxed and waned in his core where he fought to keep her caged.

My, my, my. Aren't you a hideous thing?

The blonde woman's drawl shot through the howls and screams in his head and he turned to the east.

So you think I'm helpless out here, big tough army man? Let's compare kill counts. Then we'll talk.

Frowning, he scanned the darkness until he spotted her hair bright against the barren landscape. Her back was to him so he went wide, studying her as he slowly approached from her left.

She was pretty in a way which he knew would make Rhys Kaius cringe.

He liked it. Maybe more so because she wasn't tainted by Rhys's perfecting hand. Because as much as he admired the survival instincts of the Kaius haunt's former Tender trainer, he wasn't a fan of the vampire's scathing distrust of him.

Her hair was done up in a barely-controlled mass of large curls which were held off her face with a bright red flower. They bounced with every move of her head. Tonight, she was wearing bright blue leggings and a long black shirt which hung low off one shoulder and gave him a peek of her yellow bra strap. A small purse crossed her body and rested on her hip, cutting a line between her breasts and through a bright pink design on the front of her shirt. He couldn't make out the logo unless he stared, but it didn't feel right to do that when she wasn't even aware he was nearby.

Just a little closer, buddy. Bring that nasty face a few more yards this way and kiss your ass goodbye.

He stilled while she cocked her rifle and aimed, taking the Deviant out in two shots.

While the creature lay twitching, she crept toward it with her weapon at the ready. "Why don't you things just die already?" she muttered, staying well out of reach of the Deviant's gnarled fingers but too close for Boy's comfort. "If that big guy was here, that ugly mug of yours would be tossed halfway to California."

Taking care to make his footsteps audible, he made his presence known as he walked toward her. She swung around with her gun braced against her shoulder before lowering it and giving him a bright smile. "There you are," she called across the quiet terrain. "I was just thinking about you."

Ignoring the way her words made him feel, he went straight to the Deviant, removed its head with his hands, and tossed it eastward as far as he could, tracking the faint thump when it hit the sand too far away to see.

The woman clapped and he shoved his now filthy hands into his pockets, uncertain where to look as she hopped up and down and her shirt dipped even lower. "We make a good team, Big Guy."

Keeping his eyes on the ground, he let his hair fall into his face and shrugged.

Oh my God, shut UP. Poor guy was probably out for a nice quiet walk and here I am hollerin' at him like a damn vamp groupie.

Her smile faltered and he found he didn't like it one bit. Keeping one ear open for the Deviant stumbling into view from the south, he stalked over to her and tried to appear as nonthreatening as he could while he nodded in the creature's direction.

"A new target," she said with a gleeful grin as she adjusted her stance and raised her gun. "Aren't you a gentleman?"

He can't be that put out if he's sticking around. Maybe he's lonely. Or bored.

A second Deviant appeared over the shallow ridge, followed by a third. He filtered through the noises in his mind until he locked on to the closest ones, pleased to note there were no others within their zone.

"I can take out one, maybe two if my aim is spot on, but I can't get all three before I'll have to reload." She glanced over at him. "If I wound them, will you do that cool head-ripping trick again?"

He nodded and stepped aside as she fired off three shots. Two of the Deviants toppled to the ground. The third continued its stumbling trek while they strode toward it side by side.

"It's too bad you don't talk," she mused as he

jogged ahead of her and eliminated the only imminent threat to her safety. "You could do a victory yell every time you decapitated one of those things. Like they do in the movies."

Moving on to the two creatures reaching for him with their deformed hands, he hauled one to its feet and grasped its head before looking over its shoulder at the woman.

It took her a moment to understand what he was waiting for, but once she did, she flashed him one of those genuine smiles he very much enjoyed receiving.

"Better cover your ears, Big Guy, because I'm gonna holler so loud they'll be hearing it in space."

With exaggerated motions, he tore the head off the Deviant and threw it into the distance to the sound of her victorious yell. She whooped as he grabbed the last creature, her voice even louder while he flung the final head through the darkness.

"I definitely like having you on my Zombie Apocalypse team," she announced as he loped to her side. "Are there any more out there? I know you vamps can see and hear way better than we humans can so you're probably better at finding those things before they find you."

Cocking his head to double-check what the howls in his mind were telling him, he wrinkled his nose.

Her lips turned down in disappointment. "Oh. That's good, I guess." Slinging her rifle over her bare shoulder, she walked toward her motorbike parked in the distance. "So are you planning to stay in the area long? The blockades are going up in four days—maybe three now—so if you're thinking of leaving, you'll probably want to hit the road sooner rather than later."

He nodded and slowed his pace to stay at her side.

"You should know they won't be letting anyone out after, so you'll want to make sure you have supplies," she continued, tugging her keys from the small purse at her hip. "I don't pretend to know what kind of supplies vampires need to stock up on, but whatever it is, I hope it's something you can find in Reno because I think most of the other towns nearby are already evacuated. I mean, you probably don't need soup or anything but—"

She stopped cold and crossed her arms, the pleasant smile on her face turning stern. "Let me just make this clear before we go another step, buddy. My blood isn't for the taking, so if that was part of your survival plan out here, y'all better think twice because I am not on the menu. Not for those zombies and not for you. Promise me."

He nodded his head, shoved his hands back into his pockets, and tried to appear as harmless as a vampire his size could.

"That's right," she stated, pointing a finger at him and wagging it. "I may like you, but I've got my eye on you, too. Now come on. I don't know where you're holing up but I do know those clothes of yours need a good washing. You can hang out in the barn while I put a load of laundry through if you want."

He glanced down at the dark blood stains embedded in his shirt and cargos and shrugged.

He'd been dirtier.

She straddled her bike and patted the seat behind her. "Get on, Big Guy."

With the shake of his head, he pointed in the direction of her home and took off in a sprint, his chest swelling a little when her shock gave way to awe and his mind filled with her mightily impressed thoughts.

Chapter Six

With her hands on her hips, Lexie Grace surveyed the inside of the barn in the dim light of the battery-powered lantern sitting atop a crate. "So I suppose I'll leave you to it then. I'll be back in a few minutes with something you can wear temporarily and we'll exchange. Sound good?"

The vampire nodded, his eyes and most of his face shielded by his long hair.

"Okay then. See you soon."

Every manner her grandmother drilled into her during their short time together was screaming at her to smarten up, be a good hostess, and invite the poor guy in. But mute vampires drenched in zombie blood were never addressed, so she felt confident she was making the wise choice.

Even if she felt kind of bad leaving him alone in the stifling barn while she went inside her cool home to fetch one of her granddaddy's old housecoats.

One by one, she checked the windows and locks for weakness before going into the master bedroom. Her granddaddy's collection of robes still hung on their velvet-trimmed hangers and she took a moment to set his favorite aside before selecting the largest and removing it from the hanger to size it against herself. Wrinkling her nose as she realized nothing in the house would be size Ginormous Vampire, she draped the red plaid over her arm and proceeded to the barn.

"Knock, knock," she called out as she eased the door open. "Just me."

The vamp was exactly where she left him, his broad shoulders hunched and hands shoved deep into the pockets of his filthy pants.

"This is the best fit I could find," she explained as she passed him the robe. "I know it's probably not going to be the most comfortable, but anything has to be better than those blood-soaked clothes."

He bowed his head which she took as a thank you and she motioned toward the door. "I'll wait out here while you change and you can hand me your clothes when you're ready, okay?"

She backed out and heaved the door closed, waiting all of thirty seconds to fill the silence of the still night. "I don't want to get too personal here but I'm more than happy to put your boxers through the wash, too. Or briefs. Or whatever you wear. Unless you're a commando guy. Though the chafing with those cargo pants would probably get to you after a while, especially in this heat. Never mind. You look like a boxers kind of guy."

Straining to listen to the faint rustling of fabric behind the door, she pressed her ear to the wood. "The water from the hose on the north side of the barn runs warm if you want to wash off or something. I can maybe bring some soap and shampoo out. Not that you smell or anything, but you got some of that zombie blood in your hair which is gonna dry and feel pretty gross by morning."

She heard footsteps on the old plank floorboards and she scrambled away from the door as it opened.

"Oh my."

The vamp stood there holding his neatly folded clothes, the plaid robe nowhere near large enough to fit him. The sleeves rode high on his muscled forearms while the length barely covered his strong thighs. She took the stack from him and did her best to keep her gaze on his bowed head instead of letting it drift down to the chiseled chest framed by plaid fabric cinched at his trim waist and begging for a light breeze to undo the effort the belt was putting in.

Giving him what she hoped was a reassuring—and definitely not lecherous—smile, she clutched his clothes and took a step back. "I'll toss these in right now." She gestured to the hose looped over a metal hanger on the north side and rocked forward on her toes. "I'll be right out with some supplies so you can make yourself comfortable, okay?"

She managed to make it inside the house before she erupted in a nervous giggle.

Oh my, indeed.

Shaking her head at the awkwardness of having a hunky vampire half-naked in her barn, she sprayed his clothes with a stain remover and tossed them into the washing machine to soak while she grabbed soap, shampoo, a hunting magazine, and a fresh towel from the bathroom and returned to the barn.

"Me again," she said as she balanced the shower supplies in one hand and hauled the door open with the other. "Hope you're decent."

The guy was deeper inside the barn this time, partially hidden in the shadows. Setting everything on the crate beside the lamp, she ventured farther inside and tried not to let her gaze fall to the bandages wrapped around his right ankle and extending up to his knee. "It'll take around two hours for your clothes to be ready, so I brought you something to read in case you get bored. I'll be watching TV or reading so don't you worry about waking me up if you need anything. Just give me a knock on the door, okay? Okay."

He gave a quick nod but refused to look at her, his discomfort radiating off of him in waves as she tried to ease his tension with a smile.

"Remember, it's the north hose with the warm water," she reminded him as she backed out of the barn. "The south one will freeze your balls clean off."

The door slammed shut and she cringed.

Freeze your balls clean off? Could I be any more of a creep? God, that poor guy is probably plotting his escape by now.

Stifling a groan, she pushed away from the wooden doors and went inside to start the washing machine.

****

The first time Boy felt flannel was four years ago when Bianca and Molly bought him a pair of green flannel pants he was supposed to wear when he went to bed. But having no bed in the Kaius haunt bloodslave quarters and no real need to rest for more than an hour or two at a time, he didn't see the point in changing just to change back again.

And he didn't trust the elastic waistband. If he was attacked while wearing them, the pants would become a liability both physically and mentally.

So he'd folded the pants and stored them in his stowaway bag where he kept the rest of his favorite possessions, meager as they were.

This flannel was a little thicker but just as

distracting.

He despised feeling exposed, and this robe left him as exposed as it got without being naked.

Worse, if he really thought about it.

At least if he was naked, he wouldn't be messing around fighting to keep his cock and his ass covered every time he took a step. And he'd fought bare before. It wasn't his favorite thing to do but it was manageable.

This wasn't.

Tracking the woman's heartbeat in the house across the yard, he shrugged off the robe and hung it on a nail. Her voice sang in his head while he gathered up the supplies she left for him and he wrapped the oversized towel around his hips.

The stench of Deviant clung to his skin and hair and he frowned as Khthonios's words whispered over and over until they drowned out the humming of the woman a few yards away.

Vile.

Filthy.

Depraved.

Weak.

Shoving her voice aside in favor of the off-key tune lilting quietly in the back of his mind, he tightened the towel and stepped into the yard, scouting the area before walking over to the hose on the north side of the barn and turning the tap.

With a final glance around, he removed the towel, draped it over an old barrel, and set the soap and shampoo beside it. The water was warm as promised, but it didn't matter much to him. He'd bathed in lakes and streams for most of his existence, so anything above freezing was a bonus when it came to showers.

Placing the hose aside and keeping his senses stretched to avoid being caught unawares, he lathered up his hair with the floral-scented shampoo and his body with the fruity smelling soap. He scrubbed the dirt and dried blood off his skin and reached for the hose to rinse, nearly dropping it when the woman's humming stopped and her voice echoed loudly in his head.

Hot damn. I didn't even know asses like that existed in real life.

I shouldn't have looked. Why did I look? Oh God, what if he saw me?

He probably saw me. Or he knows I saw him. He has to. He probably has some vampire sense which tells him when horny women are staring at his perfect ass.

Why did I look? Now I'm going to think about it every time I see him.

Unless I stake him.

But that wouldn't be very hostess-y, killing the poor guy just because I have zero self-control. Grandma Minda would be so disappointed.

I should check the washing machine.

Rinsing the shampoo and soap away as fast as he could, he turned off the tap, snatched the towel off of the barrel, and wrapped it tight around his hips. The humming resumed as he entered the barn and he pulled the door shut behind him, putting a fraction more distance between them.

He was no stranger to the inner dialogues of women, but it was rare one thought about him without fear. They saw him as cold. Frightening. Dangerous. He didn't blink. He didn't breathe. He didn't fidget. Long before vampires were outed to the human population almost two decades ago, women knew instinctively he was not like them, that he was unnatural. They recognized the predator in him from afar. His mere presence was capable of emptying a room faster than a fire alarm.

Bianca and Audra weren't scared of him, but they weren't scared of much aside from carpeted bathrooms and hotel bedding. And Harper, Kaius's mate, always thought nice things about him. But Molly, Lis, and Simone were still afraid of him, as were most of the Tenders trained under Rhys and still tethered to him through blood.

This woman with the blonde hair, pink lipstick, and loud voice had no fear of him. Even when she confronted him about drinking from her vein, she did so without a hint of terror in her eyes or her thoughts. Unlike Audra, Harper, and Bianca who knew him through the buffer of the rest of the Kaius hauntmates, she had nothing but instinct guiding her.

And he couldn't help but worry about her safety if her instincts didn't sound the alarm around him.

With one ear open to her movements in the house, he waited for her to return to the barn and tried unsuccessfully to block her thoughts from his mind. The singing continued, periodically interrupted by her musings about the state of his clothes in the dryer, her guilt over peeking out the knothole in the plywood, and pondering what she would've seen had he turned around.

The last one lingered no matter how much he tried to shake it and he had the sinking feeling it was the thought which would stay with him long into the morning hours while he lay alone in the cave listening to Nichol's drones circling the area.

When he heard her front door open, he took the plaid housecoat off of the nail where it hung and shrugged it on. He made a valiant attempt to make himself look a little less ridiculous in it, but knew he failed when he met her at the entrance to the barn.

Her smile was bright as she greeted him with a warm stack of clothes, but she didn't look at him and he found he didn't like not having her pretty blue eyes on him.

How terrible a person am I for wondering if he'll turn around.

He should turn around.

He should always turn around. Round and round and round like that ass.

Oh God, I'm a terrible person and this poor guy is probably wondering why I'm standing here grinning like a damn fool. But how can I not? He looks ridiculous and hot and I don't think anyone else could pull this off quite so well.

"Fresh from the dryer," she announced, holding the pile out. "I managed to get most of the blood stains out but there were a few really old ones that were too stubborn even for Grandma Minda's secret detergent recipe."

Accepting the clothes with the bow of his head, he hesitated and debated his options before turning and walking back into the barn.

I am a terrible, terrible person.

If it wasn't for the laughter he could hear in her thoughts as they filtered into his mind, he would be bothered by her self-deprecation. The door shut behind him and he heard a very soft—but very vocal—*damn*. He changed quickly, folded the housecoat and damp towel, tucked the soap and shampoo under his arm, and went outside where the woman was sitting on a barrel.

"So what are your plans for the rest of the night?" she asked, her legs swinging and her heels knocking on the wood. "I'm heading to bed pretty soon. But I guess it doesn't make sense for you to do that since you have no reason to be up with the sun. In fact, rising with the sun is probably detrimental to the whole immortal thing you're rocking right now."

Nodding, he passed her the items she shared so generously. Reaching over to a stack of crates beside the barn doors, he broke off a piece of wood and knelt down in the dirt to respond to her. *Patrolling until dawn.*

He shoved his hair from his eyes and studied the ground for a moment. *Name?*

He glanced up to see her smiling a genuine smile.

"Lexie Grace Kelly," she stated, holding her hand out and bouncing in place when he gave it a tentative shake. "And you are?"

Pausing, he contemplated making one up on the spot. The only name he'd had for thousands of years was no name at all and for the first time in his existence, he kind of wished he had one. Something with history and a story he could write out proudly. But when his mind came up blank except for the names of his hauntmates, he scuffed a clear spot in the dirt. *Boy.*

Lexie Grace Kelly tilted her head and her blonde curls moved like spun silk. "Boy. I like it. Even if there is absolutely nothing boyish about you, Big Guy."

If vampires could blush, he knew his face would be as red as Molly's became every time her temper got the better of her during her weapons training with Jagger.

"So, Boy," she continued. "Will I be seeing you around again tomorrow? I'll be heading to Reno in the morning to stock up on a few things before the army shuts this place down." She hopped off the barrel and took off in a run to her house. "Wait right there."

Her sudden disappearance caught him off-guard but he obeyed. He took the opportunity to lock up the barn, slip the piece of wood into the large pocket spanning his thigh, and scan the area for danger until she returned with a pen and notebook in her hands. "If you think of anything you need from town, write it down and leave the list in my mailbox before sunrise."

He accepted the items and she grinned as she played with a lock of her blonde curls. "I don't think I'll have the energy to go zombie hunting tomorrow night, but a quick visit before bed would be nice if you're up for it."

When he nodded, she gave him a scrunch-nosed smile that made her look all sorts of cute and sexy at the same time. "Alrighty then. It's a date."

He remained on site and listened as she disappeared inside and set her locks. He waited until the movements inside the house stopped and her heartbeat slowed to a steady pulse. Walking the perimeter of her property twice to ensure everything was as quiet as the howls in his head led him to think, he made his way back to the western mountain range, shimmied up the rocks, and sat on the ledge of his cave to ponder his newest predicament.

Chapter Seven

Nichol Kaius crossed his arms and glared at Rhys, daring his younger hauntmate to repeat himself.

Lacking self-preservation and any ability to read the room, Rhys ran his tongue along his fang and smirked. "I said, make me."

Rolling out his shoulders, Nichol removed his laptop from the communication room table, set his phone next to the printer, and took his brother down before Rhys could wipe the grin from his face.

"I. Have. A. Date," he growled, ignoring the cackling from the peanut gallery also known as Jagger, Mickey, Dominic, and Kaius. "Just do it."

Rhys feigned contemplation before patting Nichol's cheek. "Since you asked so sweetly, okay. Dominic, you're coming with me."

Dom groaned but held his hand out to help Rhys to his feet. "Fine, but this time I get to pick the console *and* the game."

Giving his brother a final shove to solidify his point, he fired off a text to Louis assuring him help was on the way. Babysitting duty for Louis and Jonathan's ten adopted baby vamps was no easy feat between feeding schedules, training regimes, and counseling sessions and the Kaius haunt was on-call to assist in the driving, pickup, and drop off on those nights when one or more of the brood was acting out.

The new vamps were all turned within the last five years and all in their early twenties. They were high energy, high maintenance, and a few of them had attitudes which were going to get them killed permanently, possibly by Nichol himself.

While the rest of the haunt discussed their plans for the evening, he returned to his seat to complete a final check of the monitors before passing control over to Kaius for the evening. Movement caught his attention and he froze. "I have eyes on Boy."

The others clambered to crowd around him and watch the grainy image on the monitor.

"I'm not seeing anything," Jagger stated, leaning in closer.

Ensuring everything was recording, he split the screen and enlarged the video from his second drone. "I swear I saw…what the fuck? Why does he fucking do that?"

The feed from the first drone went blurry as it was batted out of the air and sent spinning toward the sand. Nichol scrambled to enter recovery instructions before it hit the ground. "I'm going to stake that asshole."

While his words were harsh, the relief felt throughout the room was palpable as Boy appeared on screen again, crouched on the edge of a cliff as he tracked the movements of the second drone. Though the night vision left much to be desired, seeing the vamp alive and well eased some of the tension he and the others carried since Boy went off-grid four months prior.

The first drone recovered its path in time to catch Boy's attention and with the fluidity of a panther, he leaped from the mouth of the cave and sent the drone spinning into the atmosphere.

"Does he have any idea how much the tech he's batting around like a goddamn cat toy is worth?"

"I don't think he cares," Kaius replied with a chuckle as he tapped on the data coordinates. "Isn't this the region you've been patrolling for the last few months?"

Mickey grinned. "He's been hiding right under your nose, Nichol."

Had they been talking about a young vamp, Nichol would be feeling a little put out. But since Boy now happened to be the oldest vampire in existence, he cut himself some slack. "Looks like he wants to be found now."

All thoughts of babysitting and the issues facing the vampire sanctuary city they'd established in Denver were shoved aside while the Kaius hauntmates took a few minutes to watch while the vamp responsible for their own creation entertained himself with two-hundred-thousand dollars' worth of electronics.

"Playtime's over," Nichol grunted when his third drone reached the area and Boy started using it for rock-throwing target practice. With a few taps of his keyboard, he turned on the drone's audio. "Boy. Report."

The blond vamp shrugged and sat on the ledge, beckoning the drone closer and he dropped the pebbles in his hand.

"It's a trap," Dominic whispered. "He's probably going to frisbee it like he used to do up north."

Rhys elbowed the youngest hauntmate in the ribs and pointed to the screen. "He's holding something up, you dumbass."

All the hauntmates leaned closer to the screen while Nichol flew the drone within reach of Boy.

"Boots. Black shirts. Socks. Pants. Boxers," Kaius read off the notebook in Boy's hand before turning to Nichol. "It's a shopping list."

Pushing away from his computer, Nichol flipped open his laptop and loaded up the spreadsheet where he kept track of Boy's sizes and preferred styles, frowning when he saw no notes regarding Boy's boxer preferences. Returning to his main computer, he spoke directly into the mic. "You don't wear boxers."

Boy turned the notebook over and began writing.

"Is that a pompom on that pen?" Jagger asked quietly as he squinted at the screen.

The notebook filled the screen again. *Send boxers. And a wrist flower.*

"Wrist flower?" Nichol mumbled while he played with the steadiness of the drone. "Anyone know what that is? What it's code for?" Met with silent confusion, he rushed to speak into the mic again as Boy rose to his feet and assumed his attack position. "Expect a package drop at dusk tomorrow. I can't promise everything, but I'll ship in what I can when I can. In exchange, I want a detailed writeup of the last four months including kill count, perimeter notes, military presence, and any intel you have about the Deviant hordes moving your way. I—"

He didn't even see Boy move before the drone's video was nothing more than a whirling blur.

"One of these days, I'm going to kick his ass," he said with a huff as he made a note to himself to assemble and code a few more drones.

The others got to their feet and Kaius gave him a

tight smile. "He's alive."

"That he is."

The knowledge lifted a weight from all of them until Dominic opened his mouth and ruined it. "A wrist flower...does he mean a corsage?"

Nichol fixed him with a dead stare, hoping the youngest member of the haunt would gain a full understanding of the stupidity of his question. "Why the fuck would Boy need a corsage?"

****

Sunset couldn't come fast enough for Boy. He lay on his back inside his cramped cave with his hands tucked behind his head while he filtered through the howls and whispers to the memory of his name on the lips of Lexie Grace Kelly.

"On your knees, Boy," Khthonios snarled as she yanked his leash and dug the metal spikes of his collar deeper into his skin.

He sank to the dirt and she grasped his jaw to turn his head toward the woman they were tracking through the dark night, her face illuminated by the single candle in her hand. "Is she worth your punishment?"

Twenty-one summers tethered to her heel and hunger was a constant thrum through his body. Khthonios kept him balancing along the fine line of starvation and desperation, ensuring he was fed enough to maintain his strength but nowhere near enough to sate him. She took pleasure in teasing him with meals only to rip them away and discipline him for his body's reactions to the offerings. The descent of his fangs or the twitch of his cock guaranteed her wrath and tonight she was witness to both.

The woman disappeared inside a small hut and

Khthonios tilted his chin up, smiling with the warmth of a serpent. "Is she worth her punishment?"

He'd laid neither a finger nor a fang on the woman yet he knew her fate was sealed the moment his creator saw evidence of his desire. "It was my failing, not hers," he stated, knowing his words held no purchase but unable to stay silent. "I will bear the retribution I deserve for dishonoring you."

The chain around his neck tightened in Khthonios's hand and he felt the blood of the puncture wounds soaking into his tunic as she straightened and dropped the leash. "Very well. You may rise with the sun. Should you move from this position prior to the first rays breaching the horizon, she will pay with her life."

He stayed on his knees while pebbles dug into the bone and his wounds healed around the spikes embedded in his neck. Running was not an option, not when her blood ran through his veins to mark her ownership. She would find him as she had long ago and his punishment would be far worse for a second offense than it was for his first when he was dragged back to her side and forced to crawl on his belly for six cycles of the moon.

The whisper of dawn sent a tremor through him and he fought against his instinctual need to hide from the rays that would char his skin to the bone. When the first beam spread its light across the earth, he bolted toward the shelter, stumbling as the sun stole his vision and seared his flesh.

Pushing aside the thin curtain, he fell blindly into the woman's home and was assaulted by the scent of spilled blood and the absence of a heartbeat.

"I waited," he growled, his voice rough and low as

he rose to his feet and gazed into the blackness of his damaged vision.

"I did not." Khthonios's fingers trailed along his jaw and he fought the urge to buck against her touch. "Every part of you belongs to me and me alone. Should your memory fail, others will always pay the price."

Slivers of sunlight pierced the thatched walls and streaked across him, the pain providing him something to focus on as her lips brushed his. "You are mine, Boy. Perhaps someday you will earn the right to call me yours."

Easing one hand out from under his hair, he ran his thumb along his throat absently, soothing the phantom pains which haunted him night and day.

Few spoke his name without fear, revulsion, or irritation. Bianca did. Audra, too. But both women talked to and about him as though he were a child who required coddling and protection.

He needed neither but lacked the conviction to tell them when they were the only members of the Kaius haunt who greeted him with warm eyes.

But now there was Lexie Grace.

She didn't say his name with a mollifying or motherly inflection. She said it and thought it with a predatory growl he wanted to hear again and again.

Shifting his hips in the narrow cave, he almost smiled at the idea of the tiny blonde being the hunter while he cowered as prey in the dark. At first glance, she was the least threatening thing in the area. Unlike the Deviants roaming the land and the military vehicles patrolling the highways, Lexie Grace and her rifle should be a blip on his radar.

Except she apparently had one weapon he had no

defenses against because he'd never encountered it before. He had no immunity, no ingrained reactions. He was fighting blind and deaf with both hands tied behind his back and his ankles shackled with balls and chains.

If reality television was right about modern humans—and he was pretty certain it was because why else would people watch it endlessly—Lexie Grace had flirted with him.

Women didn't do that.

They recoiled, they avoided, they shunned, or they catered to him out of fear. They didn't tease him or give him nicknames or twirl their hair as they spoke to him.

Audra and Bianca treated him well, but sometimes he felt more like their favored pet.

The few Tenders who actually acknowledged him when they rotated through the haunt made him leery, their thoughts far too focused on dark fantasies he had no desire to experience—or relive.

And Khthonios…

Khthonios had no need to flirt or seduce him because she already owned him. She trained his responses and forced his devotion. There was no reason to entice him or court his attention when she could simply remove all other distractions from his sight.

Shaking off his memories of his creator as the sun set, he escaped his cave and sat on the ledge to listen for the drone, wondering how many of his requests Nichol was able to fill in such a short time and hoping the drone would get close enough for him to catch.

Chapter Eight

Lexie Grace flipped her head upside down and covered her face with a towel while she emptied a decent amount of hairspray onto her freshly-wound curls. A few scrunches later and she took a step back to get a better look at herself in the small bathroom mirror.

Her monthly drive to Reno was usually a highlight. She loved stopping for an expensive cup of coffee on her way to the grocery store and always left enough time to window-shop while she strolled along the downtown core alongside the tourists who flocked to the bustling city.

This time, however, she chose to forgo her perusing and picked up a coffee and a muffin at a drive-through on her way out of town. With her granddaddy's truck bed loaded to the brim with water jugs, paper products, and non-perishables, she made it home in record time despite having to stop and show her identification at the temporary barricade at the perimeter of the evacuation zone.

She was lucky her old truck held off on making that grinding sound until she was close to home because she suspected the army might not have been very accommodating had she needed a lift to the home they didn't even want her returning to.

There were chores she had to put off to make it to Reno and back during daylight hours, but the sun went down thirty minutes ago and she had all the time in the world tomorrow to top up the cattle feed and clean the stalls.

Pleased with her hair, she did a quick check of her teeth for stray lipstick, adjusted the position of her favorite push-up bra, and checked her backside to make sure her jeans still fit her like they should.

"It's his loss if he misses out," she mumbled to herself, still a little put off by the fact the vampire named Boy hadn't left a shopping list in her mailbox. "I'm the best damn thing in a hundred miles, hands down."

It wasn't like she could afford to spend any more money than she had to, but at least there would've been more of a guarantee he'd come by tonight if he was aiming to top up his supplies. What supplies a vampire in the middle of a desert might need, she couldn't guess, but he had to want something. Maybe a pillow or a book of crosswords. As it was, there was a good chance she was dolling up to sit on the couch and watch cooking shows all night.

Which might not be a terrible thing if she was being totally honest with herself.

While she had definitely spent a lot more time thinking about Boy's ass than was probably healthy, he was still a guy and her track record for spotting the good ones was, for lack of a better word, bad. Vampire or not, a man was a man and she needed to remember that. It didn't matter if he was shy and sweet and built like a Greek god, he had a dick and therefore had the natural inclination to act like one.

"Do not invite him in," she whispered to her reflection as she ran her thumb along her bottom lip to remove a little excess lipstick. "There's nothing that hunk of hotness can do for you that your vibrator can't."

Maybe if she spent her few hours of sleep dreaming about puppies or unicorns instead of fantasizing about being bent over her kitchen table by a big blond brute of a vamp she would be less conflicted. But the subconscious wants what the subconscious wants and no amount of batteries was going to help.

With one more shift of her bra, she went into the living room, frowned at the plastic bag sitting on the sofa, and second-guessed her purchase for the tenth time since she got home. She picked it up with the intent of shoving it into the hall closet when she heard a gentle rapping at her door.

Self-preservation kicked in and she inched over to the tiny peek hole she drilled into the plywood reinforcing the glass front door.

Boy stood on her doorstep, his head slightly bowed as it always seemed to be when he wasn't fighting zombies. She held off on opening the door for a moment in the hopes he would raise his head and give her a good look at his face but when he remained completely motionless, she knew waiting him out would be futile.

She flipped the deadbolt, unhooked the chain, and lifted the wooden bar before swinging the door open and greeting him like Grandma Minda would expect. "Well hey there, Big Guy. Aren't you a sight for sore eyes?"

His brows furrowed and he cocked his head. His face was still obscured by the shadows but she could feel his gaze on her, studying her with an intensity she felt low in her belly.

"It's just an expression. There's nothing sore about me except maybe my feet after all that shopping." She stepped outside, tugged the door closed behind her, and cringed when the plastic bag on her wrist slapped off the wood frame. "Speaking of shopping, I picked this up for you."

She held out the bag but he didn't move to take it. Instead, he shoved his hands into his back pockets and his shoulders hunched a fraction.

His wariness was kind of sweet, in that ethereal-skittish-creature-meets-human kind of way and it tugged on her heartstrings to think there must be a reason a guy like him felt the need to be so vigilant around a small, loudmouthed thing like her.

"You didn't leave me a list," she said as she took the first item out. "But I figured everyone needs new socks, so here."

He stared at the trio of athletic socks she bought on a whim then lifted his head to look directly at her as he accepted the gift.

"Hot damn, you're pretty," she gasped, slapping her hand over her mouth when her own voice filled the quiet night. "Sorry. But you are. You're...oh my, you are very, very pretty."

Pretty wasn't anywhere close to the right word, but her brain was too busy short-circuiting to think past a first-grade vocabulary. His face and jaw were chiseled and squared to perfection, clean-shaven with high cheekbones she could only hope to achieve with the right balance of blush and lighting. He had bow-shaped lips and a nose so textbook-straight she was tempted to hide her own slight upturn.

But it was those electric-blue eyes which kept her standing dumbfounded. At first, they appeared empty and lifeless, like those of a shark. But the longer she studied him, the more she saw swirling and writhing behind his blank stare. It was as though every word he didn't speak was laid bare and the intensity of it had her locked in place, unable and unwilling to end the connection until he bowed his head and broke the spell.

Feeling more than a little backwoods at how obviously captivated she was, she retreated a step and gave him her most carefree smile. "I bet all the girls just love those long lashes of yours, don't they?"

His attention was on the socks in his hands but his nose wrinkled in distaste as he shook his head.

"Then they're either fools or excellent liars," she stated with conviction as she pulled the other items from the bag and forced herself to stop objectifying the poor guy. "I wasn't sure if you like reading, but this was just released last week and it's supposed to be the best thriller to come out this year. And this"—she held out a tiny clip-on LED reading lamp—"was an impulse buy."

His brows furrowed as his gaze moved between the socks, the book, and the light.

"Don't you worry one bit about hurting my feelings if none of this is your thing," she rushed when he made no move to take the book or light from her. "I can always return it or—"

He held up a finger and reached down to pull her pen and notebook from the large pocket on his thigh. Balancing the paper against the porch railing, he scribbled something, stopping and starting a few times as he adjusted his grip on the fluffy pink pen she gave him last night. When he was satisfied, he turned the notebook toward her.

"The best gift you ever received, hey?" she said with a smile, not believing it but pleased he was happy with the purchases she waffled over for far longer than was probably necessary.

Nodding, he sat on the step, unlaced his boots, and patted the space next to him before he switched from his old socks to his new ones. She joined him, grinning when he wiggled his toes before slipping his feet back into a pair of familiar boots.

"My granddaddy had a pair of boots like those," she mused, leaning back on her elbows to look up at the stars. "He always said they'd outlive him and they did. They're in the barn as I speak."

She glanced over at him, her brows lifting when he bowed his head and wrote another note. Scooting a little closer to read over his shoulder, she nudged his knee with hers. "I appreciate the apology, but I guarantee he would've rather seen those boots being put to good use than sitting in an old barn until they rotted. And I'd say zombie-killing is considered 'good use.' "

Those incredible blue eyes met hers for a moment before he returned his attention to the notebook. Reading his heavily slanted scrawl, she nodded. "Yeah. Let's go."

****

Shoving his hair from his eyes, Boy locked his gaze on his destination while the motorbike beside him revved.

"You're going down this time, Boy," Lexie Grace called over the roar of the engine. "On your mark. Get set. Go!"

He gave her a three second head start this time to allow for the old motorbike's pickup to kick in, but still managed to surpass her long before the mile marker they established with his new book light.

Circling around to him, she pulled her helmet off and shook out her hair. "I think I'm seeing why the Olympic committee vetoed vampire participation in the games. Are all vamps as fast as you?"

Shoving his hands into his pockets, he shrugged.

"Oh come on," she cajoled, tapping his leg with her foot. "If all the vampires in the world ran a race, what place would you come in? And be honest." Wrinkling his nose, he held up one finger and she laughed. "I knew it. You're a super-vamp, aren't you?"

She had no idea how close to the truth she was.

And if he had his way, she would never find out.

With a sigh, she refastened her helmet. "I hate to do this, but I should get back home. Someone has to deal with the cattle in the morning and since everyone else left the region, I guess that someone is me."

Feeling as disappointed as she sounded, he jogged alongside her and scouted the area for danger while she locked up her bike and mentally debated inviting him inside her home.

As much as he tried not to tune in to her private thoughts, it was hard not to when she was broadcasting so loud and her voice was drowning out the screams and howls and whispers. He didn't even care much what she was thinking about as long as she continued to overpower the incessant noise which pummeled him hour after hour, year after year, century after century.

Khthonios's voice was the only other one which could rise above the rest with such ease, but Lexie

Grace's thoughts were nothing like his creator's. One slithered through him with dark tendrils, burrowing deep into his psyche and infiltrating his core with its depravity. The other felt like his long-buried memories of stepping into the spring sun after a long winter: a little too bright, a little too intense, and perfectly exhilarating.

"Don't forget these," she said when they reached her porch. She dropped the tiny reading light inside the bag with his new socks and book and passed it to him. "I had a lot of fun tonight."

He nodded and slung the bag over his shoulder, hoping she understood he had enjoyed it, too. Maybe more than he should since he was feeling something akin to loss with the knowledge it would be hours before he would hear her voice again.

"So I guess I'll see you around?"

Her thoughts were murkier than before, a mess of incomplete ideas and phrases he didn't understand bouncing all over the place as she stood on the top step and looked down at him. He gave her a thumbs-up and he heard her laugh inside his head.

"Oh, what the hell?" She sighed and he cocked his head in confusion moments before she leaned down and her lips brushed his, leaving him stunned and immobile.

He was an alpha predator. The supreme alpha predator since his destruction of Khthonios four months ago. He could take down dozens of Deviants single-handedly and unarmed. His speed and strength were unmatched. There was nothing in existence more powerful than he was.

Except, perhaps, a tiny blonde with a loud mouth and sweet thoughts because she was kissing him and he had no idea what to do.

You will be a god.

Khthonios's promise whispered from his core and he shoved it back into its cage.

There was no time to deal with the ghost of his creator when Lexie Grace's soft pink lips were on his and her slender fingers were skimming along his jaw. He had bigger problems in this moment, like the foreign feeling of panic he was experiencing when he realized she was about to pull away.

There were no voices left in his head, no cries or whimpers or wails. All he could think about was how little he knew about kissing, how television had failed to prepare him for this, and how badly he didn't want this to end.

Dropping his bag on the stairs, he slid his hand along her throat to the base of her neck. His fingers tangled in her hair when he opened his mouth to deepen the kiss and her tongue slid against his. The sensation was like nothing he'd ever experienced, tentative and sensual and wholly consuming. Her small hands gripped his shoulders and her sharp nails dug into his skin and ignited a hunger he hadn't felt in so long he didn't trust himself to contain it.

Pulling away, he eased his hands from her hair and dropped his arms to his side as he bowed his head to hide the involuntary lengthening of his fangs. He couldn't look at her while he scooped up the bag and backed down the steps out of the yellow glow of the porch light. There were lines and rules and limits for a reason, boundaries he didn't test because to push them meant pain and death.

Desire had no place in his existence. Not in his

past, not in his future, and not in his present.

Zeroing in on the howls of the Deviants crossing the desert to fall at his feet, he turned away from the small ranch house and went on the hunt for a new cave far from Nichol's drones.

Chapter Nine

It was official.

Lexie Grace had kissed a ghost.

There was no other explanation for the events of the past two weeks. The government placed the blockades five days ago, leaving her and a blond phantom vampire alone in the vast wasteland that was the Nevada basin. Evidence of his presence was everywhere, proof of his existence nowhere. Her granddaddy's old boots were back in the barn, the cattle feed was consistently stocked, the broken fence posts along the northern perimeter of her property were repaired, and twice now she'd found pink rose corsages on her doorstep.

Night and day, small things in her world shifted. Gates left unlatched were closed, debris she meant to clear from the path leading around the cattle pen was removed, even the rake she left against the barn was returned to its hook.

But not once did she see the skulking blond vampire.

Zombies continued to stumble across the barren earth and she spent hours on her rooftop watching them move with singular focus toward the western mountain range. Most nights, they moved alone or in pairs but sometimes there were dozens passing by below, paying her no mind as they lurched and jerked, kicking up clouds of dust in their wake. Every so often she found evidence of their slaying through the blood-drenched clothes left behind as the sludge turned to ash and drifted away on the breeze, but by her next pass by, all that remained was a stain on the sand.

Her precious ammunition was well-stocked, but she was becoming increasingly nervous about using it. If—when—Boy truly did disappear, she would be on her own to protect her home and her life, and she had no interest in wasting bullets as long as her phantom vampire was nearby doing the work for her.

Sitting on her rooftop, she took a sip from her water bottle and scanned the darkness for movement.

Loneliness was beginning to creep into her thoughts more and more. It was a different feeling than she used to experience when she was living with men who saw through her. Back then, she felt invisible and most times it was the safest thing to be because the other option was being too much. And too much meant unwanted attention. Then her grandparents tracked her down and dragged her far from Tennessee to the isolation of the desert where she felt more at home and more seen than she'd ever known.

And yet this was different still.

When her grandparents passed, there was an emptiness in her heart. The only two people who loved her and wanted her were gone. But they'd left her their home and their memories and she took comfort in it, knowing she did them proud every time she baked in their oven and cared for the cattle and defended the land. The small stipend of money left in their wills would provide for her for years as long as she was thrifty, longer if she sold off the cattle as she intended once the zombie situation was under control.

Boy's absence wasn't the same.

She knew almost nothing about him, but what she did know was enough to draw her to him. Muscled body and chiseled jaw aside, he was gentle and careful around her despite his size and obvious capacity to kill bare-handed. When they raced across the sand, she laughed when she saw dueling desire warring inside him. His stance and focus was torn between letting her win and a competitive nature he couldn't quite quash. She had yet to see him smile, but pleasure practically radiated from him when he tossed his old socks aside and put on the ones she bought for him, his huge feet wiggling almost playfully before he tugged his boots back on.

He reminded her of a wounded animal, one beaten into submission for so long it didn't understand simple kindness. His broad shoulders were always hunched and he hid his hands and face so naturally she knew it was from years of practice. The fact he allowed her to see his eyes had felt so monumental in the moment, she damn near cried with the realization he was trusting her with something she didn't think he did easily.

Of course, if he could hear the raunchy thoughts running through her head, she doubted he would've risked it.

It wasn't like she saw him as nothing more than a hot piece of eye candy. But it wasn't like she could pretend he wasn't stunning in that unicorn-meets-sex-on-a-stick way. Boy was one of those guys you didn't stare at too long because you'd either go blind from his beauty or lose all sense of reality permanently. He was handcrafted by the gods and she was only a single human woman with a stack of batteries and a vivid imagination.

A sound in the distance caught her attention and she set her water bottle down as she lifted her rifle. She strained to listen, frowning when she swore she heard a voice carrying on the gentle wind.

With her ammo strapped to her waist, her weapon in hand, and her favorite tall black leather boots with the chunky two-inch heel on her feet, she slipped down the trellis to the ground and walked westward.

She stayed tight to the road, which was illuminated by the light of the nearly full moon. The voice broke the quiet night intermittently, growing a fraction louder each time until she was close to the base of the range and she heard a clear string of growled curses.

"I swear to fucking hell, Boy, if you do that again you're on your own to find the drop."

Ducking down to avoid detection, she moved along the sagebrush until she could make out Boy's silhouette crouched on a ledge at least ten stories above her. Something small darted through the sky and he leaped toward it, sending her heart into her throat while he sailed into the air. His body twisted and turned as he struck the object and it went flying upwards before he fell to the ground and landed on his feet with the grace of a panther.

A second orb zipped over and hovered above Boy, just out of his reach judging from the swipe he took when it neared.

"Are you fucking done?" the low voice barked. "I have better things to be doing than indulging in this weird fucking fetish you have for destroying black ops technology worth more than your goddamn soul."

Boy shrugged and shoved his hands into his pockets and she slapped her hands over her mouth to stop the laughter bubbling up.

Whoever was on the other end of that flying object was not impressed with Boy's skills, but she sure was. His head cocked and she froze as he looked toward the bushes where she tried to stay hidden from view, knowing she failed miserably when his stance shifted and he jumped into the air snatching the orb from the sky. The angry voice on the other end went silent as he launched the thing to the south and it disappeared into the darkness.

"Busted." She sighed as she pushed herself to her feet and winced when dried sagebrush scraped her palm. "So this is where you've been hiding."

He stalked over to her and stilled within reach, his gaze raking over her as he slowly took her hand in his and turned it up to expose the tiny scratches peppering her palm.

Suddenly aware he was staring at the minuscule beads of blood dotting her skin, she felt her heart rate skyrocket. "It's nothing a little peroxide won't clean."

His unnatural stillness wasn't something she minded before, but being the recipient of his intense scrutiny now had her body thrumming with a strange mix of anticipation, fear, and fascination. She never claimed to know much about vampires, but she knew blood was their thing and she was the only bleeding human in the area tonight.

As her hand started to tremble in his hold, she saw his fangs for the first time.

****

Fear.

Adrenaline.

Lust.

Boy dropped Lexie Grace's hand and stumbled back, his innate agility vanishing with the realization he scared her.

The past two weeks were two of the longest in his existence and it was all because of the woman watching him with wary eyes. For an ancient vampire who'd been tethered to the most powerful, most violent, and most vindictive vamp in history, patient acceptance of the passage of time was a survival strategy. His ability to turn off his natural inclination to track each second of the clock allowed him to compartmentalize the hours, weeks, years, and decades of abuse at her heel.

And then Lexie Grace Kelly kissed him and all his meticulously honed preservation skills shattered like Nichol's drone on the hard-packed basin sand.

Part of him knew it was dangerous to continue to spend time with her. His own desire for her aside, Deviants from across the globe were making their way to him, ready to kneel at his feet and serve as his army while he fulfilled his creator's desire to be worshipped as a god on Earth. The closer she was to him, the closer she was to the Deviants.

And the closer she was to Khthonios.

The kiss had awakened more than his own numb libido. Whispers from his core where he kept Khthonios's blood locked tight were more insistent now, more frequent. Her voice slithered into his mind and wrapped itself around his memories, warping them with visions of Lexie Grace spread lifeless and bloody before him like an offering.

But he couldn't stay away.

At first, he kept his visits to deep in the night long after she went to bed. He walked the perimeter of her land, fixing what he could with the tools he found in her barn and carrying the heavy bags of cattle feed to ease the burden of her chores. It wasn't long before she started staying awake longer though, and that's when he became more reckless.

Every vampire created possessed supernatural skills. All became faster and stronger as they aged, their senses amplifying and growing more honed during each passing decade. With enough fresh blood to carry oxygen through their veins, their bodies healed at incredible speeds and their minds processed information at speeds rivaling those of Nichol's computers.

But each also gained an extra ability, one they often hid from others to use to their advantage for survival and dominance. Kaius Khthonios had the strength and speed of a vampire twice his ancient age, an ability Rhys Kaius also shared. Nichol Kaius possessed the gift of languages and could speak every one, both living and dead, complete with regional dialects. Jagger was a ghost, capable of moving with such agility and silence he was undetectable until the last head rolled. The youngest hauntmate, Dominic, was a soother who emitted a calming pheromone which affected both humans and vampires alike.

Some abilities carried with them a detriment, though. Mikhail Kaius was cursed with empathic skills. Few empaths survived their first century because the emotional bombardment from the others in their line drove them to insanity and sent them into the sun for a final relief. Louis Forbes, while not of the Kaius bloodline, was a talented hypnotist and would be hunted to the ends of the Earth should word of his ability leave the confines of their trusted circle.

And then there was him.

A soft touch grazed his arm and he shrank back, hauled out of his own head by Lexie Grace and her magnetic voice.

"I'm not scared of you," she stated, advancing on him despite the distance he tried to place between them. "If you were going to hurt me, you could've done it at any time. Besides, you don't strike me as a guy who doesn't understand consent. In fact, I suspect you understand it better than most."

She took his hand and led him to the highway, swinging his arm as though she were strolling through a park with a normal man instead of walking with a vampire bred and trained to destroy.

"You have no idea how bored I've been lately. Someone keeps coming around and doing my chores for me. It's leaving me with way too much time to read which means if he keeps it up, I'm going to need to break through the barricades and head to town to stock up my reading pile."

He glanced down and found her grinning at him.

"Come on," she said with a laugh. "You may be stealthy but did you seriously think I wouldn't know it was you? There is literally no one else it could be."

Shrugging, he slowed his pace to match hers.

"So what was that metal doo-dad you were attacking back there?" she continued as she looked over her shoulder to the mountain caves where he was holing up. "Some kind of drone? Is it a friend of yours? He sounded pretty mad at you for knocking that thing around, you know."

He nodded and listened for Nichol's drone. While his old hauntmates knew there was a woman still residing in the region, he had no desire to put her on their radar any more than necessary by drawing a straight line connecting him to her.

"Those drones are pretty cool. It would be kind of fun to play with one some time. But properly. Not what you were doing because I'm just not coordinated enough to jump like that without breaking my neck."

Frowning, he slowed to a stop and pointed in the direction of the drone scouring the darkness for him.

"What?" she asked, rising up on her toes as though it would make it easier to see the small object against the night sky. "You want me to pounce on it?"

Nodding, he motioned to a few boulders in the distance and mimed ducking behind them.

She pursed her lips and studied him for a moment before a mischievous glint sparkled in her eyes. "Are you going to draw it out and let me ambush it?"

He gave her a thumbs-up and jogged across the sand, knowing his movements would catch the drone's sensors and narrow its focus. Lexie Grace took her position behind the rocks while he pretended to follow Nichol's lead to the box of supplies dropped somewhere in the wasteland.

"One of these days I'm not going to return," Nichol warned him with a threat they both knew was empty. "You've fucked up more tech in two weeks than Rhys has in his entire existence and that, Boy, is saying a lot. Now keep your hands where I can see them and keep those feet on the ground."

Despite Nichol's bluster, Boy liked the

cantankerous vamp. He wasn't fearful of Boy and never had been because he was too busy studying him. Unlike the others who were turned after him, Nichol had a begrudging trust in him and although Boy was never seen as an equal in the haunt, Nichol seemed to instinctively know Boy would bring no intentional harm to them.

Unless it was one of the haunt's drones. Then all bets were off.

Leading the drone past the boulders where Lexie Grace was crouched in preparation of attack, he eased her pen and crumpled notebook from his cargo pants and scrawled a quick message before holding it out.

"Write larger next time," Nichol stated with as huff as the drone came closer. "What does 'hold still' mean? Goddamnit, Boy. You aren't—"

The rest of Nichol's rant was muffled as Lexie Grace jumped out from behind the boulder and, using her rifle like a baseball bat, sent it sailing through the air. They watched it tilt and tumble before it righted and zipped away as fast as it could.

"I loved that," she announced with a giggle as she grasped his hand and squeezed it tight. "Can we hunt another? I know I'm a terrible person for laughing at the poor guy controlling it but he sounded so mad and I could just picture him sitting in a gamer chair somewhere, slamming his hands on his keyboard and screaming at his screen." Her expression turned hungry. "What a power rush."

Knowing Nichol would punish him by not returning until tomorrow, he shook his head and wrote a quick note for her.

"Yes, I would love to go on a box hunt with you."

Pocketing the notebook and pen, he dropped to one knee and patted his shoulders only to be met with narrowed eyes. "What? No."

What is going through that pretty head of his? No. No way am I riding up there. I'll crush him. What if he drops me? He wouldn't do that. But no. I mean, maybe? I wonder how fast he can run with someone on his shoulders.

He held position, allowing her time to run through her internal dialogue which went on for a solid two minutes before she crossed her arms. "Promise you won't drop me."

With a nod, he reached out for her, wrapped his hands around her waist, and lifted her onto his shoulders in a single movement met by a shriek and a laugh. Rising to his feet with his precious cargo squirming above him, he took a gentle grip of her ankles and started their trek northward where he suspected his latest box of supplies was dropped when Nichol's drone went to ground to avoid detection by a military sweep of the area.

"You're crazy." She slid her fingers through his hair. "Am I too heavy? You can put me down if you want. This is so cool though. I can see everything from up here, like a whole new world."

She started singing a song he heard Molly perform when she thought she was alone in the training rooms and he felt the corner of his lip twitch up.

This was nowhere near a display of his abilities, but he liked the thoughts going through her mind about his strength and his speed when he broke into a run to cover more ground. Her mind didn't automatically flip to the danger he posed or musings about his age like it so often did when he was around his hauntmates. This was as fun for her as it was for him and he wanted more of it. He wanted to take her to the caves tomorrow night and teach her to throw stones at the drones then race her motorbike on the sand like before. And maybe he wanted to climb the side of the mountain with her on his back so she would be impressed with him again.

"Is that what you're looking for?" she asked as she trailed her fingertips along his cheekbones.

Nodding when he spotted the small box up ahead, he slowed his pace to a stop and knelt down to help her dismount.

He missed the feel of her instantly.

"So what's in there? Crossword puzzles? Shirts? Some top-secret vampire thing humans can't see? I can only imagine what kinds of things vampires get up to. You must have the most amazing history. Are you going to open it here or do you want to bring it back to my place?"

Knowing the contents would probably be more boring than she was imagining but wanting to spend a little more time with her, he patted his shoulders and helped her climb back on before he took off toward her home.

Chapter Ten

Lexie Grace grinned as she exited her bedroom in sweatpants and a pink tank top to find Boy still stalking through her home and examining her plywood reinforcements for weaknesses. "Have I passed the test?" she asked when he returned to the living room and stood in the middle, his shoulders hunched and hands shoved deep in his pockets. He nodded and she hopped onto the sofa, patting the empty space beside her. "Good. Now rip that box open because I'm dying to know what kind of things vampires have delivered."

He joined her and used his fang to puncture the tape, glancing at her as he did so.

"I wish I could do that." Holding out her hands, she wiggled her pink fingernails. "Every time I use these, I have to redo my polish."

Popping the lid open, he wrinkled his nose and lifted out the first item.

"A phone? That's pretty cool. Too bad the towers around here aren't very strong. But you could probably get some offline games and books loaded onto it if you travel west."

Shrugging, he set aside two black T-shirts, five switchblades, a wad of rolled bills, and three pairs of boxers.

"We should wash those before you wear them, otherwise they might be a little itchy," she said as she pulled the tags off out of habit and gathered the clothes in her arms. "I'll throw them in now and they'll be ready before sunrise."

Thoughts of how he would look in those black boxers entertained her as she chose the settings and started the pre-rinse cycle. She was putting soap into the rushing water when she noticed him standing in the doorway, his expression hidden by the shadows. Realizing she essentially strong-armed him into staying until his new clothes were ready, she winced. "I am so, so sorry. I didn't mean to get all bossy on you, taking your new clothes like that without asking. You probably had plans tonight. Look, it's no big deal. I'll finish them and you can get them tomorrow when we go drone hunting. If you even still want to go, that is."

Although she always talked a lot, she did more and faster when she was nervous. And experience taught her that making any decision for a guy without asking was always something to be nervous about.

Boy tucked his hair behind his ears and lifted his head enough for her to see his face. His eyes were locked on her lips as his fangs descended into view, the faint silver hue shimmering under the glare of the overhead light.

"You aren't mad, are you?" she asked, closing the lid of the washer and gripping it as he shook his head slowly and stepped into the laundry room with her.

Her heart rate picked up and his gaze moved along her body, stopping at the cleavage her favorite tank top put on display. He took another tentative step toward her and she caught a glimpse of shame behind the desire in his eyes before he looked away.

A terrible thought crossed her mind. "Are you

married?"

The horror in his expression was almost comedic as he shook his head frantically.

"What about a girlfriend?" she pressed, having been caught up in a few unpleasant situations over the years thanks to men who got hung up on semantics to explain their asshole behavior. "A significant other of any kind?"

His perfect nose wrinkled, letting her know he was very much not attached to another woman, which was good because she really wanted him attached to her. Preferably to her lips. Maybe her hands too, since it was a damn shame she had yet to get even an accidental grope of his biceps.

He lifted one brow and she bit her lip, almost feeling guilty for objectifying such a sweet guy. But guilt required her to feel bad for wanting him and she couldn't quite do it. Instead, she tilted her head and tossed her hair over her shoulder, licking her lips when his eyes were drawn to the slope of her neck.

Their silent standoff lasted through most of the rinse cycle, her daring him to make a move and him holding position just out of reach. She was dying to know what held him back, what made him hesitate when he seemed to want her as much as she wanted him. But she didn't make a move. Not this time. This time, she needed to know for certain the attraction wasn't one-sided.

The thought wasn't even fully formed when he broke their stalemate and closed the distance between them, his hands in her hair and his lips on hers before her mind could catch up.

This kiss was nothing like the one two weeks ago

when he responded so shyly it hurt her heart. His hunger vibrated through him as he caged her against the washing machine and pressed the length of his strong body into her. She grasped the collar of his shirt and wound the fabric around her fists, holding him close as his tongue flicked against her lips and she opened her mouth to him. She moaned when his fangs grazed her, growling when she felt him stiffen and try to pull away.

"More," she demanded, refusing to release her grip on his shirt and smiling against his lips when he lifted her onto the washing machine and dove back in. "Better."

She parted her legs and he stepped between them, his hips pressing into her and giving her an electrifying—and a bit intimidating—hint of just how large her Big Guy was.

The thought of using a shoehorn crossed her mind and she laughed as she arched her head away from Boy's mouth, certain she caught a brief smile before he kissed his way along her jaw and nuzzled her neck.

****

The grin on Boy's face felt so foreign he couldn't bring himself to lift his head from the veil of Lexie Grace's blonde curls.

A shoehorn.

Her laughter was still echoing in his ears while he trailed his tongue along her throat, eliciting a sigh from her as she let go of his shirt and her small hands slipped along the back of his neck and into his hair. Her fingers tangled in it and she tugged. His hips bucked involuntarily against her hot center as he sought out her lips again, desperate for another taste of her citrus lipgloss.

Her legs wrapped around his hips and she flicked her tongue along one of his fangs, sending his eyes rolling back in his head. He'd heard his hauntmates talk about how erotic it was when their partners did that, but he had no idea his fangs had a direct line to his cock which was now painfully hard.

"Oooh, you liked that," Lexie Grace said with a giggle before doing it again while she ground against him. "I think I like making you shiver."

God, I want to see him lose control.

She had no idea how close to getting her wish she was. His hunger for her was rising fast. Too fast. Between the thoughts she was inadvertently transmitting to him, the sensations ricocheting through his body, and his own desire for this woman, he was dangerously near the edge.

Squeezing his eyes shut to block the view of her hard nipples in the thin pink tank top she was wearing, he flattened his palms on the lid of the washing machine and bowed his head. He rested his forehead on hers before reaching up to straighten the thin straps of her shirt.

Is something wrong? Why did he stop? I—aw, Big Guy. You're trying to be a gentleman, aren't you? What a sweetheart.

Her train of thought eased his frustration over becoming overwhelmed by everything she made him feel after he spent his entire existence training himself not to feel, not to react, not to lose himself in the moment because it could be his last.

And yet if this moment was his last, he would have no regrets.

The realization was sobering.

Backing up, he held out his hand and helped her down while she gave him a coy smile and led him into her living room where she flopped onto the sofa and tried to drag him with her. Figuring it was safer for her if he sat under his own volition instead of crushing her, he took a seat, his brows shooting up when she grabbed the television remote and snuggled up under his arm.

"So is there a direct correlation between fang size and foot size with vamps?"

Frowning, he glanced down at his feet and shrugged.

She laughed and nudged him in the ribs before settling in against his chest and selecting a cooking show. "I'm just teasing you. I don't intend on doing any of my own research on the subject or anything."

It took him a moment but when it dawned on him she was joking about assessing the fangs of other vamps, he glared at the television screen.

Apparently jealousy was another emotion he needed to learn to handle if he intended to be around Lexie Grace. The fact there were no other vampires or men for over a hundred miles didn't make him any less snarly over the thought of her anywhere near their fangs. Or feet.

Watching TV with a woman was nothing like watching it from the corner of the common room back at the haunt. Although he kept one ear on the stillness outside her door and continued to track the closest Deviants reaching for him through his mind, there was an unexpected calm settling over him while she absently traced circles on his chest and made comments about the chef's process. Her body was warm and soft like the gentle scent of magnolias which grew stronger every time she nuzzled into him.

No other woman will ever satisfy you like I do.

Khthonios's voice whispered from her cage in his core and he tensed as memories of her "satisfaction" flooded through him before he could smother them.

His eyes snapped open in the dim candlelight of the cavern, awareness quick on its heels and dragging his fractured memories alongside.

The hunger.

The blood.

The battle.

Silence greeted him, but he knew better than to believe he was alone. He was never alone. Not when the voices of the commoners in the town were seeping into his head. Not when the depraved thoughts of his creator slithered and writhed in his mind night and day, her perverse desires playing out time and again until she turned them into his reality.

The straw beneath him was cold and heavy with blood. The scent of sex and burnt flesh hung in the still air as he fought against his lethargy to stand. The shackles around his ankles clinked when he rose, their chains rattling until his feet touched the hard earth.

"On your knees, mongrel."

His hesitation was met with a soft laugh, one which sent ice through his veins and knotted his gut.

Khthonios strode toward him, her narrow hips swaying and her red lips turned up in a serpentine smile as she stopped and lifted her hand to his face. One long talon dragged along his jaw and she pressed against him, licking her lips when he didn't react to her naked skin on his.

He knew every inch of her body.

Despised every inch of her body.

It was yet another weapon she wielded to tear him apart and drag him deeper into her warped world.

"You're angry," she murmured as she ran her finger through his blood and brought it to her lips. "You must learn to lose our games with grace."

Games.

Khthonios loved her games. She delighted in setting the rules, arranging the pieces, and handpicking the board on which they would be played. Anticipation made her giddy, the promise of new screams and fresh blood heightening her mood to such frenetic levels he was unable to fully comprehend her broken thoughts and shifting parameters until it was too late.

He continued to stare straight ahead, past her black eyes and onyx hair to the crumbling stone wall behind her. In his peripheral, he could see what was left of the game board, the woman's blood drained from her veins, her broken body no longer of any use.

Khthonios's tongue darted out and he fought the urge to recoil as she licked his blood from his skin with a purr. "Did you not enjoy the hunt, Boy? Did I not choose our toy well? Were you not satisfied?"

The dead woman's eyes stared at him, daring him to deem her unworthy.

"It was not the game board I disliked," he rasped through a voice growing more damaged with every year he spent collared and leashed to her side. "It was the game."

His insolence was met with pain but it was no less than he deserved for not being strong enough— powerful enough—to cleanse the world of Khthonios and her twisted games.

Hunger continued to pulse in his core, the blood of the dead woman having done little more than pull him from the depth of madness. He was still weak from the months of starvation he endured until Khthonios deemed him ready and placed the game board in the room with him, ordering her to stand bare and exposed and still against the wall, the sound of her thrumming pulse pounding in the silent cavern.

"You are mine, Boy," *Khthonios had whispered in his ear, letting him know the game they would play.* "Wholly mine."

The rules were simple: Khthonios was all he would see, all he would touch. Her body was his to worship as he'd been trained to do, to satisfy her every need. Should he pass her test, her vein would open under his fangs.

But the hunger had raged inside him, a beast he could no longer cage. The sound of a human heartbeat hammering in his ears could not be drowned out by moans of his creator. Khthonios's blood was not his to take at will. But the woman's...

He'd glanced at her. A single look up from between Khthonios's thighs was all it took to forfeit the woman's life, his weakness ensuring she would not live to see the sun rise.

The gentle graze of Lexie Grace's thumb along his lip hauled him from the ocean of guilt and fury threatening to breach his walls and consume him. He snapped back into the present where a warm body was pressed against his, trusting him to be the gentleman she thought he could be while the hisses and howls in his head reminded him this woman—this whisper of light and serenity—was not for him.

"Hey," she murmured sleepily as she touched one of his lengthened fangs with reverence. "Where did you go?"

Easing her up, he slid off the sofa, grabbed his box off the table, and walked to the front door where the boots Nichol's drone delivered last week were sitting on her shoe rack like they belonged there.

Lexie Grace's thoughts were foggy and uncertain but her footsteps were sure as she scampered to the laundry room and returned clutching his clean clothes in her arms. "Is everything okay?" she asked as he took the pile from her and dumped it into the box. "Boy, I—"

Her words died on her lips as she met his gaze.

Chapter Eleven

Lexie Grace sat on her rooftop and watched the sun set, her rifle at her side and a cup of tea in her hand as colors danced across the horizon and the last of the day's rays faded away. A slice of blue the color of Boy's eyes flashed along the skyline before darkening to a deep navy and she exhaled.

Vampiric irises were slightly ovaled, something televangelists pushed as a way to identify the supernatural beings before UV flashlights became all the rage. The first time she saw them, Boy's were exactly what she expected. The difference was subtle, one which registered deep in her lizard brain as something foreign and potentially dangerous, but not obvious enough to draw her attention for long. If anything, the elongation only added to his ethereal beauty, something she kept to herself because she suspected if she voiced it he would dodge her gaze more than he already did.

Except last night he hadn't. Moments before he disappeared into the night, he'd locked eyes with her and stared her down, challenge and vulnerability swirling behind cold detachment in the blue she swore was darker than it had been hours earlier.

The turmoil in his eyes didn't match the stoic mask he wore as he stood before her with his box in his hands and his fangs lying long on his bottom lip and she huffed in frustration as her mind refused to let it go.

It was like he was trying to show her something, trying to expose a piece of him he needed her to see. Except she couldn't break the code. If there even was one. He'd gone from playful and hesitant to ravenous and sweet only to end up tensing beneath her and bolting like a bat out of hell.

And she was not happy about it.

Was it her? Him? Them? Did he have some kind of vampire emergency? Because something had him hot-footing it out her front door and disappearing into the night without a second glance.

The last of the sunshine slipped into darkness. She set her tea down and lifted her rifle, locking her scope on the interloper approaching her property with his hands shoved deep in his pockets and his broad shoulders hunched. He looked up at her but made no move to stop, showed no fear of the weapon trained on him.

"Bold move for a man who left me high and not dry last night," she muttered to herself, lowering her rifle when he stopped under the motion sensor light and cocked a brow. "Right. You probably heard that with your super-senses."

She slung her gun over her shoulder, finished her tea, and hooked her finger in the handle before descending the trellis. Strong hands gripped her waist as she hit the final few feet. "Yeah, yeah," she grumbled, wishing she'd thought ahead to his possible arrival and put on something cuter than her ratty high school gym class shirt and yoga pants with zero sexy cling left in the fabric. "Such a gentleman."

Waking on the wrong side of the bed was

combining with PMS and his hot-and-cold behavior last night to make her cranky mood downright snarky. Stomping ahead to make sure he understood exactly how annoyed with life she was tonight, she flung the door open and shucked off her weapon. "Well? Come on in. I need one more cup of tea and then maybe I'll be up for playing with your friend's expensive toys."

The door closed quietly while she microwaved another cup of water and she heard him making his way around the house like he did last night, checking the security of every door and window before he joined her in the kitchen and silently watched her toss a teabag into her mug.

"Fair warning," she said as she opened a bag of cookies and took two out. "I'm in a mood. A big mood. And you're the only target for a hundred miles so if you have any sense of self-preservation, you'll walk out that door and return in six days."

His only response was to shrug as he pulled up a stool to the counter and sat down.

"Your funeral." She closed the bag, opened it, and took two more cookies out in case. "I'm a little surprised you came by tonight."

He took the pen and notebook she gave him weeks ago and jotted down a quick reply: *We have a date.*

Fixing him with a dead stare, she took a sip of her tea. "Why did you leave?"

His brows furrowed and he played with the pompom on the pen for a moment before scrawling his answer: *You scare me.*

****

Boy didn't know what Lexie Grace would read into his words, but he hoped she read the truth in them because it was all he could give her.

He'd spent the day debating the possibilities before narrowing them down to two: stay or go.

Leaving the area wasn't an option. Strategically, the Nevada Basin was an ideal battlefield to cut down the Deviants—Khthonios's army who were now tethered to him, bred to seek out the tainted blood running through his veins. The creatures knew nothing except hunger and mindless obedience to him. A hive hunting its king. He'd chosen the basin to make his stand because of the isolation, the unforgiving terrain, and the high ground overlooking the barren landscape. Prior to the American military stepping in, there were already very few humans in the region and it provided a freedom of movement he wouldn't have in a more populated area.

Of course, he didn't need to physically leave to separate from Lexie Grace. He'd avoided her before and could do it again. He could watch over her from afar to make sure none of his stumbling minions dared to bring her harm. He could continue to repair the buildings on her land and guard the perimeter from attack. He could detach himself from the thin thread linking her mind to his by allowing the voices of the Deviants and Tenders to rise up and drown her out. It was a viable option, one which would throw a wall up between him and her and keep her safe from the poison seeping into him through the cage in his core where Khthonios lay in wait.

We will be gods, and at our feet the mortals will lay down their arms and their lives.

His creator's words pounded through him like the drums of war, an ever-present call to step up to

Khthonios's final game board and play.

But Lexie Grace quieted everything when she was near and he wasn't strong enough to give up the peace she represented.

He liked her voice and craved it when it was gone. He missed it when she wasn't chattering away at his side or in his head. He liked the Tennessee twang in her accent and how much louder she got when she was excited. And he really liked the sounds she made when he kissed her and her thoughts became a jumbled mess.

So staying was truly his only option as long as he managed to keep his dead creator locked up where she belonged.

Glancing at her, he found Lexie Grace staring him down while she ate yet another cookie.

Bianca ate a lot of cookies. Molly, too. Audra didn't when anyone was around, but she snuck them in the middle of the day and quietly blamed it on Molly while adding more to the haunt's grocery list.

"I scare the Big Guy, hey?" Lexie Grace finally mused while she studied the treat in her hand. "Good. You should be afraid of me."

She turned to put the bag of cookies in the pantry and her mind lit up with a string of curses. He was on his feet in an instant, scanning her for injury while she dug her fist into her side and glowered up at him. "I'm fine."

This wasn't fine. None of it was. Not the pain etched across her face, not the way her body seemed to shrink in on itself, not her long exhale when she straightened up. Something was wrong and she didn't want him to know.

I can't believe I have to go through this for twenty

more years. This is stupid. I bet vampires don't get cramps. Unless they...oh God, what if you became a vampire during your period? Would you just bleed forever? I should ask him. No, I'm not asking that. He's a guy. What does he know about this? God, men are so lucky.

His rising panic was replaced with dread and a growing unease over the possibility she might ask the question still swirling in her mind. While Lexie Grace snatched the bag of cookies and went into the living room, he held back and wondered if the cell phones Nichol kept sending him would have Audra or Bianca's phone numbers so he could text them for advice before deciding doing so would open a Pandora's box of hell he wasn't ready to unleash.

"I'm not going drone hunting," she called to him from the sofa. "If you want this date, ya'll better plant your backside here, watch this movie with me, and tell me I'm pretty."

With orders he could follow, he tore a piece of paper from the notebook, wrote a message on it, then shoved the paper, book, and pen into the thigh pocket of his cargos before joining her on the sofa.

The movie started but he couldn't concentrate on the storyline. Lexie Grace was burrowed deep in the corner, curled into a ball with a blanket wrapped tight around her. She looked miserable despite her internal running commentary about a film she'd obviously watched often and enjoyed.

He wanted to fix it, wanted to take away her discomfort. And technically, he could. He could open his wrist as he'd done for hundreds of women who passed through the haunt under Rhys's tutelage. The healing properties of his blood would take away her pain and give her a temporary boost of energy. But it would also tether her to him. Her emotions would join her thoughts in his head. He would be able to find her anywhere.

Selfishly, it was a simple solution. He wouldn't have to be within pickup distance of her thoughts because her existence would be a constant in his mind. His body would be tuned into her night and day. More so.

And that was where the debate raged inside him.

He was snapped out of his deliberation by the rough handling of his arm as it was lifted in the air.

"Up."

Obeying, he waited for Lexie Grace to get comfortable with her head on his lap, her blanket tucked under her chin, and her knees drawn up to her chest. Once she stopped wiggling around, he draped his arm over her, contentment washing over him in a wave when she sighed and nuzzled against him.

The movie played on and she laughed a few times, her thoughts growing lighter as he stroked her hair.

He'd witnessed his hauntmates doing this very thing to their mates but never understood how their emotional streams could become so settled while their thoughts turned more and more explicit until they hit pornographic levels.

He got it now.

Playing with her hair was as soothing for her as it was for him. He liked the silken feel of it and the scent of her shampoo which strengthened with every pass of his fingers. The tension in her body lessened under the heavy blanket the longer he twirled and twisted her curls and he could practically hear a purr in his mind while she snuggled in tight to him. When she sighed and slipped one small hand out of the blanket and rested it on his thigh, he felt like a king.

And that's when he really understood his hauntmates in a way he never had before.

The moment her hand touched his thigh, his mind deviated far from the comfort his touch was providing and barreled down a track he knew he should stop but couldn't quite find the will.

Thoughts of those slim fingers sliding higher and unzipping his cargos took root and served as a launch point for his imagination. Those soft lips of hers were inches away from his cock and he thickened with the realization all it would take to feel her mouth on him was for her to turn her head and open his pants. In his mind, she would be eager to suck him, as enthusiastic to taste him as she was to kiss him. There would be no hesitation, no shyness. She would look up at him with those mischievous blue eyes and rake her nails down his chest before hollowing her cheeks and taking him deep.

A whine of displeasure drowned out the lull of the film's dialogue as Lexie Grace butted the back of her head against his stomach twice.

"Don't stop."

Noticing his hand had stilled mid-stroke, he resumed toying with the blonde locks under his hand.

The contented sigh returned and he fell straight back into his fantasy, this time wondering if he would hear that same sigh after he made her come. He could almost taste her on his tongue as he imagined burying his face between her smooth thighs, licking and sucking while she writhed beneath him and begged for more.

In his mind, she was as vocal during sex as she was with everything else and the thought made him uncomfortably hard. He wanted to hear her moan the first time he pushed inside her, wanted to feel her tug on his hair and claw at his back while he thrust into her until she screamed.

A giggle punctured through his fantasy and he snapped his gaze to the television to pretend he was at least partially paying attention while Lexie Grace rolled onto her back and looked up at him.

"Good movie?" she asked with a teasing tone.

Nodding, he tried to appear as relaxed as she was and continued to focus on the closing credits while she sat up and stretched. The blanket dropped to her waist and his eyes were drawn to the fullness of her breasts under the threadbare gray fabric. The visual did nothing to ease the pressure his cargos were putting on his hard-on, something he knew Lexie Grace had definitely noticed when her thoughts slammed into him.

Holy Mother Mary, it's even bigger than I thought. Is that a bat in your pocket or are you just happy to see me? Ha! He is definitely happy to see me. Exceptionally happy. Happy to the trillionth degree, judging from the size of that weapon. What would that even feel like? Probably a good thing I'm out of commission because that thing would break me in two. Maybe. But then again with the way he looks, I bet he knows how to wield that force of destruction like some kind of Orgasmatron God. There's probably a blog dedicated to his dick. I should check when the internet signal gets stronger. Oh hell, I'm staring. Maybe I wouldn't be if it wasn't so...big. It's his fault I'm staring. God, I want to wrap my hand around it and see if he's as thick as he looks.

No amount of willpower was going to bring his cock under control now, not when he just heard her thinking about touching him. This loss of command over his own body was foreign and he wasn't sure he liked it. Not since his early years with Khthonios had a woman managed to break past his discipline and make him hard unless he wanted—or needed—to be.

He'd mastered the ability to perform on demand long ago, but there was no demand here, no expectation or requirement. Nothing hung on the line if his body failed or, worse, reacted without permission.

Lexie Grace licked her lips and swallowed as she tore her gaze from his cock and looked up at him. "That is the biggest elephant in the room I've ever encountered. I don't know if I should be flattered or congratulate you on your superior genetics." He felt the corner of his lip quirk up and she grinned as she swung one leg over his lap and straddled him. "It's okay to smile. I'm a funny chick."

Easing a crumpled paper from his pocket, he passed it to her, pride swelling in his chest when she looked at his message and blushed. "*You're pretty*," she read with a happy sigh. "You listened. Thank you."

Her lips crushed against his and he grasped her hips as they rolled right where he needed the friction. Her tongue slid along his and she moaned softly, the sound imprinting itself in his memory instantly. She reached down and took his hand, breaking their kiss and watching his reaction as she slid his palm up her ribs to her breast. Her shameless permission had his pupils dilating with desire and need and he tried to arch his head back to avoid scaring her with the change he knew made him look almost feral.

"Don't," she whispered, nipping at his jaw and using her gentle touch to force him to look at her. "You have no idea how hot it is to see—" She swiveled her hips. "—and feel how turned on you are right now. Even if you aren't getting squat tonight."

Six nights. Just gotta pay six nights of penance and then this big guy is going down. Hopefully literally.

How she managed to laugh in her head and whimper against his throat while he cupped her breast and grazed her nipple with his thumb, he couldn't even begin to guess. Women never laughed when they thought about him. Even those with the single-minded focus of fucking him for reputation, curiosity, or with the aim of worming their way into the most powerful vampire haunt around through association carried a healthy amount of fear when they looked at him. Audra and Bianca teased him, but even they didn't associate any kind of happiness with him. Simone and Molly remained wary. Harper acted like a mother hen. But none of them had Lexie Grace's playfulness in their minds when they considered him.

A warm tongue teased the tip of his fang and his hips jerked.

I'm the most powerful woman on Earth.

Her thoughts spurred him on and he reached under her shirt, desperate to feel her soft skin while she took full advantage of the link between his fangs and his cock. Her hunger for him fed his own, the knowledge this was as far as she would let them go right now more seductive than had she stripped down and pleaded for him. Anticipation of what might be in store for him in six nights was as powerful an aphrodisiac as the scent of her arousal and the sound of her panting breaths when he ground his erection into her center.

But just as he pushed the cup of her bra down and his hand made contact with her bare skin, Khthonios's voice crept into his mind.

No, honey. I *am the most powerful woman on Earth. You're nothing more than a dead woman walking.*

Chapter Twelve

Lexie Grace felt two strong arms wrap around her and grip the handles of her motorbike before she felt the skidding of her back tire across the desert sand.

"Oh, so now you want to drive?" she called to Boy over her shoulder as he continued to steer them in a series of loops across the previously untouched ground. "Are we sending an SOS or a BYOB?"

The last five nights had been amazing and tonight was no different. For a woman and a vampire left alone in the middle of nowhere, she and Boy managed to find more than enough to do once the sun set and he arrived at her doorstep with his hands in his pockets and his head cocked to listen for sounds her regular human hearing couldn't detect. Between movies, drone hunting, a few zombie kills, and nightly make-out sessions which left her hungry for more, they were making the most of their odd situation.

The angry drone operator had kept his expensive equipment away since they used one for target practice two nights ago. From a low ledge on the mountain range, Boy had shown her how to choose the best rocks, where to aim, and coached her from grip to execution. His patience culminated in her striking the speaker mechanism on the drone and silencing the furious cursing which was amplified with each hit the tech took before being knocked speechless.

Judging by the kiss he laid on her after, Boy was impressed with her aim and more than a little happy she shut his friend up.

He steered them across the basin for a few more minutes before he worked his feet under hers, took complete control of the bike, and drove them to the base of the mountain range. He brought them to a stop, gestured up, and Lexie Grace laughed in disbelief.

"Yeah, no," she stated as he dismounted and held out his hand to her. "You go on up and wave to me when you get there."

He knelt down and offered her his back.

"I will die." When he simply shook his head, she sighed. "Fine. But if I die, I'm holding you solely responsible, so promise me I'll survive."

He nodded solemnly and within minutes, she had to admit she was impressed with how easily he was crawling up the side of a mountain with her on his back. She could feel every flex of his muscles while she clung to him like a spider monkey. And the vise grip her thighs had on his waist was more of a turn on than she thought possible while scaling a mountain.

She was almost sad she hadn't stayed on the ground for the sole purpose of freely admiring him.

When they reached the top, he knelt down just inside the mouth of a cave she hadn't seen from below and steadied her as she climbed off of him. He pointed to the ground far below and she inched onto the ledge, laughing when she saw the message he wrote with the motorbike.

"Suck this, Nicky," she read, immediately imagining the reaction of the drone operator when he came back through the area. "So Nicky is the guy with the foul mouth, hey?"

He nodded and she caught another upturn of his lips before he schooled his expression and led her back inside the cave where the moon's glow barely permeated. She took her small flashlight out of the ammo bag strapped across her chest, flicked it on, and scanned the entrance.

"Wow," she murmured, taking a few careful steps. "So this is where you hide from me."

The cave was a fascinating glimpse into his life when he wasn't with her. He led her deep inside where the sun wouldn't breach during daylight hours to a spot where boxes of clothes, unused phones, and knives of all shapes and lengths were piled in one corner and a disassembled drone was laid out in another.

She'd suspected he hid out in the mountains, but seeing it up close made her heart hurt.

"Where do you sleep?" she asked, noticing there was no bed, no nest, no soft anything indicating he rested here.

He pointed to the rock under their feet and she narrowed her eyes. "On stone. You sleep on stone." Her lips pursed as she imagined him lying here all day, waiting for the sun to set so he could set foot outside. "Why didn't you tell me? I have a guest bedroom, you know. And pillows."

He shrugged, beckoned her over to the corner where the boxes were stacked haphazardly, and pulled out a ragged coil notepad. He hesitated a moment before he handed it to her and backed away immediately.

Frowning as she glanced around the cold cave, she opened the notebook, read the first line, and looked up at him. "This is about you, isn't it? All your cool little vampire secrets?"

He nodded, bowed his head a fraction, and angled his face away from the flashlight.

She flipped through a few of the worn pages gingerly to avoid damaging them, excitement building when she realized there were stories scattered amid drawings, crude maps, and fresh notes jotted in the margins.

Closing the book, she clutched it tight to her chest. "Huge mistake, Big Guy. Two minutes ago, I was planning on luring you to my humble abode to seduce you. Now I'm demanding you take me home so I can read this immediately."

****

From the moment Boy opened Nichol's latest box drop and found his notebook inside, he'd debated whether or not he was going to give it to Lexie Grace to read. Knowing Nichol wouldn't violate his privacy by reading through an old, dirt-stained notepad, he'd asked his hauntmate to find it among the few items Boy kept in his room down in the former bloodslave quarters.

To the untrained eye, it was nothing more than a collection of memories. The details were vague, the timelines undeterminable, and the names written in a code only he knew. But with a few clarifying notes made while he waited out the setting of the sun, he turned it into something he hoped Lexie Grace would enjoy.

Unlike some of his other books which contained his own version of encrypted reports of alliances, shifts in vampire politics over time, and maps of bolt holes across Europe and North America, this one was filled with anecdotes about his hauntmates.

Lexie Grace was becoming more and more open with him, sharing selective memories of her childhood and her life back in Tennessee before she came to Nevada to help her grandparents during their twilight years. But it was the things she didn't tell him with her voice that made his decision for him.

For every cute tale she told about the shenanigans she got up to in her youth were a dozen stories she didn't speak out loud, each spiking his anger and bloodlust higher and higher until the whole of the male Tennessee population was in his sights. It took all his control not to react whenever she thought about the men who hurt her, who used her and tossed her aside. Every one had a name and a crime he committed to memory, and the desire to leave Nevada and track them down one by one was strong.

With her history in his mind, he made the decision to give her some of the stories he couldn't speak.

She clung to him while he drove them back to her home on her motorbike, his journal tucked safely inside her bag and her hands splayed across his abs. He could feel the heat of her body through her thin black tank top and the jean shorts which gave him a glimpse of her ass every time she moved.

He liked those shorts. A lot.

He locked her bike up beside the house, followed her inside, and completed his security assessment while she made herself a snack and a cup of tea. Once she was ready, she patted the sofa and he sat, amused when she ordered him to sit in such a way that she was able to recline against his chest and use his thigh as an armrest.

"If you aren't comfortable, now's the time to say

something because once I start reading, I'm not stopping," she warned, her thoughts letting him know she was as serious as serious could get. "And yes, I know you don't speak, so that should tell you just how much I don't want you to move."

He wasn't going anywhere. Her hair tickled his nose and her elbow was digging into his ribs, but she was right. He slept on stone. Having a pretty woman lying on him thinking nice things was not the worst situation he'd been in recently. He'd never had someone so comfortable with him they didn't want him to leave, someone who fought Deviants at his side one minute and kissed him senseless the next.

She was quiet for the first few pages as she read the myths and truths about vampires. Although she didn't have any negative impressions of vamps, she had so little knowledge about them he wondered if she would feel different once she knew more. She was fascinated by the haunt structure and seemed to like the idea of vampires taking on the names of their creators as a kind of family name. The existence of Tenders who were trained by Rhys Kaius and purchased by vampires looking for a companion elicited a hum of disapproval and she was annoyed to discover the creatures she called zombies were actually vampire turnings gone wrong, but it was his note about age rings which really caught her attention.

"Hey," she said, swatting at his leg. "Lift."

To the human eye, his age rings would look like little more than a thick, gray band running up the length of his calf. Exposing it would mean nothing to her, but after spending most of his existence hiding the truth, the thought of willingly showing anyone his rings had him on edge.

Not even his hauntmates knew his true age. With age came strength and speed. Rumors of increased abilities flitted through haunts with few vampires living long enough to discover the truth for themselves. His kind did not fear much, but ancients were on most lists and he was as ancient as it got.

Stretching his senses to reassure himself there was no vamp, human, or drone in the vicinity who could burst in while he revealed his secret, he reached down and hiked the hem of his cargo pants up to his knee.

Lexie Grace trailed her hands along the bandages for a moment before speaking. "May I?"

He nodded, his shoulders tensing as she unwound the gauze with the delicacy of a woman unwrapping fine china. Layer by layer, his rings were made visible until the last of the thin fabric was set aside and he felt her fingers skimming the gray lines.

"They're like tattoos," she mused, grinning when his calf muscle twitched and flexed under her touch while she counted them. "So you're fifty."

He paused.

His ability to hear the thoughts of others had been a part of him for so long, he rarely considered it anymore. The incessant commotion in his head was little more than a deafening white noise with a few voices breaking through periodically to ensure he didn't get too comfortable with the constant hum.

But Lexie Grace broke through every time. He heard everything running through her mind no matter how hard he tried to give her the privacy she deserved. His ability created an unfair balance between them, one he was increasingly uneasy about. It was the reason he wanted her to read his notebook, so he could give her a fraction of what she gave him, both intentionally and unintentionally.

Leaning over to the old wooden coffee table, he grabbed a pencil and wrapped his arms around her so he could reach the notebook and make a quick note. Putting the pencil back on the table, he sat back while her thoughts went completely silent.

"You're fucking with me." She arched her neck to look at him. "Right?"

He shook his head, thrown by the quiet coming off her mind and almost reeling when she came online again in a blast of curses in her sweet Tennessee twang.

"There is no way. That is so cool! How does that even work? You must have been everywhere. Wow, you've probably seen everything, haven't you? Is it some kind of cryogenic thing where you were frozen up in the arctic and thawed out with global warming?" she asked in a rush so quick he struggled to figure out which questions were coming from her mouth and which were hollering inside his mind. "What do you even *do* for five thousand years? I can't believe I told you I was bored watching reruns. Everything is probably a rerun for you. Oh God, you poor thing. Thousands of years of listening to the same small talk must have absolutely destroyed your soul."

It wasn't the small talk which destroyed it, but he nodded with a small smile as he grabbed the pencil and scribbled a reply: *I'm good at surviving. Never been frozen. Spent a lot of it walking. Can't stand small talk. The weather is the weather, politics are always shifting, and I'm usually fine.*

She read it and grinned. "I'm gonna ask you a

million questions when I'm not in shock."

Settling against him again, she passed him the TV remote and went back to reading from his journal while he found a true crime documentary series to distract himself by how much he liked having her lie on him and learn a few of his secrets.

Chapter Thirteen

Boy followed the path of the familiar scent deep into the woods, slowing his approach when he spotted his target crawling on his belly across the forest floor. A plump rabbit crouched in the distance, illuminated by the light of the full moon which broke through the trees overhead. The man was near silent as he inched within reach and snatched the hare mid-jump when it finally realized a predator was closing in.

The human stood with his prize and turned to face him with a smile. "I wasn't expecting you again so soon. How are you, friend?"

"I am well, thank you," Boy replied as he remained in the shadows cast by the pines. "And you? Your strength is good?"

Tying the rabbit to his belt, Kaius nodded and ran his hands over the four animals secured to his waist. "It is. Have you time to join me at the fire?"

With a nod, he followed Kaius through the thickets into the large clearing where a fire was burning low to its embers in a stone pit. A log had been dragged beside the flames for sitting and a bed of forest brush was gathered close enough for warmth but not too near as to ignite.

Kaius was quick to skin his hunts, his mind consumed with the precision of the methodical task. "Are you traveling to Athens as well?"

Boy eased his blade from its rawhide binding and set about whittling a wooden spear strong enough to support the weight of the hare. "What is it you seek in Athens which you cannot find elsewhere?"

"Knowledge. Art. Tutelage. I want to know how much I have yet to learn." Kaius chuckled and examined his handiwork. "Do you not want more than forests and fields? To know more than this struggle for warmth and food?"

Passing the spear over, he sat on the log and stared at the fire while Kaius prepared the hare to cook.

He'd been drawn to Kaius the moment he heard the newborn's cries carry on the winds twenty-four summers ago. Tossed aside by Khthonios after being forced to serve for two millennia at her heel, he'd wandered alone for centuries, unbound, untethered, and unleashed. As long as he forced his creator's parting words from his mind, he was free to feed and fuck and fight without care or restraint.

And then he heard the baby's cry and the nearly imperceptible tremor in its heartbeat.

Creeping into the family home in the dead of night, he fed the infant drops of his blood and listened as the tiny heart strengthened. He stayed close for several passes of the full moon, his ear tuned in to the thrum of the baby's pulse and his blood ready to spill the night the tremor returned.

And so it went. The baby grew strong and Boy remained near. He watched Kaius become an impetuous child without fear and later a youth with an eye for a bow, a head for strategy, and a reputation with the pretty women who gathered in the center of town and watched him with stars in their eyes.

It was during Kaius's nineteenth year that Boy realized he couldn't keep Kaius's damaged heart beating forever. The child had grown into a man, one too tall, too strong, and too active for his weak heart to support. For the next five years, Kaius traveled from the town in search of traders and teachers who would share knowledge and tales of lands he was desperate to visit. Much to the dismay of his mother and father who wished their son to marry, Kaius's wanderlust grew with every story he heard and it wasn't long before he was disappearing for days on end.

Boy tracked him every time, his persistence paying off three nights ago when Kaius's heart finally gave up. Three drops turned to twenty and the stubborn organ resumed its beat.

The man would not live to see his next summer.

"I'll be traveling south toward Athens in the morning if you care to accompany me," Kaius announced as the scent of charred meat filled the air. "The journey will be long but if we make it, it will be worth every step we take to stand in the Acropolis and listen to the orators I've been told speak of ideas which stretch the mind and stir the blood."

The steady heartbeat stuttered and Boy made his move, silently promising Kaius he would indeed stand in the Acropolis while he drained Kaius's body dry of blood, filled it with his own, and fell to his knees as Khthonios screamed her fury inside his mind.

Boy stared at the scorpion moving across the floor of the cave while the echoes of his creator's howl reverberated in his memories.

This was why he left the sweet scent of Lexie

Grace's home before dawn, why he slipped out from under her soft, sleeping form, set the locks best he could, and snuck out the door. He knew sharing his journal would stir things he'd long kept buried and he didn't want thoughts of Khthonios to haunt his time with her any more than it already did. Be it his own fears, his own failings, or his own guilt, his creator's voice was growing louder. What were once whispers were now poisonous murmurs from deep in his core. His memories of Khthonios were mixing with the present to warp his perceptions and distract him more than Lexie Grace herself.

A Deviant surge was inevitable within the month. He could hear them creeping closer in his head, the few early stragglers a warning of what was to come. Nichol's drones tracked both the movement of the horde and that of the military barricading the region under orders to allow only the Deviants in and no one out.

His army was coming for him, marching to the beat Khthonios set in motion the night he chose Kaius over her. He could hear it, could feel the tempo increasing with every passing night.

It was a warning carried in the blood of her soldiers, one he had no intention of heeding.

The sun started to dip below the horizon and he scratched absently at his throat. He brought his boot down on the scorpion before leaving the isolation of his cave for the only place where he'd ever felt welcome.

****

Lexie Grace trained her scope on the lurching figure stumbling closer across the dark terrain, then sighed in annoyance when the creature's head was ripped from its body before she could pull the trigger.

"I had that one," she called out to Boy as he tossed the head aside and stalked toward her. "You're late, old man."

He looked positively lethal in his cargo pants hanging low on his slim hips and his black singlet showing off every sculpted muscle along his arms. Something about his prowling gait had her thighs clenching in anticipation and she bit her lip.

I'm going to jump him right here, right now. I'm gonna climb that silent hunk of sex-on-a-stick like a tree and fuck him until he forgets any other woman ever existed because damn. *Damn, damn, damn. And then I'm gonna give him a tongue lashing for sneaking out this morning. And* then *I'll ask all my questions. But first, I'm gonna ride that bronco until he's purring like a kitten.*

He flung the gate open, rinsed his blood-soaked hand in the wash basin she kept fresh beside the cattle feed, and dipped her low as he kissed her senseless.

With her balance righted by his hands at her waist, she gave him a lopsided grin. "You still stole my kill."

Taking her hand, he all but dragged her through her front door. He paused long enough to secure the locks and prop her rifle against the wall before he was on her again, plunging his tongue into her mouth like he was staking claim.

"Whoa," she gasped when he hiked her up and her legs wrapped instinctively around his hips. "Don't drop me."

He lifted his head from her throat, his blue eyes dark with desire when he met her gaze with a look she read as 'seriously?'

"Yeah, buddy. Don't drop me. I'm a valuable commodity out here."

She caught a glimpse of a smirk as he pushed her up against the wall and adjusted his hold on her, palming her ass with one hand and sliding the other under her pink 'Obey the Queen' tank top. His thumb teased her nipple and she arched into his hand, exposing her throat. She felt the light scratch of his fangs as his tongue trailed along her jugular and her breath caught in anticipation.

The whole biting thing hadn't crossed her mind since the night she informed him he wouldn't be using her as his own personal juice box. Boy's fangs were simply a part of him, one small piece of the guy she was falling for hard and fast. Some would say she was foolish to trust his unspoken word long before she knew anything about him. Except, even then, she'd known he wouldn't push past the boundary she set.

But this was different. So, so different. She wanted to feel his fangs sink into her vein while he pounded her into the wainscoting. She wanted to feel him lose control and know it was because of her. She wanted him to be as desperate to explore every inch of her as she was to taste every inch of him. And she wanted to know how it felt to have her body and her blood taken by this pretty, dangerous vamp who decapitated zombies one minute and played with her hair the next.

A low rumble filled the room and he stilled, his shoulders tensing under her hand.

"What is that?" she whispered, clinging to him a little tighter as thoughts of zombies crashing through the walls danced in her head. When he remained eerily motionless, her heart stopped thumping with desire and started pounding in fear. "Boy?"

He closed his eyes and she swore she saw him exhale as he lowered her to the floor, straightened her bra straps, and shoved his hands through his hair. He looked to the ceiling for a moment and this time he definitely took a deep breath, something she knew damn well vampires didn't have to do.

"Boy," she repeated as she wrapped her arms around herself. "What's going on? What's that sound?"

He seemed to be debating his response while he shifted his attention to the living room and glared at the sofa like it was insulting his mother. His eyes were even darker than before, his pupils dilated to the point where the blue surrounding them was barely visible.

Bouncing on her heels nervously, she licked her lips. "It's getting louder," she stated, glancing at the locked door and wondering how close the sound was if it felt like it was in there with them. "If something is freaking your five-thousand-year-old ass out, I'm guessing I should be panicking, too. Which is good. Because I am."

Chapter Fourteen

Boy knew precisely what the sound rumbling through Lexie Grace's home was. He also knew it was more dangerous than whatever monsters she thought were lurking outside.

She was watching him with a mixture of fear and curiosity as he attempted to make peace with what was happening. The fact he was breathing, something he hadn't done in over five millennia, was freaking her out.

It was freaking him out too. Not as much as the low growl emanating from his chest, but enough to make him seriously consider reaching out to Nichol Kaius for help.

Before Lexie Grace remembered she had a fully loaded rifle propped beside her and wanted to hunt down the source of the sound, he took her hand and led her to the sofa. He grabbed his journal and the pencil from the table, sat, and dragged her down with him.

"Should we call for help?" she asked, settling her back against his chest like she trusted him to be on alert even while planted on the couch. "It's so loud I swear whatever is making that sound is in here."

His hand shook as he scribbled his response: *It is. It's me.*

She read his reply and twisted around to look at him. "What do you mean, it's you. It's not—" She placed her hand on his chest and he knew the moment she felt the vibration. "Well what do you know. It is you. Why are you purring?"

I'm not purring, he wrote with a frown. *It's a vampire thing.*

"I've never read about vampires purring. Is it some kind of warning signal of impending danger? Or, like, a horniness thing?"

Staring at the paper, he exhaled and jotted the simplest explanation. *It's vampire for "I really like you."*

Technically, he was being truthful. But she was also spot on. The growl was possessive, an alert to every vampire in the vicinity that Lexie Grace was claimed by a male and therefore off-limits. A holdover from their ancient roots, it was an involuntary symbol of ownership, one he recognized instinctively when he heard it from his hauntmates.

He had never made the sound. Not until tonight with the woman who had him shucking off the future he was bred to have in favor of wherever this—whatever *this* was—led.

She laid her head down and traced circles on his chest. "You're totally purring. I love it." Arching her head up, she smiled. "If I could purr, you would be the only guy who could make me do it."

And that was it.

There was no panic from her, no discomfort. All he picked up were contented thoughts as she grabbed the television remote, rolled onto her back, and snuggled against him while she flipped through the few grainy stations her signal was picking up.

While she settled on an action film he recognized

from one of the Kaius haunt's movie nights, he tried to relax and not think about the complications this new development would cause.

Being attracted to a woman was one thing. Having his core recognize her as his mate was a whole other game he was completely unprepared to play.

Except when she reached back and slid her hand behind the nape of his neck, he couldn't find it in himself to care. Her fingers looped around his hair, his cock twitched, and he decided he would mull over the rules and consequences in the morning while he lay alone in his cave, far from Lexie Grace and her gentle touch.

Dropping his journal and the pencil to the floor, he mimicked her movements and twirled her hair, pressing his hips into the curve of her ass when she sighed.

He loved that sound. Paired with the sound of his claim over her, it unleashed something inside him and he knew he wanted everything Lexie Grace would give him.

Taking his time to revel at the softness of her skin, he stroked his fingers along her jaw, mesmerized by the curve of her face and the way she turned into his touch. Her lips parted when he grazed the pad of his thumb across them and he slipped it into her mouth, swallowing hard when she flicked her tongue over it before sucking the tip.

He was hard as steel in an instant. Lolling his head back, he closed his eyes and enjoyed the sensation of her lips wrapped tight around his thumb until it wasn't enough. Opening his eyes, he inched the neckline of her tank top down with his other hand until the fabric caught beneath her breasts and put them and her bright pink bra on display. He trailed his fingers over the swells, keeping his touch soft as she arched her back and moaned around his thumb still caught between her lips and teeth.

Her impatience was broadcasting loud and clear and it both amused him and turned him on. Much like her thoughts when she watched him cross the barren desert with Deviant blood staining his hands, her desire was fueling his own and it was taking all his control not to flip her onto her hands and knees and drive into her until she screamed.

But instead of fucking her senseless on the floor like a beast in heat, he focused his attention on seducing her. He brushed his fingertips along the black lace trim of her bra and she shivered, her nipples pebbling into tight buds he exposed slowly as he pushed the cups of her bra down.

His cock was desperate for friction he refused to give it. This wasn't about him. Not right now. Right now, he wanted to learn every secret of her body, wanted to figure out what she liked, what she loved, and what made her thighs clench as she moaned and writhed under his hands.

It didn't take him long to discover she loved a hint of pain, quick pinches soothed with gentle grazes and soft touches. Her breathing became more labored and she released her sucking hold on his thumb, freeing both of his hands to tease her nipples while her grip on his hair tightened. The scent of her arousal had him rocking his hips while she ground her ass against his length. Her pulse was thrumming and his fangs ached to sink into her jugular and taste the sweet B-negative blood flowing through her veins.

He slid his hands down her body, reached the band of her jeans, and flicked the button open. Her breathing hitched as he inched the zipper down before he gripped her waist and repositioned her high enough along his body for him to ease her pants off her body. From this angle, he had a perfect view of his hands as he splayed them across her inner thighs and nudged them open for him. He took his time skimming along her smooth skin, refusing to give in every time she lifted her hips and tried to lure his fingers to the bright pink lace covering her promised land.

Her thoughts were addicting while he continued to tease her. She lost most of her words, thinking in the same hoarse moans and breathy exclamations that were coming from her lips. It gave him a feeling of power he didn't realize he wanted, the ability to make her mindless with sensation and emotion.

He wanted more.

Her skin was flushed, her breathing shallow. With a feather touch, he grazed the thin lace at the juncture of her thighs and she whimpered, both of her arms now reaching back to wrap around his neck. The shift pushed her breasts up like a gift he couldn't resist. Keeping one hand ghosting across the lace, he returned his other one to her taut nipple and pinched, eliciting another groan from her.

"Please," she finally gasped as her hips lifted, seeking the release he was priming her body for. "Boy, please."

All intentions of drawing out her anticipation longer evaporated when his name fell from her lips and he slid his hand under the lace to find her wet and ready. At this angle, he was in the perfect position to ease two fingers inside her while he sought out her clit with his thumb. Her head lolled against his shoulder as he crooked his fingers and found that spot inside her that would drive her wild.

With her nails digging into the back of his neck, he increased his pressure and speed while her body tensed and he felt the first flutters of her orgasm.

"Oh fuck, *yes!*" she groaned as she fell over the edge, completely at his mercy.

He wrapped one arm around her to hold her in place while he continued his assault, drawing a second orgasm from her before she could catch her breath. Her nails drew blood as she clawed at him and his fangs lengthened, the combined scents of his blood and her arousal threatening his impeccable control.

He had nothing to anchor him. All he could hear were her gasps and moans. He was engulfed by the heat of her body writhing atop him. Unable to look away from the sight of her spread out for him and his fingers inside her, he was wholly consumed by the need to take her, to claim her. The possessive rumble in his chest returned and he had neither the desire nor the strength to fight it as her orgasm subsided and she sighed, her ass pressing against his cock as she arched her back and stretched.

****

If anyone should be purring, it's me, Lexie Grace thought while she toed her jeans completely off and twisted leisurely to lie face to face with the guy who sent her to the moon and back twice.

She knew her hair was a wild mess and what was left of her clothes was tangled and skewed, but something about a solid hour of teasing followed by two mind-blowing orgasms had her not caring. Feeling bold now that she was no longer a tense, unsatisfied disaster, she slid her hand down Boy's muscled chest and abs until she reached the band of his cargos. Without hesitating, she popped the button, eased the zipper down, and trailed her fingers down the thick length she'd felt pressing into her while he played her body like a maestro.

His hips jerked and she smiled up at him, meeting his blackened gaze. "Turnaround is fair game," she warned as she slipped her hand inside his boxers and grazed her nails over his velvet shaft. "Do you think you could hold out for an hour, too?"

He didn't blink. Didn't look away. He simply licked his lips and stared at her with the intensity of a predator cornering his prey.

Provoking a hunter was a dangerous game, one she wasn't sure she even cared to win. If he won and he managed to control the throbbing beast between his legs for sixty minutes, she'd have a full hour to explore every inch of the gorgeous specimen laying beneath her before he fucked her hard.

If she lost, she would just be fucked hard.

Decisions, decisions.

The slight silver shimmer of his fangs caught her attention and she leaned in closer to flick her tongue across one while she continued to tease his cock with the faintest of touches. No sooner did she feel the cool enamel on her warm tongue when she found herself air born and slung over a broad shoulder.

Boy moved through her small home on a mission. He threw her bedroom door open and tossed her on the bed, his eyes completely black as he grabbed his shirt from the back and hauled it off, giving her an eyeful of chiseled perfection as he stalked toward her.

The primal need to escape kicked in and she scrambled backward before he caught her ankles and tugged her down the mattress. He hooked his finger in the band of her underwear, dragged them off, tossed them aside, and stilled as he appraised her.

Her heart was pounding under his scrutiny and the low rumble still coming from him. His hunger was a palpable force in her tiny bedroom and she was caught between feeding it or running, her decision made when his gaze met hers and she saw reverence behind the desire. Reaching back, she undid her bra and slid it off her arms, watching him as he tracked her movements. Her tank top was last to go, the fabric bunched around her ribs until she pushed it down her hips and over her thighs, her nerves settling when he took over. With a careful grasp, he slipped her shirt off and hitched her legs over his shoulders as he knelt down and kissed his way from her inner thighs to her pussy.

The growl grew louder with the first swipe of his tongue and she moaned as the vibrations hit her and moved like ripples through her body. Bracing herself to come hard and fast, she tensed in anticipation of being devoured only to find Boy had other plans.

Despite the ravenous lust pulsing off him, he ate her out leisurely as though he had all the time in the world. He kissed and licked and nipped, bringing her close to the edge over and over until she was begging him, her thighs quivering in his hands.

"I can't," she moaned as he built her up again, his tongue deep inside her. "Oh God, Boy, please. I need you."

And she did. She was aching for him to fill her, desperate to feel him push in and seek the same release he was denying her. Her fingers tangled in his hair and she pulled hard until he looked up. The sight of him watching her from between her legs was one she would be using the next time she broke out her trusty vibrator for a quick stress reduction. And the next. And every time until she died.

He scratched his fangs against the soft, sensitive skin of her inner thigh and stood. Not wanting to miss the show, she pushed herself up on her elbows and licked her lips as he shoved his cargos off of his slim hips slowly, unveiling his drool-worthy V-cut one inch at a time. His boxers were next and she inhaled sharply with the realization she was moments away from being impaled.

Seeing half a glimpse of it from afar all those weeks ago had been one thing, but coming face-to-cock was a whole new ballgame. The guy was armed with a weapon of mass destruction and she was both terrified and hungry for it.

He wrapped his fingers around his length and stroked it, forcing her to choose between watching his abs tense every time his hips flexed, gaping at the muscles moving along his forearm, or staring at the monster in his hand. Her mouth watered with the thought of taking him between her lips and she sat up, holding his gaze while she sank to the floor in front of him.

His jaw flexed as she reached for his cock and he relinquished control. It was heavy and hot in her hand while she ran her thumb across the head. She flattened her tongue and licked him from base to tip before taking him in her mouth and moaning around him when he shuddered.

Blow jobs were never something she enjoyed. They were either coerced, expected, or the easiest way to calm a raging boyfriend. But kneeling before Boy while he threaded his fingers through her hair and watched her pleasure him made her feel powerful. He was enthralled by her every move, every swipe of her tongue and graze of her teeth. What she couldn't take in her mouth she grasped in her hand, stroking him in time with the shallow thrusts of his hips and the swirling of her tongue.

She knew he was fighting to maintain his control and it amped her need to see him come undone. His muscles flexed and bunched and a slight tremor rippled through them every time she hollowed out her cheeks and sucked. His cock twitched and he tugged gently on her hair, urging her to release him.

Her confusion over being stopped was short-lived when he lifted her by the waist and kissed her while her legs wrapped around him. With his lips on hers, he lowered her to the bed, slid his hand between her legs, and sank two fingers inside her. He added a third, stretching and preparing her to take him before he lined his cock up with her entrance and hesitated.

"I want this," she reassured him as she caressed his broad shoulders. "I *need* this."

The color of his eyes shifted from black to his mesmerizing blue for a moment before the onyx returned and he pushed inside her, giving her body time to adjust bit by bit until he was fully sheathed in her heat.

She'd never felt this full or this connected. He

caged her between his arms and his head dropped forward as he held his position deep in her body. His chest was rising and falling as he breathed, something he only did when he seemed to be centering himself. She grazed her fingers along the back of his neck and he closed his eyes. His hips moved with long, deliberate strokes at a pace so slow she didn't feel her orgasm building until she was on the cusp.

She gripped his biceps and felt them tremble under her touch as her body lit up beneath him. Crying out his name, she arched as he grabbed her hands and held them above her head, his fingers lacing with hers while he continued to move inside her with those agonizingly measured thrusts. As she came down, her chest heaving, he shifted his angle and the build started again.

"I can't," she moaned, her head thrashing. "Oh God, Boy, I can't."

He paused, lifted his head, and looked down at her with a smirk.

A *smirk.*

Capturing both her hands in one of his, he sat back on his haunches and pulled her along with him so she was straddling him. He draped her arms over his shoulders and rested his forehead on hers, never breaking the hold his gaze had over her.

The change in position splayed her thighs and allowed him to push even deeper inside her, filling her more than she'd known was possible. He kept their bodies still, one hand on her waist and the other tracing her jaw with a feather touch while her body clenched around him.

His blackened eyes saw her and only her. His hips started to move at the same leisurely pace and her lids fluttered shut with the new sensations. He was worshipping her, erasing every man before him and ruining her for anyone after him. Everything he couldn't say was spoken in each graze of his hands, nuzzle of her neck, and push of his cock inside her.

The build came faster with the intimacy of their position and her body started to tighten as Boy increased the tempo of his thrusts until his hips were snapping up against hers at a punishing speed. She clawed at his back and the low rumble in his chest became almost deafening. Arching her head back, she offered him her throat as a blinding orgasm took over her thoughts and body.

His fangs sank in with barely a pinch and she cried out as his rhythm faltered and he came inside her. The sensation of feeding him while he filled her was almost too much and she whimpered as she clung to him and rode out her orgasm. The tremors wracking his body eased and he wrapped his strong arms tight around her.

He lapped at the puncture wounds on her neck before he laid her down and pulled her blanket over them, keeping her caged and warm in his embrace. She drifted off, smiling with the knowledge she'd never felt safer or more protected than she did with an alpha predator playing the big spoon to her little.

Chapter Fifteen

Boy took one last look at Lexie Grace sleeping peacefully in her bed and slipped from her room.

No matter how badly he wanted to stay, it was too dangerous to do so while Khthonios was raging in his core. Her furious shrieks reverberated in his head, drowning out every other voice and forcing him to focus on her and her alone.

He set two of the locks on Lexie Grace's door and took off across the barren terrain. The first rays of the sun licked his heels as he reached his cave in the mountainside and he crawled as deep as he could to ensure Nichol's drones didn't spot him. Then he slumped against the rough stone wall and shoved his hands through his hair.

There was no escaping what he just did. The ghost of Lexie Grace's fingers trailing down his arms was burned into his memory. Her scent covered him. His body was marked by her nails and the sounds of her moaning and pleading and gasping in pleasure echoed in the silent cave.

But above it all was the madness of his creator howling her vows of retribution for his betrayal.

Sinking to the floor of the cavern, he stared at the boxes piled in the corner.

There was too much darkness, too much poison pumping through his veins. Khthonios was alive inside him and growing stronger. He could feel her testing the cage where he fought to keep her locked away from his hauntmates, his sanity, and—now—from Lexie Grace.

Making love to her was a mistake, one he couldn't come back from. Twelve hours ago, he could have walked away and Khthonios would be none the wiser, wouldn't know the loud woman with the bright eyes managed to capture what his creator never could. Twelve hours ago, the lies he told himself were also keeping Khthonios at bay, lumping Lexie Grace in with Audra and Bianca and the handful of other women throughout the centuries who showed him a little kindness and earned a sliver of gratitude and appreciation.

And twelve hours ago, even he believed he could leave.

His creator's screams came to a sudden halt and he draped his arms over his knees and lolled his head against the stone as her whispers slithered through his thoughts.

With Kaius thrashing and snarling in his arms, he followed the call of Khthonios's blood deeper into the woodland where a single cottage sat in a clearing. The yellow blossoms along the path were deceptively cheerful, masking the depravity he could smell through the thin mud walls. The door opened and he tightened his hold on his cargo.

"The dog returns," Khthonios purred as she stepped over the threshold. "And he comes bearing the gift of a bastard mongrel."

Kaius's fangs snapped at Boy's throat, his body contorting with the raging hunger consuming him.

Sinking to his knees, Boy bowed his head.

"Please," he rasped, his throat raw from the wounds left by his protege's mangled teeth.

He tracked her as she approached him, attuned to the soft rustling of her skirts brushing against her skin with every step. It was a sound he knew well, one which woke him at high noon with memories of her coming to him while he lay bound and defenseless.

Everything in him screamed to retreat, to remove Kaius from her sights. They would both pay for his hubris. Khthonios's punishment for his disobedience would be nothing compared to the payment she would demand for the favor he was kneeling before her to ask.

But he needed her.

The Deviant in his arms howled and Khthonios snatched him, holding him high in the air as one might a feral dog.

"Was this thing worth it?" she mused aloud, the sweet lilt in her voice belying the wrath he heard howling in her mind.

He nodded but kept his head down in deference. "You are more powerful than I. Surely you can fix what I could not."

Her gentle laugh pierced the quiet of the forest. "Why would I do that? It's an abomination. A mutation. I have no desire to tether my blood to a defective animal." With the strength of a thousand men, she tossed the mangled body into the woods, sighing when Boy launched from his position to catch Kaius before he was impaled by the thicket. "That creature is as useless as his creator."

"Anything," he growled as he allowed Kaius to feed freely from his wrist. "I will give you anything you ask if you change him."

Her black eyes grazed him over as they'd done thousands of times and her lip curled in disgust. "You have nothing I want."

"I am everything you want," he countered, taking a step toward her. "Fix him."

A delicate brow lifted. "You demand it."

"No. I offer it."

He traded his soul to the devil, stepped onto her game board without knowing or caring about the rules she set. All he saw was the end where Kaius survived, and it was enough to make his decision.

But today, for the first time in his existence, he questioned whether it was worth it.

Rubbing his hands over his face, he got to his feet and walked over to the boxes of useless shit Nichol continued to drop throughout the basin, zeroing in on the one containing all the electronics his hauntmate deemed necessary for a vampire living alone amid a horde of Deviants. Cell phones, solar chargers and miniature panels, converters…each with a laminated set of instructions complete with detailed diagrams and pictures he didn't need.

It was a reminder of another untruth he allowed to spin with his silence. Nichol deemed him disinterested and incapable of comprehending the increasingly complex technology being used by the haunt, mistaking Boy's perceived indifference for boredom and lack of understanding. But he watched. He watched and listened to the resident genius for fifteen hundred years. Kaius's first changeling was formidable in both intellect and strength and Boy had taken every opportunity to learn from the shadows.

Setting aside the items he needed for his project, he

got to work, counting down the hours until sunset when he would be able to step out of his caves without the consequence a daytime sighting would bring.

****

Lexie Grace crossed her arms and glared at the distractingly gorgeous vampire crouched over a box of wires and gadgets he was placing strategically around her property. "You're being paranoid," she stated as he fastened a cell phone to the railing and angled the screen toward her door. "Or controlling."

His head dipped down for a moment in what she figured was exasperation before he tugged his notebook from his pocket and added to his *"you need security"* note he passed off as an explanation when he arrived at sunset with a box and a plan.

Looking over his shoulder while he scribbled his attempt at clarification, she frowned. "Yeah, I know there's no one around which is why this is overdoing it. Those zombie things only move at night and the few pieces that last into sunrise burn up within the hour. Since you're usually with me during their active time, what's the point in all this? And what exactly do you intend to do if something did happen to me during the day? It's not like you can just walk over here and check without turning into an inferno. So unless you're going to take me up on my offer to stay in the spare room, this whole thing is pointless."

The muscles in his jaw twitched and she reared back when she figured out what he was doing.

"Oh my God," she growled as a complete picture formed in her head, one so familiar she could envision every detail down to the way he would walk off with his hands in his pockets and his head hung like he actually felt bad. "You rat bastard. This is your way of leaving without guilt, isn't it? Making sure I feel all safe and protected so you can take off and go do whatever it is you old assholes do with your eons of time."

His eyes darkened as he rose to his feet and she knew she'd hit her mark.

That was it. She'd been a challenge for him. A game. And now that he'd won, he was done with her.

The realization slammed into her so hard she grasped the door frame to steady herself while she gathered her thoughts and tried to slow her racing pulse.

He was setting up this stupid security system to alleviate his conscience so he could disappear without feeling like the asshole he was. Boy was no different than the rest. She'd been blinded by his wounded beast act and ignored the fact he was male first, a vamp second.

When he'd shown up with enough tech to track her every move in and out of her home, she'd been uneasy with the thought he wanted to monitor her. Experience had taught her monitoring always led to control, to interrogations and accusations. But this was Boy. He'd raised no alarms in her head before; why would he now? With her past lovers, she'd always known somewhere in the back of her mind that they were dangerous. Tiny red flags would be planted in memories for her to examine once she was out from under their thumbs and she would hate herself a little more with each one, knowing she had ignored her own instincts for the sake of not being alone.

Rage bubbled up, temporarily replacing the hurt which would take over once he was gone from her sight. "Go," she snarled when he stalked toward her. "I don't need bullshit pity from an overbearing fuckboy with—"

His lips crashed against hers, silencing her mouth and stunning her thoughts. One large hand tangled in her hair while the other gripped her hip and held her flush to him. She pressed her palms to his chest to push him away, her resolve shaking when she felt solid muscles flexing and rippling with barely-contained power.

He released her instantly and the feeling of loss overtook rage as she stared up at him, trying to read the turmoil churning in his blackened eyes.

Scooping up the discarded notebook and pen, he started writing again. The paper snagged on the tip and tore but he continued without missing a beat until he was done and holding it out for her, fury like she'd never seen burning in his gaze.

The devil herself is coming for you. My weakness led her to your door and now she knows the soul I gave her was a forgery, a deception I've upheld for twenty-five hundred years. She will use her army to collect my true soul from your hands and when she does, I will be ready. If I am not, she will bring you to your knees and force you to her heel. She will destroy everything you are, everything which drew me to you. My punishment for betraying her will be your suffering as she pushes you to the brink of death time and again without reprieve. Let me install the fucking security system.

She read his words over and over, trying to imagine a being more terrifying and more powerful than the one glaring at her under the yellow hue of the porch light.

The devil herself.

She was not a religious person and never had been, but Boy was older than Jesus and his fear was emanating off of him in waves, masked by anger and frustration. Perhaps a wise woman would heed the warning and fling herself on his mercy, begging prettily for protection and forgiveness.

Lexie Grace was smart, but she was not one to fall to her knees for any man. And she suspected he needed her to be herself right now, to poke and tease him. There was a vulnerability flickering behind his anger, the same one which cracked her heart open when he came to her after running off the night he first kissed her.

"So what you're saying is I jumped to conclusions," she finally said, crossing her arms and cringing when she met his hard gaze. "I'm sorry I called you an asshole. And a rat bastard." When he remained motionless save for the lift of one brow, she slunk up to him and trailed her finger down his muscled chest. "And an overbearing fuckboy. But in my defense, I didn't know the devil existed until two minutes ago."

And there it was again, the look of exasperation she enjoyed so much from a vampire as impenetrable, stoic, and serious as Boy. Emboldened, she rose up on her toes and planted soft kisses on his chin and along his jaw until he relented, wrapped his arm around her, and ducked his head to capture her lips with his. She rubbed against him like a cat in heat, moaning when she felt him harden and he walked her backward through her doorway, slamming the door behind them with one hand while he shoved her shorts off her hips with the other.

If she was going to be hunted down by some phantom evil she-devil because of this damn guy, she might as well get off a few more times before she paid the price.

Chapter Sixteen

Against his better judgement, Boy sat in Lexie Grace's living room as the sun breached the horizon. The tremor of dawn's arrival rippled through his bones while she flitted around in a state of dismay she wouldn't be experiencing if she hadn't blackmailed him to stay.

"You'd know, right?" she demanded as she inspected the plywood blocking the large window in the dining room. "I mean, if the sun hits you, you have time to move. It's not like it would be an immediate inferno or something. Oh God, it will be, won't it? Promise me it won't."

He debated letting her fret a little longer before deciding it was his own dick which put them in this position. If his cock hadn't been so eager to feel her mouth, he wouldn't have agreed to wait out the day here. Standing, he walked over to her, took her hand, and led her to her bedroom where a single sliver of sunlight pierced the darkness.

"Get back," she gasped as she launched across her bed and used her body to block the ray. "I swear I'm not trying to kill you."

The sunlight wasn't what had him on edge. It was knowing he was a homing beacon for the hordes moving their way. It was knowing Nichol would be searching for him and might decide to widen his hunt.

He would no doubt spot the makeshift security feed Boy rigged up.

And it was knowing Khthonios was lying in wait in her cage, biding her time inside his core.

But he couldn't burden Lexie Grace with the real threats any more than he already had.

He crossed the room, nudged her aside, and passed his hand through the sunbeam to prove he wouldn't ignite in a blaze of terrifying glory. Picking a towel from her laundry hamper, he draped it over the wooden blockade and stood where the light used to be.

Exhaling, she adjusted her ponytail and swallowed. "I'm overreacting again."

He nodded and smirked.

For all the pressure bearing down on him, he liked being fussed over. Bianca and Audra used to coo and worry about him when he lived at the haunt, but theirs was more of what he imagined overprotective older sisters might do.

There was nothing familial about the way Lexie Grace fluttered around him. She spent the last hour checking and double-checking every nook and cranny of her tiny home, searching for any place sunlight might come in and stopping every few minutes to touch him or kiss him or nuzzle her cheek against him.

He really liked the nuzzling.

Pulling her onto her bed, he arranged her where he wanted her and wrapped around her tiny form. Her mind was whirring with chores she needed to do outside, but she'd gotten no sleep yet thanks to her insistence on helping him set up the makeshift monitoring system, hours of sex, and a hot shower which resulted in more sex and the depletion of her water tank.

He made a mental note to have Nichol send one of those tankless systems they had at the haunt, the one he was guilty of abusing after long hours in the sparring ring pretending he had one tenth of his strength so the others wouldn't view him as the threat he could be.

With a heavy sigh, Lexie Grace's mind slowed and he felt her relax in his arms while he buried his face in her damp hair.

He had two weeks before one of his problems arrived in the basin. Three, if he was lucky. Satellite images his hauntmates printed out and dropped in last night's box showed three masses moving as unified fronts. Between the din in his mind and the high-resolution photos, there would be upwards of eleven thousand Deviants descending on the area and he had fourteen blades, nine smashed drones, and one tiny spitfire with limited ammo.

Through Nichol's intel, he knew the military had no intent on stopping the Deviants from entering the barricaded area. Despite his best efforts to dodge notice, the government knew he was on site. They'd also linked him to videos taken months ago when he faced down his creator and drained her dry, when he took her contaminated blood into his own body to save Kaius and the haunt of vampires he'd watched over for close to two millennia.

He simply needed to remind himself it was worth it while Lexie Grace was lying in his arms, counting on him to keep her safe from the danger closing in on them.

She was a twist he never saw coming. Not a diversion. Not a distraction. Lexie Grace with her hot pink bras and nonstop chatter was now the goal, the endgame.

Kissing her hair, he tuned in to the closest Deviants moving a few days ahead of the others and let himself sink into a fitful rest.

The leather tail of the whip licked the back of Boy's thighs and he gritted his teeth, bearing the pain silently while Kaius howled and snarled from where he was bound on the opposite wall. The rustle of Khthonios's skirts gave her position away behind him and he braced himself for the next strike.

With his arms tethered to a hook secured to the wooden rafters overhead, he had been completely at her mercy for thirty nights. His feet hung an inch from the floor, too far to ease the discomfort in his shoulders but close enough to make him reach for purchase. The spiked collar was cinched tight around his neck and the metal spears pierced his skin deeper every time Khthonios tightened it. Though he couldn't see Kaius, he could hear him clawing at the stone walls and scratching into the dirt floor, his heavy chains rattling incessantly night and day.

Cool leather caressed his spine and he arched away on instinct.

"Tell me again, Boy, was it worth it?" Khthonios purred in his ear as she pressed her body flush to his flayed spine. "Was that thing worth your flesh? Your pain? Was betraying me for another worth your freedom?"

She asked the same questions every night, demanding an answer he would not give. It was an illusion of choice, a game. Khthonios wanted nothing more than to hear him relent and admit Kaius was the abomination she deemed him to be. She whispered promises of releasing him from his shackles and from Kaius's howls which filled his ears, his mind, and his core through their shared blood. Her words spun pretty tales of returning to her heel to wander the earth, feeding and fucking with abandon.

But he refused.

Even in his weakest moments when his body was screaming for an end to the agony, when blood loss was fogging his thoughts and his mind was shattering under the assault of Kaius's relentless compulsions, he couldn't accept his choice was the wrong one. Everything inside him had locked onto Kaius, as though he knew on the most primitive levels that this man would be his greatest achievement. He couldn't explain it, didn't understand it, but he'd known then and he knew now.

All he needed was for his own creator to uphold her end of their bargain. And for him to survive long enough to ensure she did.

Her skirts rustled as she came into view, dragging her whip across his shoulders before wrapping the tail around his cock. "Was it worth hurting me?" she whispered as she trailed her fingers down his filthy chest. "I gave you freedom and you chose another. You walked away from me and linked yourself to him for eternity."

"I returned," he countered. "I returned and lay myself at your feet."

Her nails dug into an open wound at his hip. "Because you had no choice. You know only I can save that mutation."

"And yet you haven't," he spat, his rage boiling

over. "You set the rules of our trade. I hang here at your mercy, tethered to you through my word, but the game has yet to begin."

She met his gaze, her onyx eyes revealing nothing. She locked him in a silent standoff until her red lips turned up in a smile that sent ice through his veins.

"It begins now."

Boy's eyes snapped open as phantom pains rippled across his throat through his core. A warm body wiggled against him before resettling and he pulled Lexie Grace in closer, needing her heat as an anchor while memories assaulted him, dragging him back into the hell of the night that set the course of his existence for twenty-five hundred years.

The collar fell from his neck into Khthonios's hands and rivulets of blood streamed down his body as she stroked his cheek.

"Tonight, I create the players. Tomorrow, you make your move."

She disappeared behind him and Kaius growled low, instinct alone making the Deviant wary of the predator advancing on him. Chains rattled and Khthonios laughed as she hauled Kaius over and lifted him effortlessly.

"Do you see yourself in this beast?" she demanded, shaking Kaius as though he weighed nothing more than a silken wrap. When Boy refused to answer, she tightened her hold on Kaius until the Deviant screamed. "I ask again. Was it worth it?"

Looking away from his damaged protege, he stared down his creator. "You ask what I see in him, demand to know his worth." He paused to filter through Kaius's insanity to lock onto Khthonios's thoughts. Then he grinned when he heard her fears through her fury. "His existence scares you."

"I fear nothing," she snarled.

"You fear him," he replied, his voice scratched and graveled. "You may own me. You may use my body and break my will and destroy my mind, but a piece of me exists in him and you are terrified of what piece I gave him, what I refused to give you. End him if you so choose, but know that piece will die with him. You will never possess all of me and in that, I have already won the game."

Khthonios drained Kaius of his Deviant blood that night, cutting Boy's link to him and filling his veins with her own, tying Kaius to her for eternity. The change altered the smell of their blood, uniting them under a single line while Boy was shoved aside, a lone bloodline.

But he still scented himself in Khthonios's new child. Somewhere deep in Kaius's core was that piece Boy promised would remain and it did. When he could no longer feel Kaius's existence, when Khthonios claimed Kaius as hers, when she coated the spikes of the collar with mercury and drove them deep into Boy's throat, some part of him lived in Kaius.

The mercury poisoned his blood, weakening him for months and permanently sealing the damage to his impaled throat. He never again spoke words of insolence and truth to his creator, but she still heard him. His silence screamed every time she laid eyes on him, reminding her she might continue to play but his victory was already claimed.

Centuries passed and Kaius became everything Boy knew he would be. The strength and power of

Khthonios's blood was reflected in his every move but balanced with a calculated stoicism Khthonios lacked. Kaius replaced Boy as her favored pet and Boy was banished to the shadows where he stood guard in silence, hiding his own growing strength. He was a ghost lying in wait for the night Kaius would rebel, would hold that piece of Boy hidden inside him and push against Khthonios as Boy had.

But the night never came, not in a blaze of fury and glory. Kaius was smarter than Boy. His rebellion was mere whispers amid his obedience while he played both sides of the board. He changed the game and added his own players, creating a haunt that would one day stand against Khthonios.

And Boy watched.

He stayed in the shadows under Khthonios's threat to end both of them should Kaius ever know he had once been linked to Boy. It was a threat he knew she would make good on, her ego as strong as her desire to own him. He appeased her with his compliance, allowing her free rein over his body and helping to create the ancient army of Deviants now descending on him.

But he did not give her everything.

He hid his abilities from her, from Kaius, from the haunt where he lived as a servant. His age was guarded along with his secrets, an undercover assassin hiding in plain sight. He bided his time on the battlefield throughout the ages, concealing his strength until he drained his creator and put an end to the war.

Except he'd been wrong. The final battle was yet to come.

Chapter Seventeen

Nichol Kaius sat alone in the communication room, spinning a pen between his fingers while he tried to make sense of Boy's request for a tankless water heater, ammo for weapons he didn't have in his possession, and a selection of cookies.

The vamp was living in a cave, feeding on cattle blood, and decapitating Deviants when he wasn't being an intolerable asshole knocking military-grade stealth drones out of the sky. Nothing about his current situation led itself to needing a water heater, ammunition for gun he didn't own, or cookies vampires couldn't ingest.

"Audra," he barked into the hall when he heard the telltale clicking sound of her heels. "In here."

She snorted inelegantly and stopped in the doorway, her manicured brow lifting. "Yes, master?"

Grumbling an apology for his abruptness in case she told Simone he was "acting like a tyrant" again, he rolled his chair over and passed her the last image his latest drone sent before it met the same fate as its predecessors. "What do you make of this?"

A faint smile graced her lips as it always did when she saw proof Boy was still alive. "He wants long, hot showers?"

"He lives in a goddamn cave."

"Then obviously he wants someone else to have

long, hot showers."

Grunting, he snatched the paper back from his best friend and greatest pain in the ass. "There is no one else. It's him, nine hundred military personnel patrolling the perimeter, and eleven thousand Deviants on their way."

Audra pulled up a chair and sat, giving him a look he knew well. "Nichol. Think. There was a single holdout to the evacuation of the area."

Scoffing, he opened the file he assembled on the woman in question and read from the PowerPoint he put together for simplicity's sake. "I'm well aware. Lexie Grace Kelly. Two misdemeanors for petty theft, one for vandalizing a car, and three for trespassing. Two dismissed charges of resisting arrest. Records show she spent her childhood in foster care, youth in and out of group homes. She took ownership of the Nevada property upon the death of her grandfather and her online presence consists of two accounts, both of which have been neglected for three years. Tagged videos show a loud, abrasive personality with little respect for authority and a tendency to talk and argue too much, hence the resisting arrest charges. This woman is not our concern."

He moved to the next slide of photos he located online, leaned back, and waited for her to agree with him.

"Nichol, Nichol. Nichol," she gasped as she swiped her phone to life and tapped out a quick message. Her phone pinged moments later and the sound of women running through the halls echoed in the quiet haunt while Audra loaded the slide of intel next to the pictures. "Ladies," she called when Molly, Harper,

Simone, Bianca, and Lis barreled into the communication room. "This woman is the lone holdout in the basin."

The room went silent while five sets of eyes read Lexie Grace Kelly's info and compared it to the photo of a petite woman with blonde hair pulled into a high ponytail and tumbling in bright curls over tanned skin. Her neon pink shirt sporting the phrase "Make me a sandwich, beeotch" hung off her shoulder, displaying a leopard print bra strap. Tiny jean shorts frayed within an inch of their life left her legs bare down to the black combat boots on her feet.

Bianca was first to crack a grin. "Oh my."

"Right?" Audra squealed while Molly cackled and Lis giggled.

Harper, Kaius's mate, bit her lip and her eyes lit up while Nichol's own lover, Simone, slammed her hand down on her thigh repeatedly and bounced in place on her heels.

Bringing a chair over, Bianca opened video footage of the woman's second arrest and turned up the volume.

"All y'all are morons," Lexie Grace Kelly hollered, her volume and tone piercing his eardrums. "That rat bastard over there's the one you should be cuffin'. I didn't do squat. I...aw, sugar, you don't want all this hassle, do you? Look at me. I'm five foot nothing. I couldn't scare a fainting goat, let alone bring a huge guy like him down, could I? But even if I did, he would totally deserve it, you know. Guys who get off on stalking their girlfriends should have big ol' warning signs tattooed to their foreheads so sweet things like me don't get all caught up in their webs. Webs of lies, officer. That's what he spun, you kno—"

Nichol closed out the video with a growl while six women howled with laughter.

"Nichol," Audra stammered as she sucked in gulps of air to calm herself. "Tell them what you said about her. Go on."

Meeting the gaze of his beautiful mate, he pled his case. "Boy made a few strange requests for his next drop and I merely asked Audra what she made of them."

Waving her hand in front of her tearing eyes, Audra shook her head. *"This woman is not our concern,"* she mimicked with her weakest imitation of him to date. "Now, ladies, what do we say? Setting aside the tankless hot water system and cookies Boy requested, what do we say about Lexie Grace Kelly?"

Bianca was first to bring herself under control while Nichol fired off a discrete SOS to his male counterparts. "I say she is most definitely uncultured. Untamed, really."

Simone nodded. "Wild. Unpredictable."

"Probably dangerous too," Harper added with wide eyes.

"And short," Molly pointed out. "Like a little, angry doll."

The rest of his hauntmates filtered in to the room, staying tight to the outskirts to get a read on the situation unfolding in the crowded com room.

"Cowards," he muttered before turning to Simone. "I relent. Fill me in on the joke."

"It's no joke," Lis dared to reply, shrinking back a bit when Nichol glared at her. "I mean, it's funny but it's probably the biggest problem you have right now."

Pinching the bridge of his nose, Nichol looked to

Kaius. "What say you, Almighty Leader? Boy is requesting ammo for guns he doesn't have, a tankless hot water system, and cookies. Specifically, chocolate dipped wafers."

Kaius's usually stoic expression morphed from shock to horror as Rhys flopped into a chair and tried to slide his hand between Lis's thighs. "Sounds to me like Boy has a honey," the haunt's former Tender trainer stated. "A honey with a small water tank and monthly cravings he's learned to prepare for."

"There's no hon—" Nichol froze as he caught on to what was going on. "No. Absolutely not. No."

"Yes," Audra countered. "So start prepping those contingencies."

Shaking his head, he rolled over to his computer and pulled up every piece of drone footage he had. "We have eleven thousand Deviants moving across the western states, ready to converge on the Nevada Basin with nothing but a single vampire to take them out while we sit on our asses and monitor from the air. All this on Boy's orders, with *single vampire* being the key fucking words." Slamming his hand down on his desk when the image he dreaded to find was located, he gestured at the computer where a lone frame filled the screen, a moment so quick he missed it during his nightly tracking. "That mute asshole had thousands of years to go on a goddamn date and *this* is when he decides to put himself on the market and get himself a *honey*?"

The hauntmates gathered around him to study the grainy black and white still of Boy looking to his left.

"He's smiling," Jagger stated, his voice reflecting the stunned expressions of everyone in the room. "Holy hell."

"Holy hell, indeed," Kaius echoed, meeting Nichol's gaze. "Start planning an extraction, because if those Deviants descend and the honey dies…"

He trailed off, but everyone heard what he didn't say: The honey dies and Boy's vengeance just might make Khthonios's rampages look like child's play.

****

Lexie Grace trained her scope on her mark. "You better be as good as you claim to be," she muttered as she exhaled and squeezed the trigger. The shot was clean and true, ringing through the silent air while her target played the part of the dying swan in the distance.

Rolling her eyes, she slung her rifle over her shoulder and sauntered across the sand, nudging the immobile form lying sprawled in the sand. "Show me." Boy's fingers unfurled to reveal the bullet he caught mid-air and she crouched beside him. "Has anyone ever told you you're nuts? Because you're nuts."

He nodded as he hopped to his feet and held his hand out to her to help her up.

They'd been practicing her target practice and his agility for hours under his reassurance more ammunition would be arriving soon. Her initial reluctance to shoot at him was tempered the first time she actually shot him and the bullet lodged itself in his shoulder. With tears in her eyes and frantic apologies falling from her lips, she watched while he dug the ammo out with the stoicism of a monk, dropped it to the ground, and forced her attention to the wound which sealed itself within minutes.

After that, it was game on.

Staying clear of the cattle range, they alternated

between moving target practice and surprise attacks. For a guy his size, Boy was surprisingly stealthy. He managed to sneak up on her three times before she realized he was using the low-lying brush, crawling on his belly at a snail's pace until he would rise like a phoenix behind her and kiss the back of her neck.

She nearly shot him twice for that move alone.

He led her back toward the house, set her rifle on the stoop, and handed her a large knife.

"Uh, no thanks," she said, holding the blade gingerly. "I'm a distance killer. None of that up-close-and-personal stuff for me." When he refused to take it back, she frowned. "Boy, I'm serious. I don't need a knife."

His lips drew into a tight line as his brows furrowed before he took out his ratty notebook: *Please. If a Deviant makes it past me, I need to know you can use this if you have to.*

"Deviant?" she read. "Is that what you call those zombie things?"

He scribbled his reply and she waited impatiently, anxious to know anything and everything about what she deemed Vamp Culture.

Deviants are vampire turnings gone wrong. Usually unintentional. These were not.

Her eyes widened. "You mean someone actually made these things on purpose? Why? Are they like those bullfrogs imported into Australia where they were intended to eat some bug destroying their crops but couldn't jump high enough and had no natural predators so they became a virtual plague?"

He cocked his head and stared at her for a moment before returning his attention to his notebook. *My creator, Khthonios, made them to serve as her army when the time was right.*

She blinked.

Boy's creator?

She'd never thought about the fact a vampire as old as him had to be made by a vamp who would have to be older than him. It was mind-blowing. But not as mind-blowing as the other tiny detail she noticed. "*Her* army? I didn't know women could be vampires. Why haven't I seen any on TV?"

He took the knife from her hand, led her to the twin rocking chairs her grandparents used to sit on in the evenings, and opened his notebook to a fresh page. While he worked on his response, she got comfortable and watched the stars twinkle and flicker in the night sky.

"I don't know what would be harder," she mused. "Losing days or losing nights. I mean, I feel bad you can't just sit here and watch the sun rise but at the same time, if you were some kind of reverse vampire who could never see the moon and stars, that would be equally sad."

He shrugged but continued to write.

"I don't think I could live without either. I suppose the good thing to come out of this whole Deviant zombie thing is I've had a reason to spend long hours outside in the dark with nothing to do but admire the night sky until one of those stanky things stumbles close."

His lips quirked up and he passed her his book: *Female vampires are rare because they are a threat to the existence of both humans and vampires. Their strength and abilities develop at record speeds, making them uncontrollable, unpredictable, and extremely dangerous. Should one be turned, they are hunted and put down immediately before they become too powerful to be contained.*

Thinking about this along with what little she knew of him, she drew her legs to her chest and wrapped her arms around her knees. "One obviously lived long enough to make you. Do you remember anything about her?"

She could see a debate raging in his blue eyes before he replied: *I remember everything. I put her down eight months ago.*

Guilt flooded her as she realized the poor guy was probably dealing with loss this whole time and she'd not once asked him about his family, going off the misguided assumption he wouldn't have one. But before she could gush her apologies, he tore a paper off his pad and passed it to her: *I do not mourn her. She was the devil. She* is *the devil. And when she returns, I'll do everything in my power to ensure she cannot harm you. Including teach you how to wield a blade no matter how stubborn you are about it.*

The dots connected in her head and she dropped her feet to the wooden decking with a thud. "You're telling me your creator—your female vamp creator—is the one you think is gunning for me?"

He nodded and scrawled a reply: *She chose me with the intention I would someday be powerful enough in my own right to walk at her side.*

Holding her hands up, she shook her head. "The 'female vamps are stronger and more deadly' creator who also happens to be older than you and therefore, if I remember correctly, already going to be more powerful? This is who you want me to fight with a kitchen utensil?"

Her voice was becoming shrill, but she couldn't help it. She had a natural aversion to death and dismemberment and torture, especially at the fangs of an ancient, scorned vamp seeking vengeance against his new girlfriend.

"I'm gonna die," she stated as she paced the short length of the porch. "You two had a bad breakup and now your old-as-shit ex is going to come back to life and take all that rage out on me, isn't she?"

Two large hands stopped her in her tracks and she looked up at him. His face was a mask of determination and barely-concealed anger and she squeezed her eyes shut, knowing she was getting worked up and was bound to say or do something irrational if she didn't bring herself down a notch or ten.

"Okay." She exhaled. "Okay. I'll learn how to stab if you promise to tell me something good. Something that doesn't involve Deviants or psychotic vampires who want me to suffer a thousand deaths."

Chapter Eighteen

Boy ran his fingers through Lexie Grace's hair as she lay naked on his chest. Her small hands skimmed up and down his ribs while he contemplated what he was about to reveal.

His entire existence was wrapped in layers of secrets which were being revealed one by one, exposing him a piece at a time. First was the revealing of his connection to Kaius—and by extension the rest of the Kaius haunt—to the others. Next, his lineage, and ties to Khthonios. With that came approximations about his age and strength from hauntmates who never knew the totality of his strengths and power. Then his ability to manipulate his blood was revealed during what he believed would be the final battle against his creator.

But none of those would earn Lexie Grace's trust. For that, he needed to share something he spent a thousand lifetimes hiding from his haunt and his creator. It was a risk, one he would have to take if he expected her to trust him with her safety, her life, and— if he were lucky—her heart. But thousands of years in the dark had him on edge with possibilities.

Reaching deep into his core where Khthonios lay motionless in her cage, he threw up the strongest barrier he could between her and him, one he knew would not hold for long.

Nudging Lexie Grace out of her post-sex daze, he

slipped out from under her, yanked a pair of boxers over his hips, grabbed his notebook, and walked into the kitchen to start the coffee he knew she would need for this.

"What are you doing?" she asked as she joined him at the small farmhouse table in nothing but tiny pink shorts and a threadbare lime-green T-shirt, her eyes brightening when she saw the coffee pot brewing. "I like the way you think."

Taking his opening, he flipped to a fresh page: *I like the way you think, too.*

She grinned in that lazy, sleepy way he loved to see, when she was sated and tired and her mind was filled with happy thoughts and naughty flashbacks of everything he did to her earlier. Her blonde hair was wild and tangled, her makeup smudged, and she was stunning. Stunning and sweet and currently wondering if there was room for her to duck under the table and suck him off.

Shoving his hand through his hair to refocus before he abandoned his admission in favor of feeling her hot mouth wrapped around him, he laid it out as simply as he could: *I'm a mind reader.*

Her eyes moved over the words and she scoffed. "Okay, I'll play along. What am I thinking right now?"

He waited for her thought to fully form before he blinked twice.

She sat back, crossed her arms, and sent a new intentional request his way. When he stood and struck a flexing pose he'd seen Mikhail do when he managed to get the jump on Jagger during a sparring match, she exhaled.

"That's impossible," she stated, her face paling.

"Anyone could've guessed those. What am I thinking right...now?"

He sat down and recorded her thoughts word for word: *There's no way he can do that. It's some kind of funky little trick like a Vegas act or something. Okay, think of a number. Eight. No one picks eight. Or one. One is better. Eight is too close to seven but one is perfect. No way he'll get—is he writing this down? Holy shit, he is. He's writing it while I'm thinking it. Boy, stop. You're freaking me out.*

She slammed her hand down on the paper and ripped it from the notebook. "I said stop. Why—how? I mean, can you hear everything I'm thinking? Is it just me or can you hear everyone? Oh God, you're doing it right now, aren't you?" Her eyes widened and she stood up abruptly, pushing her chair back. "How could you hide this from me? I mean, these are my private thoughts. It's...it's an invasion of privacy."

He met her furious, frightened gaze before turning to a new piece of paper: *The ability manifested itself almost immediately after I was turned. Yes, I can hear everything and everyone but I try not to focus on any particular voice unless there's a threat. And I didn't hide this from you. I've been hiding this from everyone my whole existence. If vampires found out I could hear their thoughts, there's no doubt they would unite en masse and I would be hunted and slaughtered. I don't even trust my own haunt with this information because it makes me a bigger danger to them than my age or power ever did.*

Her thoughts were jumpy and scattered, their disorganization pulling his attention more than usual as she paced the floor.

He hated this, hearing her sense of betrayal ringing loud and clear above thousands of Deviants voices. Gone were the sleepy, wicked ideas of what she wanted to do to him and what she wanted him to do to her. In their place were memories of their interactions through her eyes as she examined each for signs he was using his ability to confuse or toy with her. She was hunting for any exploitation or manipulation and it tore at him.

"Why would you tell me this?" she demanded, coming to a stop in front of him and putting her hands on her hips while she waited for him to write his response.

I trust you.

The hardness in her eyes softened a fraction and even without hearing her thoughts, he could see the debate raging in her mind. A part of her was melting over his declaration, but there remained too much uncertainty and annoyance. Knowing he could listen in had her switching between thinking about how to handle his revelation and trying to hide her thoughts by repeating lyrics to a song he knew from Molly's vinyl collection.

He learned early on that vampires hid their exceptional abilities from each other. Exposure took away their edge against a species designed to kill. But his was a particularly deadly skill, one for which there was no chance of defense or escape. If he wanted to listen in, he could, and there was nothing anyone could do to stop it. It was both a blessing and a curse, the ability to track the plans of his enemies countering with the silence he had to uphold to keep his mind reading a secret.

Had Khthonios known, he never would have

survived his first year.

Lexie Grace resumed walking the short length of the kitchen for a few minutes, paused to pour herself a coffee, then sat back down at the table. "You can hear those Deviant things, can't you?"

Nodding, he filled her in on another secret no one but he and Khthonios were privy to: *I can hear them, yes. Anyone within a thirty-mile radius is within range if I zero in on them. But I've heard the Deviants since the night they awoke and emerged from the earth because my creator and I turned them. Her, because she thrived on mayhem, me because I was at her heel. I'm connected to the Deviants through blood which means they are always in my head.*

"That's hundreds of voices," she stated, concern lacing her tone. "Can you hear them all, all the time?"

Thousands, he corrected her. *There are thousands descending on the basin. And yes, I hear them as well as the Tenders tethered to me.*

Her brows knotted. "What are Tenders?"

Women trained to be courtesans in vampire society. Rhys Kaius would prepare them and I would link to them through blood to ensure they were treated well. My role was to monitor them, to check on their wellbeing in case any were being mistreated.

"And you still hear them?"

Those who have not had our link overridden by their masters, yes. But they are little more than a whisper.

Sipping her coffee, she stared past his shoulder to the wall behind him as she considered her next question. "Can you hear your creator? Is that how you know she's coming?"

Once upon a time, yes. Now, she whispers into my mind through our blood.

A shiver went through her and she sighed. "What am I thinking now?"

Zeroing in on her voice, he translated: *You want to go to bed. You don't know if you want me to join you.*

****

Lexie Grace lay in her bed, snuggled deep under her blanket but still unable to shake the chill in her bones.

Boy's revelation was fresh in her mind, a mind he could listen in on at will. The whole concept of it was terrifying and mortifying. But the reality…

She couldn't imagine what he must be going through as he sat in her living room where she heard him go after she left him in the kitchen. The noises Deviants made were grating on the nerves, the howls eerie in the night. For Boy to have thousands in his head? She couldn't begin to imagine it.

And she didn't want to think about the women he heard. She heard rumors about the women who served vampires thanks to one coming forward a couple years prior. Lis Bruckner made international news for exposing the way women were trained and sold between vamps, only to end up living with the very vampire who did it. Lexie Grace didn't understand the ins and outs of the whole thing, but she knew she didn't like the idea of Boy being caught up in it.

If only he could speak, even for a moment, to answer the millions of questions she had.

She heard footsteps in the hall and she sat up as Boy appeared in the doorway, notebook in hand. He waited until she motioned for him to come in and he slunk inside her room, passing her the notebook.

I promise you will get your answers tomorrow night.

She took a deep breath and exhaled slowly, wondering if he could feel how much better she felt when he was close. "So now that your big, bad secret is out, you're just going to respond to the questions I think instead of waiting for me to ask?"

He shrugged and scribbled a quick note: *Sorry.*

One look at him told her he wasn't sorry. If anything, he appeared almost pleased, as though he was liking their unspoken conversation.

"Oh my God," she said with a huff as she lay down again and patted the empty place beside her. "You're enjoying this, aren't you? Not having to listen to me talk so much?"

His nose wrinkled but he didn't hesitate before climbing into bed and writing in his ragged notebook: *Your voice is my favorite sound. I just like us having our own language.*

****

Lexie Grace sat on her sofa fidgeting nervously with the hem of her shirt and wondering when Boy would return.

The note he left behind when he snuck out sometime before sunrise was cryptic, and she was in no mood for cryptic from a mind-reading vampire with a vindictive ex-whatever and a gang of mindless Deviants gunning for him.

Be back tonight. Bringing company.

There was no company to be had in the region unless he intended on inviting the military. And she didn't foresee that happening anytime soon since every time she mentioned the border patrol his nose wrinkled in disgust.

Nonetheless, she spent the last two hours scrubbing the house and then herself, smoothing out her legs, teasing up her hair, and brightening her eyes. Her wardrobe left much to be desired, but she figured whoever was fool enough to land themselves in the basin during Deviant season had no right to judge, so she happily donned her favorite threadbare jean shorts with the lace trim, a lime-green tank, and her bubblegum-pink *Fragile like a bomb* crop top.

And then she waited.

The television was no help to pass the time. The signal was so weak she barely got a picture let alone sound. The mystery romance she was halfway through required too much concentration to consider reading when she was this impatient. So she sat and fiddled and shifted, tucking her bare feet under her ass and then changing position like it would make time pass faster.

She was so prepared for Boy and his mysterious company that his knock at her door startled her.

"Coming," she called as she smoothed the lace hem of her tiny shorts and scampered to the door, plastering a wide smile on her face as she swung the door open. "Well hey there…Boy?" Frowning, she glanced over his shoulder to see no one. "Do not tell me I shaved my legs for nothing."

His gaze traveled down the length of her body slowly, lingering on her thighs before he tugged on her belt loops, pulled her in tight to him, and kissed her.

"That's all fine and dandy," she said with a breathless huff when he finally released her. "But I cleaned the kitchen because you said company was coming and all I see is a hot vamp with boundary issues."

He reached over her shoulder and plucked her motorbike keys from their hook. Relenting, she opened the closet, tugged on her boots, and slung her rifle over her shoulder. "You aren't messing with me about this whole company thing, are you?"

With the shake of his head, he took her hand and led her to her bike, commandeering the driver position and giving her a slight smirk when she straddled the bike, scooted up tight to his ass, and wrapped her arms around him.

You're a horn dog, she thought, grinning when he shrugged and nodded. He skimmed his palm across her bare thigh and revved the engine before easing onto the narrow road heading west. The bike stayed on the pavement for a few miles, veering into the hard-packed sand once they neared the mountains. He looped them at a leisurely pace and it didn't take long for her to realize he was writing another message in the earth.

"Did you seriously bring me all the way out here to introduce me to the cranky guy flying the drone?"

He placed his large hand over hers and held tight while he drove them back toward her home, parked it beside the barn, and led her to the rocking chairs on her porch.

"So you're, what, luring him here?" she asked, wondering who the miserable tech was to him. When Boy nodded, she settled back in her chair and watched the dark sky. "Have you known him long?"

His response was quickly scrawled on the cardboard back of his notebook: *1500 years.*

"Fifteen hundred." She grunted inelegantly.

"Showoff. Is he part of your little group?"

He drummed his fingers on his knee for a moment then hunched over his book, the scratching of his pen the only sound in the still night. She liked watching him write. The way her pink fluffy pen was dwarfed by his large hand. The way he focused so intently. And she loved how his penmanship was such a mashup of printing, handwriting, script, and an almost calligraphy style.

He glanced up at her while she mused about his writing, fixing her with a dead stare until she shifted her thinking to the flex of his forearm which seemed to appease him as he finished up and passed her a chart.

"A family tree!" she exclaimed. "So this one up here, K…Khthonios? That's your creator?" He nodded and she dragged her finger down the line. "You and Kaius are brothers but you're kind of his dad, too?" With the wrinkling of his nose, she moved on, noting it as a question for another time. "Kaius has a girlfriend named Harper and five kids? Turnings? You guys prefer turnings, right?"

He nodded again and she scanned the rest of the lineage and the few details he provided.

Dominic was the youngest, a little over three decades into his vampire life, spoiled, and engaged to a woman named Molly. Mikhail was around two hundred and twenty, moody, and dating the haunt's psychologist, Audra. Next was Jagger who was four hundred and fifty, deaf, a weapons specialist, and partnered with Bianca Schumann. The fourth on the list was a name she recognized from the news, Rhys. He was closing in on eight hundred, living with Lis, and Boy's notes indicated the guy was an arrogant ass.

Last in line was Nichol, his age letting her know this was the vamp she would be meeting tonight. Nichol was the brains, the organizer, and dating a former vamp killer.

"Can I ask Nichol anything?" she inquired, her excitement building as she passed his notebook back. "About you, not him, obviously."

Anything is fair game, he wrote. *I'll be here to let Nichol know he has permission to share.*

Rubbing her hands together, she turned her attention to the sky. "This is going to be fun."

Chapter Nineteen

Boy felt a tension headache coming on. His first tension headache ever. And it was all due to a hostile vampire with control issues and a stubborn blonde with a diamond backbone and a death wish.

"I'm sorry, did we enter a time warp and land in prehistoric times? Because I'm pretty damn sure y'all just threatened to whack me on the head and haul me out of my own home because you can't accept the fact I'm an asset," Lexie Grace snarled at the drone hovering inches from her face. "Suck it, Fang Licker. I'm going nowhere."

"Asset," Nichol's voice growled through the speaker. "You're a distraction, an obstacle, and soon you'll be a detriment. If Boy's going to insist on doing this on his own like the obstinate son of a bitch he is, he can't afford to be watching your back as well as his own. I—"

Her eyes flashed and she leaned in closer. "You did not just call him a son of a bitch."

"We all know it's true."

There was a beat of silence before Lexie Grace grinned. "On that, we agree. Tell me everything you know about her. Be as nasty as you need to be."

The drone backed up and the camera angled toward Boy, waiting for his approval which he gave with the weary wave of his hand.

"None of us knew who Khthonios was until two years ago," Nichol began. "Kaius used to disappear for long stretches, which is why I ended up taking on the role of pseudo-leader trying to wrangle the rest of these assholes. We knew Khthonios was his creator, but none of us knew she was female or even still alive. I don't know what Boy told you about female vamps, but they're the devil incarnate. It took seven vamps in their second millennia to take down a three-hundred-year-old female a few centuries back and even then, two of the males met their end."

Lexie Grace pulled her feet up under her and her chair rocked. "So you've met her?"

"Met her, fought her haunt, and won," he pronounced with a tight clip. "Long story short, we caught word there was a danger coming for us so we met the threat head on at a neutral territory. Imagine our surprise when the two ancient vampires we were expecting to fight turned out to not only be sired by a female vamp, that female vamp was on site and Kaius was at her side ready to fight on her orders."

"No," Lexie Grace breathed, her eyes wide in anticipation. "What did you do?"

"Rhys, Boy, and I met Kaius and the two others on the field under her eye as the game master. The other two were eliminated swiftly but Kaius—" His voice trailed off and Boy knew he was reliving that moment Nichol took down his own creator. "I took Kaius out. A kill shot. Except he didn't die. He turned Deviant, and that's when we discovered Boy was not only Kaius's original sire, he was also created by Khthonios."

She was enthralled, her eyes wide and her lips parted. "You poor thing. I can't imagine how stressful that must have been, trying to lead the rest of your family with all that upheaval. And the betrayal! The betrayal you must have felt finding out Boy and Kaius were both keeping such dangerous secrets from you. Secrets which could have killed you."

Boy slumped in his chair and glared at the drone, wishing he'd never had the bright idea to introduce his hauntmates to his lover. Had he stopped to consider how much Lexie Grace seemed to enjoy her mystery romance books, he might have foreseen she would skip past the information digging and dive head-on into the treachery.

She was loving the treachery.

"This is just like a movie," she stated, shaking her head and looking over at him. "She made you stay quiet, didn't she? I just can't imagine you hiding something like that because you felt like being a jerk."

He nodded, but she was already focused back on the drone. "So what happened? Did you have to kill Kaius? I mean, I know he's still alive so you didn't succeed but what happened? Did you fight Khthonios right there and duel it out?"

"Khthonios loves games. The bet was her haunt against ours. We came out victorious, and she walked away," Nichol continued. "Boy took Kaius and disappeared. Went north. After some research and study on the re-Deviating phenomenon, we sent a convoy to join him and Boy managed to change Kaius back. Khthonios came for him and Kaius and you probably know how that turned out."

"My Boy slaughtered her ass," Lexie Grace stated as she stretched over to pat his knee. "So what now?"

He could hear the shift in Nichol's tone from

informative to strategic. "Now there are eleven thousand Deviants heading your way and Boy is refusing assistance from us. While we are still the Kaius haunt sired by Kaius Khthonios, the revelations over Boy's lineage now gives him the power to make decisions on whether or not we participate in his war."

She frowned. "But you're all family and lived together forever. Didn't he have a say before?"

There was an uncomfortable pause before Nichol responded. "Up until the moment he revealed Khthonios to be his creator and him to be Kaius's sire, we believed Boy was not of our bloodline and he was treated as such within the haunt."

Lexie Grace's frown turned into a glare, her blue eyes narrowing as her thoughts flashed to several foster homes where she was deemed lesser for not being a biological child. "What did this treatment look like?"

"Over the centuries, he took on the role of sentry, servant, runner of the bloodslave quarters, and backup when our numbers required extra strength in our court."

With her lips pursed, Lexie Grace sat back in her seat and crossed her arms. "You used him for what you needed and didn't give him choices until all y'all decided he was worthy. And he only became worthy when you found out Khthonios was his creator and he was Kaius's. Is this correct?"

"It is."

Boy could hear her mind churning with sad and angry thoughts before she settled on one of determination. "Well then, getting back to your position on my presence here, I'm staying right by his side whether you like it or not. Boy made his decision and it sure sounds like once again you're not giving him his voice."

"He is being reckless with that voice," Nichol growled. "He has power, strength, skills, and access to tech the military would die to possess, yet he's digging in his heels out of the stubbornness inherent to our bloodline."

Lexie Grace looked over at him. *Being reckless isn't in your nature. You're protecting them, aren't you?*

With his eyes shielded from the drone's camera by his hair, he gave her a slow blink of agreement and she turned her attention back to Nichol and shrugged. "Looks like he made his call. Thanks for the box drop offs and answering some of my questions, but we have plans tonight so unless you want this sexy little drone to be in on my target practice, you're probably going to want to head out for the night."

Done with being brushed off, Nichol's focus shifted. "Are you sure you don't need reinforcements? With forty-eight hours' notice, I can free up whomever you need to stand against the Deviants."

He pointed at the drone's camera.

"We're fine," Nichol stated. "The sanctuary city is going strong and we're seeing a settling on both the human and vampire fronts. A few territory disputes, but between me and Kaius, we've managed to resolve them enough to keep the peace. I—wait—"

There was a rustling and Lexie Grace's ears perked up as Boy caught Audra's voice rising in the background.

With a growl, Nichol returned to the drone's speaker system. "Audra says hello and she's demanding a separate meeting with Ms. Kelly along with the other women who feel I'm being negligent in giving Ms. Kelly a proper welcome. I'll make the arrangements and include optional time slots in tomorrow's drop."

The drone sped off into the night sky, leaving him and Lexie Grace alone in the stillness and silence.

"He's a real charmer," she snickered and he lolled his head against the backrest of the rocking chair. "Seriously though, he seems pretty upset you won't accept their help."

Flattening his crumpled notebook across his thigh, he scribbled out his reasoning: *Khthonios will sense their presence. I can hold my own against her assaults because I'm accustomed to having my mind invaded. They will not fare as well.*

"You're worried she'll hurt them."

I'm worried she'll use them to hurt me.

Understanding filled her eyes and she bit her lip. "They're your weakness."

As are you. Let's work on your hand-to-hand combat skills.

****

Lexie Grace linked her arm in Boy's and skipped along at his side, pleased as punch with her ability to take him down into the sand. "I warned you I knew how to fight."

The lift of a brow let her know exactly what he thought of the back alley fight skills she picked up during her teen years, trained by two of the older girls in the group home. Her methods weren't fair, they might not even be legal in some states, but they were effective, as proven by the six-foot-four vamp beside her with dust embedded in his cargos and shirt.

She nudged him in the ribs, bopped her head

against his bicep, and grinned. "You're just mad I got the jump on you. Didn't even see it coming, did you?"

As much as she wanted to brag she managed to plan and execute her attack without him knowing, it was instinct driving her reactions when he came at her as a Deviant might, his movements unpredictable and jerking. He might have been able to foresee the throat punch if she hadn't startled him with her screaming, but her run and his subsequent chase did him in. As he closed in on her, she dropped to the ground and turtled, he stumbled over her to avoid crushing her, and she booted him in the ass.

It wasn't graceful. It wasn't pretty. And it probably wouldn't work on an attacker who wasn't holding back because he thought she was cute, but she won that round and she was crowing her victory.

"I deserve a belt. A big one with *Ancient Vamp Destroyer* stamped right on the gold buckle. No, wait. *Boy Blaster*. I want *Boy Blaster* on it so every time you look at me, you'll remember not to screw around because I can whoop your ass."

She hadn't even realized he'd lifted her up and tossed her over his shoulder until she was dangling upside down and staring at his very nice, firm, dusty backside. Taking the opportunity, she brushed the sand off his cargos while he carried her into the house and set the locks.

He set her on her feet, holding her by the waist as she regained her balance, smiled up at him, and backed up toward her bathroom. "Are you listening to what I'm thinking now?"

His blue eyes were darker tonight than they were yesterday and her thoughts had his pupils dilating as he stalked toward her.

For all his patience, control, and stoicism while he trained her, she loved it when he looked like this, like he was one thread snap away from going completely feral on her. He was predatory, a hunter with his prey in his sights. His movements were more serpentine as he followed her into the tiny bathroom and she started the shower, his gaze locked on her while she shimmied out of her clothes and stepped under the water.

"I saw that heater thing," she called over her shoulder as she turned into the spray. "Do you think we could install it tomorrow?"

Nodding, he stripped his own clothes off and she lost her teasing edge.

The vamp was just too much. Too gorgeous, too strong, too sculpted, too tall, and too big.

And it just so happened she was developing a taste for excess in the form of a sweet silent blond with fangs that made her thighs clench every time she thought about them sliding into her.

She waited for him to join her but he didn't. Instead, he leaned against the wall, crossed his arms, and watched as though expecting a show. So she gave him one.

His eyes tracked each movement of her hands as they slid her magnolia body wash over every inch of her skin. It was both exhilarating and nerve-wracking to be observed with such intensity, like he was biding his time for the perfect opportunity to strike. His fangs lengthened, digging into his bottom lip when she slid her hand between her thighs and lingered.

"Enjoying the performance?"

He responded by wrapping his hand around his

cock and stroking himself slowly, his gaze locked on the movement of her fingers as they slid through her wetness. She teased herself, biting her lip when his eyes grew darker, tension rippled across his pecs, and his abs tightened. A low rumbling from his chest was the last sign of how close to snapping he was, the sound echoing off the tile.

Deciding to take advantage of his little ability, she switched from thinking about what she was doing to what she wanted him to do to her. She spoke directly to him, leaving no doubt she wanted him to listen in.

I want to feel the cold of the tile on my back while you fuck me. I want you pounding me into the wall until I'm screaming your name. Oh God, Boy. I love the way you fill me. I need your hands on my skin, your tongue on my body, your fangs in my veins. I'm so fucking close but don't want to come unless you're inside me.

The growl changed, growing more territorial as he advanced on her with blackened eyes. He lifted her as though she were a feather and pressed her against the cold tile, his lips crashing to hers in a punishing kiss as he thrust into her with one powerful stroke.

"Oh fuck yes," she moaned while he fucked her hard and fast, the speed and angle making her helpless to do more than wrap her arms around his neck and hold on tight.

Her orgasm coiled in her belly and her body tightened around him as he nipped at her throat. The feeling of his fangs sinking into her sent her over the edge with a wail. He continued to pound into her at a brutal pace before his tempo became erratic and he released inside her, his body shuddering under her fingertips.

The cooling water sent a shiver through her and he carried her out from under the spray, turning off the faucet with one hand while balancing her with the other. He draped a towel around her and took her to bed while she smoothed his wet hair down and nuzzled into his neck.

"You're like a giant teddy bear," she sighed as he tossed the wet towel across the room and joined her under the covers. "Like a giant, growly, killer teddy bear with a pretty hair and a talented dick."

His unimpressed expression made her grin and she burrowed against him, sated, happy, and loving the feeling of his arms around her as she drifted off knowing this couldn't last but unwilling to imagine returning to a life without him.

Chapter Twenty

Boy watched from a distance, a feeling of satisfaction rushing through him while Kaius led Nichol through the dense forest toward a shelter where they would be protected from sunlight when dawn came.

"The mongrel has spawned a line of its own," Khthonios mused behind him as she slid her hand up his spine and grasped the back of his neck. "He believes himself ready to lead."

His skin crawled under her cold touch but he held back his instinctive need to recoil.

She was here for him under the guise of calling Kaius to her, a game she enjoyed immensely. Outwardly, she remained indifferent to his existence, cutting him off from her name and ignoring his presence in the shadows while she toyed with Kaius, promising him a freedom he would never have should he simply carry out her unending strings of orders. Her voice dripped with disdain whenever she chose to acknowledge him, but her thoughts spoke her intentions loud and clear.

She was merely biding her time.

Even now, with her nails drawing blood and her attention on Kaius's first turning, she was assessing Boy, waiting for him to show her the power she suspected he hid from her. She wanted to take him for a mate, but only once he proved himself worth more than his body which he handed unencumbered access to her long ago. Superior strength, speed, and stamina weren't good enough for her, not when she desired a perfect specimen to stand at her side.

He refused to be that specimen.

Khthonios owned his body and commanded his strength, but she didn't possess his mind and she never would.

"Sometimes I regret silencing you," she purred in his ear when Kaius and Nichol disappeared inside the small cottage where an underground cellar served as a perfect place to wait out the sun. "I miss hearing you moan when your body rebels against you, the sounds you make when you finally succumb to the pleasure I give. It was a victory I've now denied myself."

She turned toward the hills beyond where a castle lay in disrepair and he followed.

He would catch up with Kaius and Nichol after Khthonios took her fill, and he would continue to watch while his former protege built himself an empire capable of ruling the world. But until then, he would appease their creator the only way he could and hope it was enough to sate her blood thirst.

Boy snapped awake to the sensation of Khthonios's cool body pressed against his, rippling through his conscious. Momentarily caught between cognizance and sleep, he could still feel her fangs in his throat and her hands on his skin and he tensed.

"Hey," a sleepy voice murmured beside him as the warm hand on his chest grazed him gently. "You okay?"

Nodding, he tightened his hold on her and let himself sink into her contented, borderline incoherent thoughts while she straddled between sleeping and waking. Over the last week it had become a guilty pleasure he indulged in, hearing single words from her mind as she snuggled up to him before giving in to reality. She liked waking up to him in her bed as much as he liked being in it, and hearing her happiness only made it better.

I will enjoy watching you end her almost as much as if it were my own hand delivering the blow.

Khthonios's voice slithered through his head and he pushed against it, shoving her back toward the bars no longer containing her power as they once had.

He felt her growing stronger inside him. Her whispers sounded closer than they did mere days ago. She watched Lexie Grace through his eyes when he trained her to fight. She murmured her hatred of the human. She filled his head with her blood-drenched fantasies of how Lexie Grace would die in the coming days.

But it wasn't her words he feared anymore, not when her wishes were starting to meld with his own one shrouded thought at a time. She struck when he was at his weakest, when he was too busy focusing on Lexie Grace and not paying attention to the places where her poison traveled as it leaked from her cage. His ability to keep Khthonios contained deep in his core where she had no power was failing him while she grew stronger. He was starting to second-guess every move he made in a futile attempt to separate her desires from his own, slowing his responses and forcing his hesitation.

The Deviants were closing in on them on three sides, five nights away at best. He couldn't afford to be distracted, not when Lexie Grace was at his side. She was a spitfire, an excellent student, and had great aim with the old rifle she insisted on using despite Nichol sending over a new semi-automatic, but she was human and therefore very, very breakable.

The more he considered Nichol's rationale for removing Lexie Grace from the region, the more he understood it. She was an asset in a lot of ways, but his hauntmate was correct. Her presence was putting both of them at risk, just not in the way Nichol may have thought.

Peppered throughout Khthonios's whispers of Lexie Grace's weaknesses were others which fed the Deviant voices in his mind. She spoke of power, of control. The approaching army was not there to decimate him.

They were his to command and the basin was an ideal stronghold from which to rule.

Ignoring those murmured promises of never returning to anyone's heel became harder as Khthonios burrowed into those dark, deep recesses of his mind where his resentments and rage lay buried and hidden. The small army was mindless and lethal, ready for him to lead. With thousands acting on his word, he could lie in wait as Khthonios had done, hide in the caves and bury his soldiers in the sand until they were forgotten. He could build his numbers in the shadows.

Easing his arm out from under Lexie Grace, he slipped out of her bed and stalked to the shower, shaking off his grim plans under the cold water.

It was time to do what he should have done weeks ago. He needed to end all of it before there was no turning back. Because although he was no saint, he wasn't his creator.

****

Lexie Grace crossed the property to the cattle pen, relieved to see Boy filling the feed barrels and water. "So this is where you've been hiding," she called out as she approached the wooden fencing. "Waking up alone wasn't one bit fun, you know."

It wasn't the waking up which worried her as much as what she woke up to.

Her new tankless water system was installed, her rifle along with the heavier semi-automatic she disliked were propped beside her ammo bag and an old, empty suitcase belonging to her granddaddy. The kitchen was spotless. There wasn't a single dish in the sink and the trash was emptied. In the bathroom, her toiletries and makeup were lined up on the counter for easy access. Her laundry was washed and folded and set in piles on her dresser.

The whole house looked…prepared. As though he were expecting her to leave at a moment's notice. And that didn't sit well with her at all.

She watched him ignore her while he finished up the chores, any annoyance she might have felt under other circumstances overshadowed by worry, apprehension, and a hefty dose of confusion.

Since the night she spoke to Nichol, she and Boy had been a team. It was something she'd never experienced, being one half of a pair who stood on equal ground. She loved waking up with him, loved having her lunch while he wrote out amazing tales of things he'd seen over his long life, loved curling up with him on the sofa while he suffered silently through rewatching her favorite movies.

They were inseparable, but it didn't feel forced due

to their proximity in an area where no other person dared walk. If anything, she felt chosen, knowing he could be anywhere doing anything with anyone and he chose to organize her barn and play the role of moving target for her shooting practice.

But she wasn't stupid, nor was she oblivious.

She'd seen the slow shifting of his eyes. Ovaled irises which were once electric blue had shifted to a more muted gunmetal before darkening to navy. With the change had come a different quiet from him. While she rarely noticed his mutism amid his overwhelming presence and quick pen, the silence was heavier now, weighted by things he didn't share with her.

She knew he continued to listen in on her own thoughts and she used it to nudge him out of his head when he went still for too long. The slight lift of his lips or brows was a victory every time, a half smile more rare but enough to make her do a little happy dance.

But tonight wasn't the time to entice him with thoughts of what she wanted to do to him or stupid jokes she picked up during her waitressing years. He was moving with a stiffness she'd never seen in him. The muscles across his bare chest and shoulders taut with tension. The slouch was back, as though he were trying to fade into the shadows, and her heart ached to see it.

We have to talk, don't we? she asked him wordlessly and he nodded without looking her way.

I'll be on the porch.

She hesitated before turning away. He looked lost. Damaged.

Defeated.

Fear started to rise up inside her as she walked to

the house and climbed the steps to the veranda. Boy was a force of nature, silent and stalking and lethal. No matter how many times she saw his strength and speed, she was left speechless, her blood heating with the knowledge such a powerful guy looked at her the way he did.

There was only one name that she knew could break him.

Her fury toward Boy's creator knew no bounds. Saying it, she spat it from her lips. Thinking it came with curses and disdain. Knowing the vampire was the reason Boy had no voice, that she hurt him and continued to beyond her death infuriated her.

Khthonios was one sadistic bitch.

But Lexie Grace was discovering she might be too, given the right circumstances.

Sitting in her rocking chair, she watched Boy cross the barren terrain with his head bowed.

Prior to meeting him, her protective instincts had kicked in for precisely two people: her grandmother and granddaddy. Both were now dead and gone and all that energy was channeling into the vampire advancing on her with dragging feet.

He pulled his shirt from his back pocket and tugged it on as he sat in the rocking chair she now considered his. His notebook was already out, the few remaining pages wrinkled and torn as he opened it slowly and started writing.

"I should warn you if you tell me it's not me, it's you, I'll stab you with a sharpened broom handle," she stated, sighing when he paused, tore the page out, and crumpled it.

She waited until he began again before continuing.

"No matter what your reasons are, I'm going to be upset. But I guess you know that, don't you?" He nodded but kept his head down while he turned the page and made deliberate strokes of the pen. "This is probably the first time I've been resentful about you being able to read my mind because no matter what I say, you'll know how hurt I am. I can smile and pretend it's all fine but you'll know it isn't. And that sucks, Boy. It sucks because you get to hide it all and I don't."

The silence stretched out between them as he folded the notebook and held it in a clenched fist, his attention on the vast emptiness beyond her property line. Her eyes pricked with tears but she didn't speak and didn't move because when she did, he would and it would be over.

She wasn't ready.

So when he passed the notebook her way, she shook her head and tucked her hands under her thighs. "I don't want to read that."

But vampires didn't survive as long as he had without patience. His arm remained extended toward her without a single twitch of his muscles, the words he wrote waiting for her to read them. Knowing she was merely prolonging the inevitable, she exhaled loudly and took it, steeling herself for whatever rationale he felt he needed to make.

She unfolded the first page to find two words: *I'm sorry.*

Swallowing, she nodded and tried to blink back the tears already rolling down her cheeks. "I know you are."

She flipped to the next page, expecting to see a wall of text and unable to hold back the floodgates when she read the words written in the middle of the paper: *I love you.*

Everything was blurry when she looked over to find him still staring into the darkness. "If you love me, don't tell me to go. Because I won't. I saw the bags, Boy. I know what you're planning. But this is my home and I'll be damned if you or anyone is going to push me out of it to make their lives easier."

He didn't blink, didn't glance at her, didn't react.

Slamming the tattered notebook onto the small wicker table between them, she stood and stormed over to him. "Look at me," she growled. "You want to end this by sending me away? Well it's not happening. You can walk away, but I'm not leaving. You have some hero complex you're feeding by ending us under the excuse of protecting me, so at least have the balls to look at me while you throw me away, you coward."

That got a reaction.

Boy rose to his feet so fast she stumbled back a step. Then another. He advanced on her with his head bowed, his hair shielding his face as he forced her up to the railing and caged her against it with both arms.

Her heart was pounding, fear and anger and desperation and heartache all tossing and mixing together into a combination lethal for a woman with a loud voice, a big mouth, and nothing left to lose. "Yeah, you heard me," she said with a snarl. "Do you know what kind of guy tosses aside the woman he loves, a woman who loves him too? An asshole. An asshole and a coward and a jerk. You have someone willing to stand with you against those Deviants and your creator and you don't trust me to handle it. Well let me tell you something, Mr. I Love You But I'm Sorry, all you had to do was actually pay attention to those thoughts of mine you've been listening in on to know I wouldn't do that. We were supposed to be taking a stand together, you and me against the Deviants and Khthonios when they came. It was supposed to be me and you, and you're ruining it."

The low rumble from his chest grew from a barely detectable hum almost into a howl and he lifted his head as he shook his hair from face to reveal his black eyes. There was a torrent of frustration, sorrow, and pain churning in them, but behind them was something new, something she couldn't read.

He released the railing and cupped her chin gently, hesitating as though he expected her to flinch or scream. When she merely narrowed her teary, red eyes, he dipped his head down and kissed her with such softness she wasn't sure it was real until he deepened it with the desperation of a starving man.

And while she wasn't foolish enough to think he changed his mind when he lifted her and carried her to bed, she needed this last moment as much as he did.

Chapter Twenty-One

Boy didn't know if this was right, but it was necessary. He was losing himself to Khthonios more and more with every passing hour and he needed one more night, one more chance to leave Lexie Grace with no doubt about how he felt about her. At the rate his creator's influence was spreading through his mind and his body, he had two, maybe three nights left before he lost all control. Tonight was for him. For them. Tomorrow he would put enough of a distance between them so she would be safe from the hell he feared he was about to unleash.

But tonight she was here with him, her legs wrapped around his hips while he carried her down the hall to her bed.

Her thoughts were killing him with a thousand tiny spears embedding in his heart but he welcomed this pain. He felt every broken word she formulated in her mind while she kissed him and clung to him, wondering if the piercing edges would be strong enough to anchor him when the time came. Because this was what he would hold to when he allowed Khthonios out of her cage. He would have an eternity of memories from mere weeks with one woman and he was counting on those memories to fuel him.

He laid her on her bed and hovered over her as he kissed the tear tracks streaking both cheeks. His chest ached with the knowledge he was the one to do this to her. It didn't matter if it was the only way he could keep her safe from his creator's wrath. He hurt her. Every tear was because of him.

A small part of him reveled in it.

No one cried for him. He wasn't one to be missed or craved or desired the way Lexie Grace missed, craved, and desired him. Throughout his existence, Khthonios was the only one who ever sought him out and wanted to claim him for herself, but it came from a dark, disturbing need to possess and control him. Lexie Grace didn't want to keep him as a pet or a guard dog. To her, he was the guy who made her feel secure and happy while she ate popcorn on the sofa and slapped his knee to make sure he was paying attention to her favorite part instead of studying her perfect profile. He was the vamp who showed off his speed and strength to impress her and organized her barn to help her. He lifted her heavy things and opened her jars and entertained her with stories about the most epic pranks his hauntmates pulled.

And he was an asshole, a coward, and a jerk.

Sitting back on his haunches, he undressed her slowly, running his tongue along every inch of skin as it was exposed to him.

He held out no hope he would come out the other side of this battle. The army of Deviants was his to control only under Khthonios's will and she could pull their loyalty back to her with her blood, the blood still running through his veins and theirs. He was becoming little more than a vessel for her now, a body to house her power. Her ability to manipulate her blood was more refined than his. His limited experience was no match for hers, not when he only knew how to go in full-throttle, and tired quickly from the exertion. Khthonios, on the other hand, was capable of a subtlety so refined even he hadn't known she was lodged deep in his core until he drained the last of her blood from her body and he didn't feel the full hit of her final death.

For now, she was once again contained in her cage. It had taken hours to pluck every tendril of her influence from his mind and corral her, but he managed it before joining Lexie Grace on the stoop where she sat rocking in her grandmother's chair, watching him with an expression of such sadness and worry he'd almost abandoned his plan.

But there was too much at stake.

He moved farther down the bed and slid her black cotton panties off of her hips. They were his favorite pair and he tried not to think about the fact this would probably be the last time he peeled them from her body. Parting her thighs, he kissed his way from her ankle to her center and she sighed. Her fingers found his hair and tangled into it as he licked and sucked and nipped at her until she was breathing heavily and panting his name. He took his time, savoring her taste and keeping her on the edge until she was writhing in desperation for release.

"Don't tease me," she whimpered as he circled her clit with his tongue in a long, leisurely stroke. "Please, Boy. Not tonight."

Pushing himself off the bed, he stripped without hesitation. He was desperate to be inside her every time he made her come tonight, craving the feeling of her body tightening around him moments before she cried out. It would be another memory to cling to, another anchor he would need if he had any hope of surviving the next few nights.

Their gazes locked as he climbed back onto the bed and caged her between his arms. He needed to see her eyes as he entered her, needed to know she would feel the loss of them as intimately as he would. She lifted her hand to his face and grazed her fingers along his jaw, drawing in a shuddering breath when he kissed her palm and pushed inside her.

In this moment, while she lay beneath him trusting him with her body and her mind, he wished he had a voice, some way to tell her how he felt with more than a drying pen and a tattered notebook. He would lay everything at her feet and beg her to understand, plead for her forgiveness on his knees.

But he had no voice and no words. All he could do was make love to her and hope she heard everything he wanted to say before sunset tomorrow.

****

Lexie Grace straddled Boy's hips and clutched his shoulders as he thrust up into her with his arms holding her against his chest. Her skin was slick with sweat and her hair was falling in a tangled mess down her back, but she couldn't think about how she looked while she was riding the crest of another orgasm. The low, possessive growl rumbling from him filled the room as he increased his speed and sent her tumbling over the edge for the fifth time. His hold on her tightened and his rhythm faltered as his fangs sunk into her throat.

The mixture of pleasure and pain had her crying out, her voice hoarse and her breathing labored. Boy pounded into her a few more times before his body stiffened beneath her and he came hard as he unhooked his fangs from her skin and crushed her to him to ride it out.

His lips were on hers moments later and he kissed her softly while he twisted and turned, lying on the bed and arranging her on top of him.

"Are you staying?" she asked in a whisper, knowing dawn was near. "Please?"

He nodded and brushed her hair from her face while he studied her face like he was memorizing it. His onyx eyes followed the path of his fingers grazing her skin and traveling from her jaw to her lips to her cheekbones. He twirled her hair and watched it fall, then skimmed his palm over her bare back.

The sun rose outside but they stayed cocooned in her bed, neither falling asleep but both pretending they did. She listened to the faint rumbling still reverberating from his chest as he stroked the pad of his thumb along her throat where her heartbeat could be felt.

Every movement was a goodbye and they both knew it.

Sorrow had given way to numbness by high noon and she wrapped her leg and arm around him a little more to keep him close as long as she could. Thoughts of what nightfall would bring swirled through her mind, each new worry easing a fraction when Boy would kiss the top of her head as though trying to reassure her she would be okay.

And she would be. Physically.

Even when she was unleashing on him, she knew Boy wouldn't force her from her home. But the alternative wasn't much better, staying while he walked away. Either way, he would be gone at sunset and she would be alone.

His chances of survival were higher without her and while it pained her to accept it, she knew Nichol was right. He hovered over her whenever they were outside, one eye on her at all times even when he knew they were alone in the basin. His concentration could be broken by a scrape of a cactus against her leg or a stumble over rough terrain. Even her thoughts were a distraction no matter how aware of them she was. Thinking about how hot he looked when he was shirtless could draw his attention almost as fast as a simple *"what was that?"*

And then there was Khthonios.

She didn't pretend to understand how the dead vampire managed to survive, but she knew the bitch was the reason she was losing the guy she loved. Khthonios was gunning for her somehow and Boy wasn't going to let it happen.

It would be sweet if she wasn't torn between missing him already and wanting to throttle him to prove she was strong enough to kick some decrepit female vamp ass.

He nuzzled his cheek against the top of her head and she knew he heard her.

Boy?

His arms tightened around her and she took a deep breath before asking the question she'd been scared to think about, let alone ask.

When you finish annihilating everyone and everything is safe, do you promise you'll come back to me? When you survive?

His only response was a nod and a soft kiss on her temple before he closed his eyes.

****

Boy hefted his rucksack higher onto his shoulder and continued his ascent along the unforgiving rock toward a peak where he would have an unencumbered view of the valley. Nichol's drone hovered just out of reach, the tiny camera scouring the terrain below for signs of movement and finding nothing but nocturnal rodents.

He kept his focus on his grip and his balance, memorizing the location of each loose stone and calculating the time it would take once he was more familiar with the climb. His hands were raw and bleeding and he used the discomfort to center his thoughts on what he needed to do, not where he wanted to be.

For all he knew, Lexie Grace was still sleeping fitfully in her bed where he'd left her hours ago. He waited until she finally succumbed to exhaustion and then slipped from her bed and dressed, refusing to indulge in more than the brush of his lips across her forehead before he walked away.

The drone rose above his head while he scaled the final stretch to the peak. The clear night gave him a decent view of the terrain on both sides of the range and he began mentally cataloguing the best positions for attack, retreat, and where he could stand his ground.

"You have a plan," Nichol stated through the drone's speaker and he nodded, cocking his head to study the access points to a narrowing in the range. "The com room is cleared and it's just me, Boy."

Testing the strength of a ledge jutting north, he stepped on to it and knelt down to check its proximity to a cave opening.

"You've served as my sounding board in the past," Nichol continued, his low voice rumbling against the granite rock of the mountain. "You've stood behind me—behind all of us—for centuries. Let us do the same for you. I can be on site in three nights."

He shook his head and stood, tightening the straps of his bag across his chest and taking another look around before he dropped off the ledge, catching the lip with both hands and swinging into the cavern's narrow opening.

Nichol's words gave him pause.

Century after century, he stood behind his hauntmates while they clawed their way into the position as the most powerful haunt in North America. Arguably, the most powerful anywhere. They were loyal to each other to a fault, taking huge risks to protect their own.

He'd never truly been one of theirs, though. And he hadn't wanted to be, not when the one he needed protecting from was Khthonios. She was a demon he would need to battle on his own if there was any chance of his hauntmates and Lexie Grace to survive.

"You need eyes on your six, Boy." The drone hovered closer. "I hacked into the makeshift security system you set up for Ms. Kelly." His eyes narrowed and he stilled as Nichol's voice went quieter. "You can be pissed at me all you want, but she's important to you so she's important to us. I have ears on the military surrounding you and I'm not liking the silence on their end. You don't have to do any of this alone. I just need you to tell me what you need and I'll make it happen. You need bodies, we have them. You need weapons, tell me."

He hesitated then set his rucksack on the ground and pulled out a pen and a stack of pink sticky notes he swiped from Lexie Grace's kitchen junk drawer: *I need one thing.*

"Name it."

This isn't a favor or a request. It's an order and it's the only one I'll be making. Prepare a protection plan for Lexie Grace, complete with a minimum of four contingencies, ready to implement within twenty-four hours. Once the threat is eliminated, take care of her for me.

"I can have her out by dawn—"

She stays in her home unless there is no other option. He glared at the pink paper and added to it. *Her stubbornness is somewhat aggravating in times like these.*

There was a long pause before a grunt of acknowledgment came over the speaker. "I understand a thing or two about stubborn women. It will be done."

Satisfied Nichol would carry out his command, he scribbled a final note, set it on the edge of the cave, and went inside to prepare.

This will be my final declaration. Consider all future communication with me to be compromised. And thank you.

Chapter Twenty-Two

Lexie Grace sat on her roof with her rifle at her side, the faint smell of gunshot hanging in the still air while she stared at the motionless Deviant lying dead on the sand. The heat of the desert wasn't as stifling at night as it was during the day, but it was enough to cause beads of sweat to form and drip down the small of her back.

Scrunching her heavily sprayed curls to keep them somewhat buoyant, she stared into the darkness for any sign of the blond vampire who snuck from her bed before she woke.

She knew she looked ridiculous sitting on her roof with her hair and makeup done, wearing the pink camouflage print tank top which put her cleavage on display and drew his attention, and the lace-trimmed jean shorts he seemed to prefer. It was stupid to think he would return, that he would double back on his insistence on staying apart, but that small glimmer of hope remained.

And she'd be damned if she was going to run the risk of Boy coming to her while she looked as bad as she felt.

She hadn't been surprised to wake alone, but the emptiness of her bed and her home struck her hard all the same. There was no trace of him anywhere. No single socks in her hamper, no crumpled notes in the trash. No knives tossed onto counters or tables. The only sign he'd been there was the full cattle feed and water.

But she shouldn't have been surprised to see his existence wiped from her home so easily. He never left anything behind when he walked out the door, whether she was at his side or not. It was almost as though he were a ghost only she could see and when his physical presence was gone, so was all evidence he ever existed.

The thought made her heavy heart ache.

To her, Boy was larger than life. No matter how stealthily he moved or how hard he tried to slip into the shadows, she saw him. She sensed him. She knew instinctively when he was near. Even when they were training in the desert and she couldn't see him, she felt him close. It was like there was a thin rope connecting her to him, like something inside her was constantly scanning for him, ready to lock on the way ships found lighthouses in the dark.

But tonight, she couldn't feel him anywhere and she knew no matter what that tiny spark of hope wanted, he was far from her now. He wouldn't have returned to the mountain cave where she could track him down. He didn't want to be found, not by her anyway.

Running a finger along her eyelashes to prevent her mascara from running down her cheeks, she scanned the horizon for lurching Deviants and came up empty with the exception of a small black drone approaching her with a tiny box dangling from thin claws. It slowed and dropped in altitude until it was inches from the stairs of her porch. Slinging her rifle over her shoulder, she shimmied across the rooftop and crawled down the trellis while the drone rose into the sky and hovered above her.

The box was heavy for its size and she ran her nail along the tape to slice it open, frowning when she opened the flaps to see a phone.

"Well what am I gonna do with this?" she asked with a huff while she eased it from its packaging. "The government cut cell service out here, in case you didn't know."

The drone lowered but stayed out of reach. "Charge it," Nichol ordered and her hackles rose with his command. "I'll call you on it in ten minutes."

Rolling her eyes, she went inside and did what she was told solely to prove him wrong when the phone would be unreachable.

Ten minutes later it rang.

"Turn your camera access on, Ms. Kelly," Nichol's gruff, clipped voice greeted her when she answered. "I have some quick introductions to make before we discuss extraction procedures and expectations of both your behavior and your role."

Her brows shot up and she scoffed at the brusk tone as she fiddled with the settings. "I don't know what Boy told you but I'm not going anywhere and I certainly don't care about your opinion about my behavior, thank you very much."

The camera turned on and she blinked as the face of a young, handsome man filled the screen. He looked no more than twenty-three, with auburn hair, amber eyes, and a sprinkling of freckles across the bridge of his nose. He repositioned his lens, giving her a view of his broad shoulders encased in a tight black T-shirt showing off a muscled chest and hints of the abs under the fabric. The scowl was her only clue this cutie was Nichol Kaius, drone king.

"In case no one ever informed you, your miserableness doesn't match your appearance," she stated as she sat on her sofa and adjusted her phone to show off her best angle.

The image jostled and the faces of two women took over. One was a stunning brunette with black hair with turquoise tips brushed poker straight, incredible cat-like eyes, and full lips pursed in annoyance. The second looked like her—blonde, petite, and bright, but with flawless makeup, an obviously expensive minidress, and a warm smile. Nichol's grumblings faded as the blonde woman took over.

"Bianca Schumann," she said with a little wave. "It is so amazing to meet you, Lexie Grace. I wish I could say Boy told us all about you but you know how he is, so secretive and sly. Oh my, Audra, she's even more adorable than I thought."

The brunette was appraising her through the screen and she felt instantly on edge, as though she were being probed while the woman nodded and blinked slowly. "I'm Audra Verdi, Kaius haunt psychologist and best friend to the miserable twit trying to make our first meeting unpleasant. I'll introduce you to the rest of the table before I turn the camera back on Nichol, but don't worry. His mate is on her way and she won't let him go full Power Tripper on you."

Before she could speak, Audra moved the camera, stopping on a gorgeous brunette with a bright smile and a guy with his ball cap on backward and the most intense turquoise eyes she'd ever seen. "This is Molly and Dominic Kaius." The screen rotated again to a handsome, dark-haired vamp with tattoos along his temples and a hot blond one who looked an awful lot like Boy, but more relaxed judging by his grin and warm blue eyes. "Jagger Kaius and Mickey Kaius."

The pair waved and Audra spun the camera further, landing on two guys who looked like they just stepped off a battlefield, one wiry with fire-engine red hair and the other with long brown hair, a sexy smirk, and his arm slung around the redhead's shoulders. "Louis and Jonathan. They won't be here long since they have seven kids running amok somewhere around here."

She barely had time to give them a tight smile before a familiar couple she'd seen on the news filled the screen, the gorgeous vamp's mischievous grin disappearing into the rose-gold hair of the woman who looked more like a fairy or pixie than a human. "Lis and Rhys Kaius."

"I think I see why Boy chose the desert over civilization if he's getting to tap that every night," Rhys stated as Lis swatted his chest with a growled apology toward the screen.

The camera moved again, this time settling on a pretty woman with friendly brown eyes. Her fingers raked softly through the short blond hair of the hot vamp who looked like a CEO on his day off. An air of ancient power seemed to surround him, much like she felt around Boy and she knew his name before Audra spoke. "Harper and Kaius. Kaius Khthonios."

"Kaius Boy," she mumbled under her breath, remembering the rhythm of the last name.

Someone offscreen snorted, another agreed, and Audra turned the camera back to herself. "Sorry about overwhelming you with everyone, but you're a woman and Boy is Boy and the two concepts have never existed simultaneously in the same realm before, so everyone was curious about you. That, and we're worried, which is why Nichol and Kaius will be leading the discussion right now."

The screen filled with Nichol's grumpy expression and Kaius's stoic one so similar to Boy's it was eerie. A pretty woman with brightly dyed curls passed by the camera and planted a quick kiss on Nichol's head before disappearing and she bit her lip. "Are you worried about the Deviants or about Khthonios?"

Neither vampire blinked, moved, or did anything to indicate they heard her, yet her question was met with such complete silence from the whole group that her anxiety shot through the roof.

Taking a deep breath, she clasped her hands tight. "I'm guessing it's Khthonios."

Kaius was the first to respond, tension in his voice. "Khthonios was ended months ago."

She drew her legs up under herself and glanced at her boarded-up windows. "Well, yeah, I know. But, um…I don't think she actually died. Completely. Like, there wasn't total death, if that makes sense? I don't know how much I'm allowed to say here—"

"We're going to need you to say everything," Audra called out. "Lexie Grace, honey, I know it might feel like a betrayal to Boy if you tell us things he told you, but this isn't the time to hold secrets. Especially if Khthonios is involved."

Nichol disappeared from the screen for a moment, returning with a laptop turned toward her. Without a word, he pressed play on a video taken from one of his drones and her heart clenched at the sight of Boy standing inside the mouth of a cave, scribbling on a tiny pad of paper before he held it out to the camera.

I need one thing.

When Nichol responded through the drone's speaker, Boy continued to write, his pen moving with measured loops.

This isn't a favor or a request. It's an order and it's the only one I'll be making. Prepare a protection plan for Lexie Grace, complete with a minimum of four contingencies, ready to implement within twenty-four hours. Once the threat is eliminated, take care of her for me.

He looked different, more feral and lethal. His shirt was torn, his expression hard and his jaw tense as he held up another message.

She stays in her home unless there is no other option. Her stubbornness is somewhat aggravating in times like these.

Tears burned behind her eyes and she ran her thumb along her lashes to stop them from falling. Before Boy, her grandparents had been the only people who ever understood how desperate she was to have a place of her own, one no one could rip out from under her.

The next message filled the laptop screen and Nichol paused it.

This will be my final declaration. Consider all future communication with me to be compromised. And thank you.

"This is a problem," the cranky vamp growled. "During his time in our haunt, Boy gave nothing away of his strength or his abilities. He was a servant and mercenary and all along he was the strongest of us all, hiding behind his silence. We commanded him because he allowed it, but only one ever had any true control over him. With his ending of Khthonios, Boy became the most powerful being in existence. There is no other who can match him, let alone hold enough influence to compromise him."

"Except Khthonios," she stated, her fear for Boy growing with the realization she was speaking with a room full of vampires doing their best to hide their own freak-outs. "She hates me. The feeling's mutual."

Kaius's lips drew into a thin line. "Khthonios hates you," he echoed. "She told you this?"

"She told Boy," she replied, shifting in place and stretching one leg out to relieve the stiffness in her knee. "I don't know for certain, but I think she talks to him in his head. She sounds to me like a vindictive ex-girlfriend, but I don't really understand the whole creator relationship thing, so maybe more like an overprotective mother?" When no one spoke, she cleared her throat. "It's even worse than it sounds, isn't it?"

Nichol ran his hands through his hair, the grinding of his teeth apparent in the movement of his jaw. "Khthonios believed Boy to be her soulmate, for lack of a better term. From what we've managed to piece together since her demise, it is likely she was connected to Boy from the start but chose to wait to claim him until she deemed him worthy in both strength and power."

"Connected?" she asked, unwelcome jealousy rearing up.

"When a vampire becomes connected to another, they're driven by an invisible force. Think of it like imprinting," a lazy drawl replied and the screen moved to Dominic, the youngest. "I'm connected to Molly and let me tell you, it's physically nauseating to be away from her and vampires don't get sick. It's a borderline obsession, so strong that when it first hit, I damn near went insane. Lucky for me, Moll here decided I was cute and stuck around otherwise I'd be talking to you while hanging from manacles in our cell downstairs. Again."

Nodding despite her confusion, she sat back. "So Khthonios was connected to Boy. Was—or is—he connected to her?"

There was a chorus of scoffing and snorts before the beautiful Bianca replied curtly. "No. Boy most definitely did not return her affections."

"But this may explain some of the current situation we're in," Nichol added, his tone wary. "Khthonios had the ability to manipulate her blood, whether it was in her own body or passed down through her blood line. If she managed to sink the essence of her core into the blood Boy ingested—"

"She would continue to exist," Kaius finished, his stoic expression faltering. "Given the lengths Khthonios went through to keep Boy tethered to her, it wouldn't be out of the realm of possibility. She waited thousands of years to possess him. Perhaps death wasn't the hurdle we all assumed it would be."

Her eyes narrowed. "That bitch doesn't own him."

Kaius and Nichol exchanged a look she didn't like one bit before Nichol spoke. "If she's managed to survive through her blood, she's inside him, Ms. Kelly. We'll need confirmation from Boy before we can address the issue, but if what you're saying is true and she's speaking to him, we can assume she really is coming for you."

"Let her come," she growled. "I have more than enough ammo to knock her clear off the planet."

Kaius leaned in closer to the camera. "If Khthonios comes for you, it will be in Boy's body. The only way to eliminate her existence entirely is to eliminate Boy."

She stared past the screen to her front door with its paltry locks nowhere near strong enough to keep a determined vampire from her. "And he knows it, doesn't he? He knows she'll use his own hands to kill me," she whispered, her heart dropping when Kaius gave a terse nod.

Nichol cleared his throat while she blinked away the tears threatening to fall again. "We also have an added complication, one which will make your protection on site significantly more precarious."

Laughing humorlessly, she swiped at her eyes, not caring what her mascara was doing. "What could possibly be more complicating than vengeful vampires and zombie armies gunning for me in the middle of nowhere?"

"Our surveillance of military communications in the region has uncovered their plan to destroy Boy through any method required once he ends the last of the Deviants. This in itself is a non-issue given what we suspect Boy will do if Khthonios is indeed lodged in his core, but the United States military has video evidence of you with him," Nichol stated, his voice strained. "You've been charged with Voluntary Association with Vampires and Treason to the Species and will be arrested for sentencing the moment Boy dies or you step foot out of the quarantined region, whichever comes first."

Chapter Twenty-Three

Boy surveyed his growing army with a mixture of interest and disdain. Interest in the remarkable stillness his presence above them wordlessly commanded and disdain for the mindless obedience of his legion.

Their power rests not in their abilities but in their strength and numbers, Khthonios whispered in his head. *They are loyal through death, to death. My gift to you so you will never again be forced to return to the shadows.*

The Deviants stood in a horde while he studied them before willing them into formation.

They hear you.

Thousands of bodies lurched into rows and dropped to one knee in perfect synchronicity.

He felt Khthonios watching them through his eyes and he retreated back into his own mind to allow her this moment.

Their soldiers were tattered and filthy as they howled and screeched inside him, their fealty earned solely through the blood running through their veins. Eleven thousand large and growing, they would not be the most formidable to walk the land, but they would be the most lethal once they were unleashed. Despite lacking much of what made a vampire an apex predator, Deviants still gained strength through age and judging from their clothing, many were two or three centuries old and therefore significantly more difficult to kill.

We will grow their numbers together, Khthonios murmured, her voice a caress above the Deviant chaos in his mind. *This will be our fortress and from here we will take the land. The towns. The sanctuary. We will bow to no one. We will answer to no one. We will raze our path, leaving nothing in our wake until every step we take echoes across the globe.*

Her words were a madness above the meager band of mercenaries yet he could see her vision, taste the promised freedom on his tongue. With her blood running through his veins and her power uniting with his, they would be unstoppable. Unreachable. Unbreakable.

There would be no more hiding, no more pretending. He would no longer have to rein in his strength and speed or mask his abilities for fear of discovery. There would be no more banishment to the bloodslave quarters or cast aside into the corners, brought out when needed and forgotten as fast.

From a ghost to a god, Khthonios purred. *They will all see what I saw in you, Boy. And they will beg for the benevolence they do not deserve while they grovel at your feet.*

His mind was flooded with images of his hauntmates, memories snatched from troves buried for months, for decades, for centuries. Their voices were as clear as ever while their thoughts were dredged up and spread out in the moonlight.

Fuck you, Boy. Fuck you, fuck you, fuck you.

One of these nights I'm going to stake that mute bastard.

That old fucker could snap at any time.

He saw visions of the women staying tight to the walls when he passed, of his own hauntmates regarding him with suspicion and wariness. He heard every muttered word dripping with disdain and annoyance, caught each disparaging thought about his silent presence. His mind flashed with scenes from the last fifteen centuries, all the times his own hauntmates turned their backs on him, dismissed him, and outright ignored him because the scent of his blood was not the same as theirs. Every hushed conversation questioning his presence and his loyalty, each sneer when he stepped into a room, even the looks his hauntmates exchanged when he was brought into the fold churned inside him.

He was unwelcome among the very vampires his bloodline spawned because they couldn't smell his blood in Kaius, not when Khthonios's overpowered it. But he could. He scented his in every one of them while they rose to power and he remained in the corner, out of sight.

A faint wind drifted over him, the breeze breathing through his hair as though Khthonios herself were running her talons through it.

Tonight, we revel, she whispered in his ear. *Tomorrow, we strike.*

He nodded as her blood wrapped tighter around his own and squeezed.

****

Lexie Grace paced her living room floor while Nichol reviewed his plan for the fifth time, each reiteration becoming infinitely more complicated and bringing about another round of issues he hadn't considered earlier.

"I've noted possible hideouts along each of the possible routes you'll be taking," he stated with a mumble she'd learned meant he was already distracted, seeking out a backup solution. "I'll continue to drop location pins onto your phone but you'll need to add them to your rough sketch in case you lose signal or battery power. The last thing I want to be dealing with is you losing your bearings if the military decides to send out an EMP."

"Yeah," she snorted, looking at the terrible map of Nevada she'd attempted to draw on his orders. "My bearings are top priority."

"They are if they mean the difference between getting you to one of the extraction points and driving that death trap bike into a ravine. Do you have your bug-out bag prepped?"

Slumping onto the sofa, she crossed her arms. "The bug-out bag you told me to pack once we were done reviewing the plan? No, Nichol. I haven't."

His irritation was palpable through the screen as he glanced to his right with a scowl before returning his attention to her. "Our drones have been launched and should be in your proximity within seven hours. Plug in your phone, pack, and remember to turn on your television before you leave. It should pick up the signal I'll be transmitting to make it appear as though you're still on site. Questions?"

She blinked and straightened.

She had thousands of questions. Millions. None she could remember as his amber eyes locked on her and he ground his teeth, but she knew there were plenty.

"What if he comes for me before I can get out of the area?" she blurted out, grasping for anything to keep him on the line for a few more minutes. "Boy. Or Khthonios. Whatever. What do I do if he finds me?"

"Lie," Nichol replied. "Tell him you've changed your mind about waiting out the Deviant occupation and you'll be back in a few weeks. Say whatever you need to say to send him away and alter your path to counter his presence."

She exhaled loud and long while she debated betraying Boy's secret to the guy working his ass off to get her to safety.

It weighed on her all night while Nichol took control and the others popped on and off the screen with updates and suggestions. Plans were being made. Contingencies, emergency backups, and tertiary situations were all debated and assessed while she listened in awe at the speed with which the vamps analyzed each aspect of every idea. Despite her protest, they determined what they called their endgame right out of the gate: get her to safety. Second priority was saving Boy. When she attempted to argue, she was shut down with a single uttering from Rhys Kaius: *"Your life is Boy's top priority and that makes it ours. Trust me, angel, we know this drill all too well."*

And so she'd reluctantly agreed, her heart aching every time she thought about Boy putting her life before his own when every other man she'd thought she loved had placed her happiness and security somewhere above that of their beer-stained, secondhand sofa and below their dogs.

But all it was going to take was one stray thought through her mind in Boy's vicinity and it would all go up in flames.

They would all go up in flames. Or down in a blaze

of glory. Or however Khthonios decided she and the others should pay.

Squaring her shoulders, she shook her head. "I can't."

The vampire clasped his hands on his table, leaned forward, and glared at her. "I didn't give you a choice, Ms. Kelly. If Boy finds you, Khthonios finds you. Once they come for you, they'll come for us. Your survival instincts may leave much to be desired, but I assure you ours do not. We have not lived through the shitstorm that's been our existence for the last seven years to end up slaughtered by your boyfriend's obsessive sire."

Mimicking his pose, she stared at him, chose her loophole, and hoped he would pick up what she was throwing down. "Boy will know if I lie to him, Nichol. He'll know before I even say the words."

If vampires could pale, Nichol definitely did as he straightened his posture and rolled out his shoulders. "You better mean because you two are lovestruck soulmates who know each other so well you finish each other's sentences or some other bullshit, Ms. Kelly."

When she stayed silent, he slammed his fist down on the table and his laptop bounced, shaking the image while he cursed in no less than eight languages. "This is not fucking happening," he snarled as he jumped to his feet, hollered for Kaius out the door of his office, and started pacing. "I'm going to need exact words, Ms. Kelly. What are you telling me?"

Licking her lips while her anxiety rose, she swallowed. "I won't betray his trust and speak exact words but I can think them. If you were Boy, there would be no difference."

He ran his hands through his hair and sank back

into his chair as Kaius entered the room. "I'm going to kill your true sire, Kai," Nichol stated without emotion. "I have access to eleven nuclear launch codes. I'm using them all and then I'm going to watch a movie with Simone and forget this night ever happened."

Kaius's face appeared on the screen and he gave her a quick, tight smile. "As much as I wish I knew what I just walked in on, I'm going to need context. I'm not a mindreader."

"No," Nichol stated. "But Boy apparently is."

For the second time in five minutes, a vampire paled in front of Lexie Grace and she realized how right Boy was to keep his secret.

Kaius reacted with complete stillness and it was even more unnerving than Nichol's rant. His eyes were glazed, his expression stoic and unreadable for so long she was tempted to shake her new cell phone to see if their connection dropped.

"Fuck," Kaius finally said as he sat. He looked at Nichol then back to her. "I…fuck."

Twisting the hem of her shirt, she laughed. It was a nervous twitch left over from navigating some of her more volatile relationships, one she hadn't needed around Boy but apparently had yet to shake when she was starting to panic. "Not to complain, but shouldn't I be the worried one here? I mean, you two are old and know your way around mayhem and I'm just some dumb human out here trying to shield my thoughts from a five-thousand-year-old vampire."

"Five thousand," Nichol echoed, his expression shifting from furious to complete apathy as he stared at Kaius. "Did you know that?"

Kaius shook his head and both vamps looked

through the screen into her soul as she shrugged. "Maybe he assumed you knew." When they narrowed their eyes simultaneously, she sat back. "Or maybe he didn't want you to know because you didn't deserve it. Not with the way all y'all treated him. You probably would've kicked him out or used him like a weapon or something."

She knew she hit a nerve when Nichol broke his stare down with her and Kaius cleared his throat before he replied. "He was wise to conceal his age and his ability. Unfortunately, we're now in the unpleasant position of knowing our chances of total success in this undertaking are statistically nil. We have an ancient who will know our every move before we make it, who is likely being influenced by a female vampire even older and stronger than he is, and an army of Deviants drawn to his blood. We will do everything in our power to extract you, but it would be suicide for us to go up against Boy."

Nichol was solemn as he nodded his agreement. "I'll alert the others our endgame has changed to exclude Boy's survival. Ms. Kelly, go prepare for your departure. The sun rises in three minutes."

Chapter Twenty-Four

Boy stalked across the desert sand, the footsteps of thousands of Deviants lumbering at his back and the sound of Khthonios's voice in his head as he approached Lexie Grace's home to find her scent weak on the wind.

She has run from you, his creator murmured as memories of her tongue flicked against his ear and sent a chill into his bones. *The hunt begins.*

The faint smell of magnolia hung in the air and he latched on to it, refusing to think about how strong it was the last time he buried his head between Lexie Grace's thighs and heard her moan while she writhed beneath him. The cattle were where he turned his attention and his fangs lengthened as he approached the pen where his next meal stood and watched him with empty brown eyes.

You will not feed off that beast, Khthonios snarled. *We are not animals.*

Ignoring her protest, he placed a staying hand on the steer's back and sank his teeth through its thick hide to the vein below.

The taste wasn't wholly unpleasant in its blandness. In terms of effectiveness, it was an adequate substitution for human blood and had been serving his purpose well for the last few months.

But vampires were, by nature and their own

culture, a prideful group. Feeding off anything that wasn't human was considered uncivilized and uncouth and Khthonios's disgust over his meal choice was transmitting loud and clear while he got his fill.

Never again will you soil us with filth, she hissed and he fought the urge to recoil when the sensation of phantom nails dug into his skin and raked across his spine. *We are deities, Boy. Once we take our place, the mortals will line the streets with their wrists held in offering and their bodies bared. That woman made you believe this is what you are destined for, drinking the blood of cattle for sustenance like a rogue foundling and living in a shack like a pauper. But I know you, Boy. I know you as no other ever has.*

Her voice took on the smooth, serpentine quality which had led him to her heel thousands of years ago when he knew nothing of the corruption her tone hid with ease. His fangs unlatched from the beast and he walked toward the front door of Lexie Grace's home. Every movement was propelled by the strength of Khthonios's blood as it clutched to his own.

He didn't fight it.

We are not so different, you and I, she purred as he put his fist through the door and the plywood reinforcement now hanging by a few bent nails. Kicking the weakened splinters to the floor, he stepped inside and walked through Lexie Grace's home to find her drawers ajar, her closet ransacked, and her bathroom counter cleared.

A familiar unmarked box lay open on the living room floor and he growled, feeling Khthonios's glee reverberating in his veins.

We both long for a freedom denied us by Kaius and

his spawn, she hissed. *It is I who placed it in our reach. In your reach, Boy. The woman aligns with them. She has chosen them over you. Together we will hunt her down and show her what happens to those who ally with those mongrels.*

He stared at the box for a moment longer, his nostrils flaring as a hint of Nichol's bloodline hit him. Crushing the cardboard beneath his boot, he skulked out to the veranda and locked on to Lexie Grace's scent without acknowledging the drone hovering above the barn.

****

Swiping her hand across the dusty table, Lexie Grace plunked her backpack down and began the process of shucking her rifle, hip sack, and strips of bullets strapped to her waist and across her chest. Her legs were rubbery from walking the last eight miles after the fuel in her bike dried up, leaving her stranded short of her destination. Her hair was a tangled mess from the unexpected windstorm which rose up while she tried to make up for the time she lost securing the cattle and locking up the barn before she left. She licked her lips to counter the dryness as she scanned the large space once more before calling Nichol.

"Here," she whispered cringing at how loud her voice sounded in the underground bunker as his hard, amber eyes filled the screen. "What is this place?"

"It's an abandoned gold mine you were supposed to reach before sundown," he grunted in response, his annoyance with her late arrival coming through clear. "Timing is an essential component of our extraction plan, Ms. Kelly. Prolonged snack breaks have not been factored into the schematics."

"It was two stops for maybe ten minutes each," she countered with as much vitriol as she could summon with grains of sand embedded in her teeth.

"It was three, clocking in at eleven, seventeen, and fifteen minutes respectively. Your departure was an additional fifty-seven minutes late."

Glaring at him, she crossed her arms and shrugged. "I'm here and I'm alive. Now what?"

"Now you prepare for tomorrow's hike and go to sleep."

She snorted. "That's your big plan for keeping me safe tonight? Don't I get any weapons drops or special sprays or something?"

Kaius's face replaced Nichol's, his tone less aggressive as he adjusted the angle, giving her a glimpse of their swanky computer setup. "If Boy is capable of reading your thoughts, the less you think, the less you give away. Deeper inside the tunnels are beds and showers. The water will run cold but it should suffice. We anticipate the depth will provide a bit of a buffer should Boy make it this far north in his search for you—"

"Thirty miles," she interjected. "He has a thirty-mile radius."

Something almost like sadness or regret passed across Kaius's face before he looked away from the screen to confer quietly with Nichol. "That's good intel. I'm glad he shared it with you, especially since we can include the information in our plans. Boy is a little over forty miles from your current location right now and it's doubtful he'll make it within reach by sunrise. We'll need to widen the gap tomorrow though."

Her heart rate picked up. "Are you tracking him

now? How does he look? Is he okay? What do his eyes look like?"

"What do you mean, his eyes?" Nichol barked from somewhere behind Kaius.

She frowned and met Kiaus's piercing gaze. "Boy's eyes started going blacker and blacker a few weeks ago. Just a bit at a time, but definitely noticeable and got worse until there was only the odd flash of blue."

Kaius rubbed his temples and she knew her observation was a revelation. "I witnessed the same the night he drained Khthonios. There was a shift inside him, something I can only compare to a possession. Bianca spoke to him through a phone and managed to ground him long enough for him to finish the job, but I know the blackness you speak of and I believe we have concrete confirmation she is alive and well inside Boy."

"Fucking awesome," Nichol muttered as he appeared on camera with a laptop in his hands. "You two watch this while I go slam my head off the bricks a few times to rid myself of this goddamn Boy-induced migraine."

One of them tilted the camera so the computer screen filled her own and she inhaled sharply when the live video came into focus.

Boy was walking across the vast, barren terrain, his movements fluid and powerful as he stalked across the sand with his Deviant army lurching and stumbling behind him. His long hair hung in his face and his shoulders held a predatory hunch as though he were primed for attack. His gait was steady and rhythmic.

He knew exactly where he was going.

"He's coming for me, isn't he?" she asked, unable

to tear her eyes off the screen.

The image shifted to an overhead angle and she wrapped her arms around herself to ward off the shiver building deep in her bones. The eagle-eye view of Boy's minions moving en masse was equally stunning and terrifying. He strode as a lone figure ahead of them and they followed, adjusting their trajectory as a single, mindless hive.

"He hears them." Taking a deep breath, she watched as Boy stopped and cocked his head before shifting his path a fraction. "Every one of those things is in his mind all the time. The same goes with those women y'all made him share his blood with. He hears them, too. And each of you."

The aerial footage was removed from her sight and Nichol's fierce, handsome face filled the screen. "You're telling me he has thousands of voices in his head?"

She nodded and opened her backpack to pull out a sleeve of soda crackers. "More if he's in a city I'd reckon. It's a miracle he hasn't snapped."

Nichol's snort was his only response before he changed the subject. "All but two of my drones have made it into the area and each is tracking different aspects of this extraction. I'll be maintaining a constant surveillance on Boy but I'm going to need you to be prepared to move on my word so go get ready now while we have some flex time."

Nodding, she moved to end the call, pausing when Nichol barked a final instruction.

"Keep your ringer turned to max, Ms. Kelly. You have Black Ops military holding the line in front of you and a pissed off ancient closing in behind you. This is not the time to be unreachable."

Chapter Twenty-Five

Lexie Grace burrowed deeper under the scratchy blanket in a futile attempt to ignore the horrific sound coming from somewhere beside the hard cot where she was attempting to get a few more minutes of sleep. The noise stopped for a moment, the silence blissful until she remembered there was only one reason that god-awful ringtone would be blaring.

Scrambling to her feet, she rifled through the haphazard mess on the floor and found her phone, her pulse ratcheting up when she saw nine missed calls from Nichol Kaius. Before she could call him back, the screen lit up and the high-pitched squeal resumed as she fumbled to answer.

"Here," she stated, breathing heavily while she tugged her boots on with one hand. "I'm going to die, aren't I? Oh God, that's it. That's why you keep calling. He found me."

"He," Nichol replied with an ennui only a billion-year-old-vampire could convey, "went to ground forty-five minutes ago. I keep calling because you lack the discipline to adhere to the alarm I programmed into the phone and you have ten hours to walk as far as you can without detection by the US military. So yes, there is a good chance you are going to die."

There was a rustling on his end of the line before another familiar voice took over. "I am so sorry about him," Audra growled in such a Nichol-esque manner Lexie Grace stood a bit taller. "You aren't going to die. We have drones deployed to drop points with food and water and I'm sending an updated map of possible stopovers."

"Her lack of attention to time is counterproductive to her survival," Nichol barked in the background. "I refuse to allow this mission to fail because the female wants her beauty rest."

"Ignore him," Audra instructed as the phone pinged and Lexie Grace glanced at the screen to see a color-coded map pop up. "Simone cut him off from sex unless you make it out alive so the stakes for him have risen on a personal level. Get ready and call us when you're topside. You'll be heading east out of the mine."

East.

East?

The adrenaline blast to her sleep-fogged mind had her replaying the odd phone call over and over while she packed her bag and prepared to leave the cool safety of the underground bunker. As she heaved the heavy iron door open and stepped into the sunlight, her head finally caught up and she took a moment to scan the still terrain and nod to the drone circling above her before setting off east and calling Nichol back.

He answered with a statement. "What."

Stifling the urge to cock her rifle and split his precious drone in two, she appeased her temper by flipping it the middle finger and injecting as much syrup into her voice as she could muster under the early morning sun. "Tell me everything I need to know this morning."

And he did. He laid out her trek with explicit

detail, providing precise locations and numbers of both the military ahead and the Deviants at her back. His instructions and descriptions were clear and concise and she reluctantly admitted to herself that if anyone was going to be walking her through his nightmare, she was almost glad it was him.

"Questions?" he finally demanded.

This time, she was prepared with two, neither of which she wanted to vocalize but knew she needed to for her own peace of mind. "I know you said Boy wouldn't…" She paused and swallowed back the tears she didn't have time to shed while she hiked through the dried brush. "But is there any way he might, you know, be okay?"

The drone lifted higher into the sky for a minute and spun slowly before lowering within her reach. "I'm working an angle but its chance of success is slightly above impossible and six degrees below hopeless. That's all you need to know."

The ache in her heart eased a fraction. "How did he look last night?"

There was a long silence on his end before he responded, his voice low and gruff. "He walks with the stride of my nightmares. Pick up your own pace, Ms. Kelly. I'll be watching from above."

Alone with nothing but her thoughts and a silent drone circling overhead for company, she marched across the sand for six miles before stopping to rest on the deserted highway intersecting her route.

The drone dropped beside her while she ate half a sleeve of soda crackers and downed a full bottle of water.

"The convoy is on site and ready to retrieve you

when you make it through the line," Nichol stated, his voice tight and agitated. "The gap in the perimeter security remains, but we can't risk sending anyone in so you'll be on your own until you make it to the rendezvous point."

"On my own to dodge elite Black Ops forces in the dark," she scoffed as she got to her sore feet and resumed her trek. "You may not have noticed, but I'm not exactly the silent, sneaky type."

"You will be," he stated without argument. "Because my partner and the partners of three of my hauntmates will be risking their lives to hold position until you're secured."

Her steady pace faltered. "You sent your girlfriends?"

Even through the drone speakers, she could hear his teeth grinding softly. "The women are more than capable of ensuring your safety. And I did not command their compliance. They volunteered and informed me and my hauntmates our objections were noted and subsequently discarded."

A fleeting thought danced through her mind and she walked a little faster.

Boy would probably never know the lengths his friends were going through to fulfill his request to get her out and keep her safe. Maybe it was out of guilt over their treatment of him over the years, perhaps there was a hefty dose of obligation and a touch of fear of the mute, ancient vamp, but she suspected there was more.

"Nichol?"

"What."

She smiled at the lack of question in his clipped response. "He'd appreciate what you're doing. You,

Kaius, the others…he'd thank all y'all if he could."

Nichol cleared his throat. "We owe him this. You have thirty miles total left to go with an overnight stop in twenty. Providing Boy maintains the pace he set last night, you should remain out of reach of his ability to hear your thoughts until shortly before dawn when he won't have time to catch up." *And end you.*

The unspoken words hung in the air beside the drone.

****

Boy shook the sand from his hair and continued heading east while his army dug themselves out of the ground and joined him.

Lexie Grace's scent wove across him in weak tendrils, teasing and taunting him with memories he had neither the time nor the freedom to indulge in as long as his creator's claws were firmly entrenched in him.

She has made her choice, Khthonios spoke softly in his ear while the sensation of her cold hands slipped under his shirt and skimmed across his skin.

He marched on while she filled his head with promises of power and idolization. Visions of bodies strewn at his feet flashed through his mind, the faces of every human and vampire who dismissed him, discarded him, or ignored him staring up at him with their lifeless eyes.

One of Nichol's drones tracked him from above, the last link to his former haunt hovering out of reach.

They fear you, Khthonios stated with a gleeful laugh. *They fear us. They know they cannot stop us, that retribution for their betrayal comes—*

Ew. They cannot seriously think I'm sleeping here.

His steps faltered as Lexie Grace's voice carried

strong over Khthonios's.

Screw this. I don't want to survive if it means spending the night in a place that smells like ass and used sweat socks.

His creator's excitement was a palpable thrum through his veins. *Run, Boy. Tonight, she dies. Tomorrow, we reign.*

****

Lexie Grace lay curled up on the floor of the abandoned bomb shelter, her body exhausted enough to overpower her mental refusal to stay in the cement tomb. She shivered from the dampness of her hair, her bones still chilled from the cold shower she took upon her arrival and the cool concrete beneath her.

The room held no furniture, no indication anyone had ever inhabited the space or even prepared it in anticipation of needing it. The bathroom was separated from the main room with a rough cement wall, the shower a pipe arching from the ceiling and the toilet a cold metal bowl with no seat.

But it was, as Nichol barked when she muttered her discontent, functional. And functional was the best she could hope for as she tried to rest her body for the final stretch of her escape.

Her phone lay at her side within reach, the volume at max in anticipation of Nichol's call.

There was a peculiar silence surrounding her, heavy and constricting in the bunker which felt more like a tomb than a fallout shelter like the cranky vampire professed. The air smelt of dust, stale and suffocating as she lay alone listening for signs of life above her and knowing if she heard any, she was as good as dead.

Everything ached. Her backpack beneath her head was lumpy, the concrete under her body hard and unforgiving against her sore muscles. Her legs and feet cramped periodically, yanking her from the sleep she desperately needed to clear her mind and refocus her thoughts back to survival and away from Boy.

It wasn't working.

Every time she closed her eyes, she saw his blue ones as they were before the poison of his creator seeped in. Her mind brought up memories of him scaling mountains, sitting at her kitchen table watching her fill her coffee pot with rapt interest, hovering over her moments before he kissed her. She could almost feel his lips on hers, the way he trembled every time he fought off his own release to bring her over the edge once more.

With a shuddering breath, she rolled onto her back and lifted her phone to check the time, sighing when she realized she had an hour before sunrise and her thoughts of Boy were going nowhere fast.

But as much as it hurt to think about him, it hurt more not to. The unfairness of it all swept over her, crushing her lungs until she sat up and gasped for air as her fingers clawed on the cement.

She'd survived before him. She would survive after him. But survival wasn't living.

Before Boy, she hadn't known what it felt like to wake up excited and hopeful without the shadow of fear lurking in her periphery. His large hands were gentle, his imposing presence reassuring as he watched her with desire and treated her as both a goddess and his equal. After a lifetime of being deemed too loud, too brash, and too much, he not only accepted her as she was, he loved it.

Loved her.

Steadying her breathing, she wrapped her arms around her knees and stared across the room lit with a single bulb.

He was an apex predator, a hunter at the top of the chain, yet she'd felt safer with him than with anyone. Ever.

And that was what hurt most of all, knowing his creator would use his hands to destroy her if she failed to escape.

Her phone vibrated against the cement, the shriek of the ringtone piercing her eardrums as she swiped it to life and Nichol's clipped voice filled the room.

"We have a problem, Ms. Kelly," he stated without introduction. "I'm going to need you to get topside. Now. And then I'm going to need you to run."

Chapter Twenty-Six

Nichol rolled out his shoulders and opened another tab to ensure he was catching every angle of the nightmare unfolding before his eyes. His hauntmates were silent behind him, their attention on their own laptops while they monitored the global feed his drones were transmitting to every computer, phone, and television across the planet.

The world was watching.

"There's no way in hell she can make it, not with the speed he's going now," Kaius stated while he paced the same short path over and over behind him. "We underestimated Boy again and that woman is going to pay with her life."

"I'm fucking aware, Kai," Nichol snarled as Lexie Grace emerged from the underground bunker and paused to scan the dark terrain. Running his hand through his hair, he enlarged the color video feed from the drone hovering above her and compared her location to the two advancing forces closing in on her. "I put Boy's ETA at five minutes and the military's at six. I'm going to send her toward the army and hope to hell they control their trigger fingers until she's out of the line of fire. We can negotiate for her freedom later."

Bringing the drone down so he could speak to her, he reined in his frustration and channeled every ounce of calm he could before he spoke. "You're going to head north, Ms. Kelly. The military is advancing faster than anticipat—"

"Then I'm better off going south," she countered and he clenched his teeth to keep from snapping. "It's only eight minutes until sunrise and I have a good head start on Boy so it won't matter if I have to backtrack during the day."

"Boy is now four minutes from you," he stated, watching the screen as her expression morphed from determination to fear. "I'm sorry, Ms. Kelly. We underestimated him and now the soldiers coming over that berm are your best chance." *Of surviving.*

There was not a doubt in his mind she heard what he left unsaid.

He despised the tremor he could see in her hands as she tightened her hold on her old rifle and bolted across the sand, the dust kicking up behind her. Turning toward the others, he rubbed his chin. "How many views are we up to?"

"Closing in on ninety-seven million," Dominic called out. "Jagger turned off the comment sections on each of the feeds before they crashed the servers."

Rhys entered the room with his phone tight to his ear. "Lis wants to know what we need the women to do."

Nichol glanced over at Kaius and returned his attention to his computer while the haunt leader made the decision.

Boy was never supposed to catch up. The army wasn't supposed to move. They had contingencies for each, but not for both sides to advance simultaneously. Now they had tanks on the move, a vampire crossing the desert at twice the speed of the fastest vampire on record, and a woman caught between both.

"Tell them to retreat." Kai stopped his pacing to watch as Boy's speed picked up the closer he got to his target. "Immediately."

"They won't walk away, not while there's still the possibility she can make it," Jagger stated quietly.

"Boy signed Ms. Kelly's death sentence the moment he handed her his heart knowing full well Khthonios wasn't truly dead," Kaius replied, his expression locked down. "Their mission is over."

Rhys passed on the message while Nichol brought up the overhead feed of the area and readied himself to witness the bloodshed.

****

Lexie Grace ignored the burning in her thighs and kept her focus on the dozens of headlights cresting over the hill ahead. Her lungs were heavy with the dust she inhaled in every gasping breath, her muscles screaming as she pushed her body to go farther and faster into the lion's den.

Nichol's drone traveled ahead of her, the single red light reassuring as it led her toward enemy lines.

"Drop the rifle," his voice growled from above. "Give them no reason to open fire."

"I will," she panted, her pace slowing a fraction as she risked a glance over her shoulder. "When I'm closer."

"This is as close it you're going to g—"

The red light disappeared into the sky and she skidded to a stop, her grip on her weapon tightening as she locked gazes with Boy.

He was motionless as only Boy could be, his head bowed and his black, empty eyes trained on hers. The lights of the military vehicles in the distance illuminated him from behind, making him appear even more imposing than he already was with an aura of cold power radiating off him in waves she felt in every cell of her body.

"Let me pass," she whispered, searching his onyx eyes for any hint of the blue she loved. "Please."

He cocked his head and continued to assess her like one might a circus animal, a curiosity of mild interest. Her heart hammered as she took a hesitant step to the side, her breath catching when he mimicked her with a smirk. Staring him down, she tried again, her stomach sinking when he simultaneously matched her and closed the distance between them until the muzzle of her rifle was pressed to his heart.

"Don't do this," she pled, not caring how desperate she sounded while her finger trembled against a trigger she couldn't bring herself to pull. "Please, Boy. Don't let her do this to us. This isn't how we're supposed to end." She drew in a shaking breath. "You're more than this. More than her."

There was a flash of electric blue across his black irises, the remorse in his eyes breaking her heart all over again moments before his fangs tore into her throat.

****

Nichol's hazel eyes moved between the seven video feeds, the clock, and the stoney expressions on his hauntmates' faces as they watched Boy feed off the very woman he demanded they protect.

Their failure would be a bitter pill to swallow later when the monitors went dark, the streaming videos were cut, and the com room was no longer filled with the live feed of the haunt's inability to carry out the sole request Boy made of them.

"Sunrise in forty-two seconds," he announced as he pulled up the image of the military holding position four hundred yards from Boy and Lexie Grace.

Jagger reached over his shoulder and tapped on the upper left corner of the screen. "What the hell is he doing?"

Zooming in on the video, Nichol opened his drone control panel in a side bar and leaned into the mic. "Get on your goddamn feet and run," he hollered at Lexie Grace as the sun crested and Boy dropped her to the sand.

His hauntmates muttered in disbelief as she scrambled backward, putting as much distance between her and Boy as she could before she grasped her head and froze, her scream piercing through the room moments later.

****

The heat of the sun warmed his back as Boy brought the blade to his wrist and dragged its serrated edge deep across his veins. Khthonios howled her rage in his head while he exorcised her poisoned essence from his body and watched it form a black pool in the sand at his feet.

Lexie Grace's blood was sour on his tongue, her terror pungent and nauseating. But he couldn't spare the time or energy to focus on her right now, not when he was using her blood to fuel the elimination of his creator from his body and using his blood manipulation to hold his army under the powerful rays of the morning.

The flow of black sludge pooling under him began

to slow and he bared his fangs, ripping his wound back open and spitting out the drops of Khthonios's toxin before he shredded his other wrist and forced her out into the sun.

Shouts and commands from the military in the distance blended into the howls of his Deviants as they started to ignite behind him. Nichol's drones barked orders while Khthonios's curses wove through the din, her voice growing weaker as his blood clashed with hers and purged her tainted existence from his veins. Her essence bubbled on the sand, the sludge thickening and roiling.

And through it all, Lexie Grace stumbled to her feet and watched him, her eyes widened in terror and her small hands grasping her rifle as she backed away from him.

One by one, the growls of the Deviants were erased from existence as they burned, their bodies turning to ash and blowing on the gentle wind crossing the terrain. With the final death of each one came another small reprieve against the weakness beginning to take hold as his ability to control them wavered. Lexie Grace's blood had provided the boost he needed to start the fight, but only he could finish it.

She will die alongside me, Khthonios screeched inside him as he reopened his wrists. His own blood splashed onto the ground as he pitched forward, reaching toward Lexie Grace and falling to his knees to the sound of her scream. His body expelled the last of his creator's poison as a bullet tore through his gut.

****

Nichol sat in silence while his hauntmates whispered shocked curses at the nightmare unfolding

241

on his monitor.

For a second, he had a sliver of hope. As the Deviant army ignited in an inferno at Boy's back and the blood of Khthonios ran black from his veins, Nichol allowed himself to believe the woman would be okay. Maybe even Boy.

But the moment her shaking hand fired her weapon, all hope drained from him, leaving him numb as he bore witness to the myriad of bullets which wracked her small body. The restraint his drones held over the military by bringing millions of eyes onto them was erased in a single heartbeat and there was nothing left to do but watch Lexie Grace crumple to the ground.

The room stilled as everyone's attention turned to Boy's form hunched on the sand. The drone footage zoomed in close enough to make out the streaks of blood in his blond hair. None of them wanted to see the final moments of the vampire who was responsible for their very existence, but each of them refused to look away, refused to disrespect Boy by turning their backs while he ignited in the sun.

The seconds ticked by as they scoured his body for the smoke and flames sunlight would surely bring, knowing Boy's age would fight off the effects longer than most but accepting his end was inevitable.

It was Dominic who broke the silence when Boy's prone form rose up, his body unblemished from the rays which were annihilating his Deviant army. "What the impossible fuck is going on?"

Kaius crouched at Nichol's side, staring as Boy lifted his head and his eyes locked on Lexie Grace's bullet-riddled body. For a moment, the world seemed to stop. Not a single noise came from the motionless military. The wind which always hushed through the drone mics stilled. Not a breath was taken as understanding settled into Boy's blue eyes a split second before the silence was broken by an anguished howl heard across the world.

Chapter Twenty-Seven

Boy fought the urge to crush Lexie Grace's broken body to him as he hunched over her and angled his wrist over her bloodied mouth. Desperation took hold when her flutter of a heartbeat shuddered.

He sensed the military inching closer and he bared his fangs at them, ready to eliminate each and every human in retribution until Nichol's voice sliced through the quiet of the dawn from the drone hovering in the blue sky.

"The world is watching," Nichol snarled at the stealth force creeping in from the north. "Every television, every computer, every phone, every fucking screen on the planet watched you gun that woman down and they're watching now, courtesy of the Kaius haunt."

Lexie Grace's blood soaked the thick fabric of his combat pants and seeped through his shirt to his skin, its warmth cooling in the early morning breeze. In his peripheral, he could see heads tilt, ears listening while he reopened his wound and held it to her pale lips.

"We played the game your way," Nichol continued on, his voice powerful and steady against Lexie Grace's weak, faltering heart. "We retreated from the streets of your cities and established a sanctuary away from those of you who sought to exterminate us. We fought for you against our own, hunted them in the shadows, and erased them from existence. We adapted to your society. We acquiesced to your laws."

Boy brushed his lips across Lexie Grace's forehead as a terror unlike anything he'd ever known rose fast with the knowledge he hadn't enough blood left in him to repair the damage to her broken body.

"But we're done playing," Kaius's voice growled through the air. "You may know our names. You may know our faces. You may even know the rumors of what we've done over the centuries. But none of that is going to matter if that vamp dies at your hand because I will personally, meticulously, and leisurely disembowel each and every one of you with the patience and skill of a vampire who has had thousands of years to perfect his technique. I will come for you while you sleep, hunt you like an animal, and string you up by your Achilles' tendons before I open your gullet and revel in the sound of your organs sloshing onto my boots."

Rhys's smooth baritone took over as Boy picked up a small scuffle somewhere in the distance. "And if that isn't enough to convince you to back the fuck up and drop those weapons, you see that vamp you think you can overpower? The one guarding the woman you gunned down? If her heart stops, I guaran-fucking-tee you'll be praying for Kaius to come for you by the time he's done because he is the oldest, baddest bastard in existence and you guys made his honey bleed."

Familiar scents danced on the wind and Boy's head snapped up as Molly and Simone broke away from the military line and raced toward him with Bianca and Harper hot on their heels in a black SUV. Their thoughts came at him too fast, his blood loss weakening his ability to filter through the keening howls of the last of the Deviants left to perish in the sun.

The vehicle skidded to a stop and Bianca jumped out and dropped to her knees as she shoved her exposed wrist into his face. "Bite," she ordered. "You need to save yourself before you can save her."

His fangs pulsed with hunger as he sunk them into her vein without hesitation. No sooner did he take what he safely could from Bianca when Simone took her place.

Tearing his own wrist open again, he held it against Lexie Grace's mouth. Jagger's voice cut through the air from the drone above while he monitored her shuddering heart. "This is for all you government types listening in right now. It took us less than twenty-four hours to orchestrate this broadcast into every video system across the world. Your boys on the ground here make one more wrong move and we might be forced to turn our attention to the banks. Maybe dip into your security defenses. We have, what, ten launch codes already?"

"Eleven," Nichol growled and Boy picked up a collective curse from the minds of the nearby soldiers.

"Eleven," Mikhail echoed, and he could hear the feral smile in the blond vamp's tone. "Hear that? Eleven launch codes from around the globe."

Dominic's rumbling laugh came through the speaker, humorless and taunting. "And knowing Nichol, those nukes were strategically chosen, gentlemen. You better pray to whatever deity you believe in that Lexie Grace and Boy survive because we have no problem wiping this whole slate clean and we don't give a flying fuck if we go down with the ship."

The military took a collective step back, their

weapons lowered when a barked order rippled through the ranks.

The women's thoughts were clearer now. His own heartache echoed in their unspoken words as Harper knelt at his side and held her arm out to him when he released Simone's. He looked over to see her watching him, her expressive eyes too intense for him to hold her gaze.

Lexie Grace wasn't getting better despite the influx of fresh blood he now had in his system. Try as he might to listen, he hadn't heard a single whispered thought since she fell to the sand in silence, the shock of the assault on her small body too great for her mind to process.

And he was desperate to hear her. He needed her to tell him what to do, what she wanted while he held her on the cusp of death. Her injuries were too numerous and her blood loss was too great. But he couldn't let her go, so he selfishly clung to her and dripped his blood down her throat, keeping her in a purgatory she didn't deserve because he was too weak to release her.

He unhooked his fangs from Harper's wrist and slid them into Molly's as Nichol's drone approached him and hovered within reach.

"Let her heart stop," Kaius said quietly through the speaker and he squeezed his eyes shut, refusing to accept what he already knew. "Get her into the backseat and take her home."

"Boy?" Bianca's voice was soothing. Too soothing. He didn't need soothing and comforting, not when he was barely holding on to the rage and grief swirling inside him and threatening to break free of his brittle control. "Listen to Kaius and he'll guide you through this. Everything will be okay."

Releasing Molly's wrist, he clutched Lexie Grace to his chest and snapped his fangs at the woman who dared try to placate him while the woman he loved lay dying in his arms.

"Don't you even fucking think of turn feral now, Boy," Kaius shouted through the speaker. "Your mate needs you to hold it together if she has any chance of surviving the transition."

The words pierced through the black cloud of fury surging through his mind and Boy stilled.

Female vampires were a scourge, hunted and culled before they became too strong to be contained. His own creator was a testament to the threat female vamps possessed and no one in their right mind would sire a protege the whole of vampire society would seek to eliminate, his own hauntmates included. Turning a female was considered traitorous, akin to an act of war.

He lifted his gaze to the red light of the drone's camera.

"You heard right," Kaius stated with the tone of unquestioned authority Boy knew well. "I hope to hell you're as powerful as we think you are because you're going to have your hands full with that one."

Chapter Twenty-Eight

Boy's hands shook as he pulled the last bullet from Lexie Grace's body and dropped it onto the floor of the SUV before he smoothed her bloodied hair from her throat.

"It'll be okay," Bianca whispered softly beside him as she tucked his own hair behind his ears. "You fixed Kaius. You can fix her."

Abomination.

Squeezing his eyes shut, he tried to ground himself in Lexie Grace's irregular heartbeat while the vehicle, driven by Molly, bounced and jerked across the sand.

Mutation.

This time, there would be no Khthonios to fix things if he didn't succeed. There would be no second chance, no backup plan, no one stronger and more powerful to make it right if he failed.

Was this thing worth it?

Khthonios's words spun round and round, drowning out everyone and everything else until Nichol's voice barked clear from the drone held tight in Harper's delicate hands.

"Any day now, Boy. I'd like to know if I'm planning global annihilation or a movie date this weekend."

Reaching behind her, Molly gave him an awkward pat on the knee, her thoughts a jumbled mess of worry for him, fear for the dying woman in his arms, and concern about the curling iron she wasn't sure she unplugged before joining the rescue convoy.

Determination surged with the realization his hauntmates dropped everything and were ready to rain hellfire down across the globe for him.

Yes, it was all fucking worth it. Every one of them.

His eyes snapped open and he sank his fangs into Lexie Grace's throat as he monitored her weak pulse. Beat by beat, her dying heart pumped her blood into his mouth until the final shudder wracked her body and the taste of death hit his tongue.

Re-opening his wrist, he pressed the wound to her lips and ducked his head down to rest his forehead against hers.

"Should we cover her with a blanket or something?" Simone asked behind him. "You might be a daywalker, but what about her?"

"Once it starts, it takes hours for the transition to complete and for the body's cellular structure to become hyper-sensitive to UV rays," Kaius called from the drone held fast in the front seat before his voice became muffled. "Nichol? Where are we standing on an official ceasefire? I want that platoon retreating within the next ten minutes."

Boy ignored his hauntmates, blocking out everything while he waited for the telltale flicker to bloom in his mind, the stream which would connect him to Lexie Grace for eternity. Seconds to minutes and he sliced his vein open again while he channeled his energy into his own blood, willing it to fill her still heart and ignite the spark in her core.

Bianca remained tight to his side while Molly

drove with Harper perched on the center console. Simone hung out the passenger window with her gun drawn while the military started their slow withdrawal. As the last of the soldiers disappeared over the berm behind them, another of Nichol's drones held speed beside them.

"Anything?" Kaius asked and Boy could picture him and the others sitting in the com room with their hands clasped and brows furrowed while they waited for the outcome of their latest mission.

He was about to shake his head when something detonated in his mind. The intensity of the blast rippled through every muscle in his body as though he'd been electrocuted. Tightening his grip on Lexie Grace, he heard himself panting as he drew in unneeded air to steel himself until the aftershocks subsided.

He's breathing.

The words froze him in place as he took in the enormity of hearing her voice.

Why is Boy breathing? Vampires don't breathe unless...oh God, he's dead. No. I'm dead. One of us is dead. Maybe both of us are dead. More dead?

He brushed her hair from her face, his heart in his throat until her eyes opened. Her gaze was unfocused as the telltale vampiric ovaling of her irises started to take hold and he trailed his thumb across the pale skin of her cheek down to her lips. His instinctive drive to check her over battled with his need to reassure her she was going to be okay. Better than okay, if she embraced what he made her.

He couldn't think about what he would do if she didn't.

"Blue eyes," she murmured, a small smile on her

face moments before the deep sleep of her turning took hold again. "I missed that."

The SUV sped up and the back tires kicked up a cloud of sand as Molly shrieked with an excitement he felt blasting from every woman in the car save for the resting vamp in his arms. "We'll be at her house in two minutes, Boy," she hollered as though they weren't all sitting within inches of each other. "I can't wait to watch my first vampire waking."

The others started chattering with the relief and anticipation he heard clear in his mind until Kaius cleared his throat. "I don't believe an audience would be a good idea. Mikhail has already negotiated your safe return through the barricades and we expect you back on site here immediately."

Simone huffed from the front seat while Boy continued to track his blood in Lexie Grace's body. "She won't eat us. Boy's here and we have three dozen bags of blood in coolers in the hatch."

"And we want to meet her in person," Harper chimed in, arching her neck to give Boy a smile. "She's one of us now."

One of them.

If the stress of the day wasn't caging every emotion he had, he would be grateful. Happy. Maybe even touched. But until Lexie Grace woke and he knew for certain she was okay, he couldn't afford to allow a single crack in the prison where he was keeping every feeling threatening to explode out of him.

Kaius sighed and Boy could picture him rubbing his chin as he chose his words. "From what I've witnessed and heard over the years, female vampires do not wake like males do. They require more—" He paused. "Attention."

"So we'll give her attention." Molly laughed, pulling the SUV to a stop and grabbing her own weapons as she hopped out to join Simone and Bianca in protecting the short walk to Lexie Grace's door. "Harper and Boy handled you on their own, Kaius. The five of us can handle one fresh vamp."

The drone lifted from Harper's hands as she exited the vehicle and she opened the door for Boy to carry his precious cargo out while Nichol's voice carried on the breeze. "What Kai's saying is when we male vamps wake, we take our time. We stretch, growl a little, eat. The urge to hunt comes online over the course of a few nights. Other...urges...follow. We wake feral but there's an adjustment period for sires providing they address the newborn's insatiable hunger."

Rhys cut in, the smirk in his voice coming through loud and clear as Simone pushed the broken front door open and Boy stepped inside. "And what Nichol's saying Kai is saying is females wake up needing it all at once and there isn't enough bleach in the world to cleanse your eyes if you witness what Boy's going to be doing for the next few weeks. Say your goodbyes, get in the car, and get your asses back home. Boy, good luck to you, your jugular, and your cock. You're gonna need it."

****

Boy paced outside the small bathroom of Lexie Grace's home. Simone and Molly stood guard at the door and refused him entry while Bianca and Harper cleaned the blood from Lexie Grace's skin and hair.

He's so adorably nervous.

Glaring at Molly, he quashed the urge to bare his

fangs and show her how *adorable* he could be right now.

Although the Kaius haunt vamps were insistent the women depart immediately, they hadn't. And he was beginning to wonder if they ever would. The contents of the fridge had been emptied and replaced with bags of blood organized by type and date. A load of laundry was in the washing machine. Fresh clothes were set out on the bed for both him and Lexie Grace. Bianca's suggestion for him to shower was more of an order than her sweet tone implied.

"Okay, Boy, we're ready for you," Harper called through the door and he tamped down his desire to give Simone a triumphant grin when she reluctantly stepped aside and let him in.

With a large towel draped over her body to preserve her modesty, Lexie Grace lay asleep in the bathtub much as he'd left her twenty minutes ago. Her wet hair hung over the side of the porcelain, as clean and sweet-smelling as her skin now that the blood and dirt was washed away.

"We can help lift her," Bianca offered, trailing off with a laugh and the shake of her head when he growled. "Or not. Carry her to bed, honey. Harper and I will dress her there before you tuck her in for the next few days."

Ensuring the towel remained in place, he gingerly scooped her up and cradled her to his chest. The absence of a heartbeat hit him hard when he instinctively tried to tune into its soothing tempo and he stilled.

"Hey," Harper said softly from the doorway, her long brown hair pulled back into a ponytail and her clothes damp. "You did the right thing, Boy. I may not have met her officially yet, but that woman is a survivor. It might take some time for her to adjust, but she'll be grateful for this opportunity. I just know it."

With a stiff nod, he carried Lexie Grace to her bed, laid her down, and resumed his pacing. Bianca and Harper slipped in and dressed her with such care he wished he could speak and thank them for doing something he wouldn't have thought to do, not when he was too focused on monitoring his blood while it worked its magic inside her. As much as it pained him to admit, he wasn't firing on all cylinders right now despite the relative quiet in his mind with the final deaths of so many Deviants left to ignite in the sun. His fear for Lexi Grace was too encompassing and his need to contain that fear required too much of his depleted energy to allow him to think past survival.

But Lexie Grace wouldn't want to sleep with her skin and hair caked in filth. She would want to rise clean and beautiful, with no reminders of her final moments of life marring her. Bianca was buzzing around him, arranging Lexie Grace's makeup on the bedside table while Harper took a brush to her damp hair. Simone and Molly continued to patrol the house and the grounds under the watchful eye of an agitated Nichol hovering above.

And he waited. Waited and worried and hoped he remembered to express his gratitude to all of them once Lexie Grace was alert and safe and—hopefully—his.

Chapter Twenty-Nine

Boy picked up the television remote and sprawled out on the sofa to select a movie from the multitude of options Nichol's recent drone drop provided in the form of a little black box. He spent four hours fighting with the new tech until Lis called him and walked him through the process with the patience of a saint.

After five nights with nothing to do but watch over his resting companion, he was grateful for the distraction. Nichol's drones patrolled the area and fed the video footage directly to the cell phone he left plugged in beside the bed where Lexie Grace continued to sleep the sleep of the dead.

Or former dead.

Either way, he couldn't think about it too much, not when he was still holding his figurative breath.

Turnings rarely took longer than twenty-four hours with a few going well into a second night. Between Kaius's reassurances female vamps were a different breed entirely and Nichol's statistical analysis of Lexie Grace's injuries in relation to her recovery time, he was keeping his head.

Barely.

With his senses open to pick up any movement both in and out of the house, he chose a dystopian film, settled in to watch it, and gave up after ten minutes.

Of all the things he needed during the past five

nights, eyes on Lexie Grace was number one. It didn't matter if he could feel her existence in his mind; he had to see her. He needed to prove to himself time and again that she was here, she was safe, and she was as alive as a vamp could be.

Slipping into her bedroom, he took up his position with his back against her door.

And that's where he was sitting in a state of half-sleep when she pounced.

Had he been fully awake, he would have caught the flash of life through their link moments before familiar thighs straddled him and tiny kitten fangs slid into his jugular.

Lexie Grace's thoughts were a wild mess of single-minded need as she took her first draws from his vein. Her ravenous hunger pulsed into his head like a bass drum pounding through a wall of speakers. In this moment, he was nothing more than a meal for her, a nameless, faceless food source.

And he was so fucking relieved he could've cried were he not so focused on the sensation of her small teeth piercing his flesh and the moans of pleasure coming from her as she fed. Her first swallows were uncontrolled and messy and he could feel his blood dripping down his neck and pooling in the collar of his shirt before her initial thirst was quenched and her feeding became slightly more restrained. He stayed motionless beneath her, allowing her time to sate her hunger until the frenetic thoughts bouncing through her mind started to shift and her soft tongue flicked his healing wound twice before her lips grazed his ear.

"Run."

She leapt to her feet as her desire to hunt surged to

the forefront, spurring his own. With a feral growl, he jumped up, tore through the small house, and sprinted out the door into the darkness. He could feel her elation as the thrill of the hunt rushed through her veins and he smiled as he shimmied up and over the roof, dropped silently to the ground, and slipped into the barn. She moved with stealth, relying on instinct instead of her heightening senses as she crept around her property in her search for him.

He couldn't wait to train her, to teach her how to scent the air and filter through the noises of the night to pinpoint her prey. While he stood tucked deep in the shadows, he tracked her movements and her thoughts, his pride in her soaring when she noticed barn door was slightly ajar.

Lavender's blue, dilly dilly—

Anticipation rose, electrifying every nerve in his body as she slunk inside and closed the door tight behind her.

Lavender's green—

Inch by inch, she moved deeper into the barn and breathed in the stale air, her head tilting.

When I am queen, dilly dilly—

In a blink, her small form was pressed flush against him. "You shall be king." Her fingers grazed his jaw and she smiled up at him, giving him a glimpse of blue in her predator gaze and his first look of her delicate viper fangs. "You came back for me."

I promised I would, he thought to himself while she explored his face with her hands like she was relearning it, memorizing it.

"You did." Her eyes blackened again and her humanity took a backseat. Her vampiric core roared to the surface and a fresh hunger crashed over her and slammed into his mind.

All shock over her response evaporated as she dug her nails into the back of his neck and yanked his head down. Her fangs sliced his bottom lip as she kissed him and she growled while she lapped at the blood before nipping at him again. She tore at his shirt, ripping it open and sliding one hand down his chest while the other tugged at the button of his cargos and snapped it, sending it skidding across the wooden floorboards.

Her thoughts were a frenzied tangle of cravings and desire and he fought through the mess as she wrapped her fingers around his cock and pumped him. Squeezing his eyes shut to rein in his unraveling control, he dug into her mind, desperate to know if her actions were driven purely by her changing biology or if she truly wanted him.

"You," she panted against his skin as she sought out his jugular again. "I want you, Boy. I need you. Now."

Spinning her around, he pushed her flat to the slatted wall, shoved his hand under the soft cotton of her yoga pants, then past the cool silk of her underwear to find her slick and wet.

Flashbacks from his own turning attempted to break free from the cavern where he kept them sealed and locked away. He remembered the insatiable hunger, the all-encompassing need to hunt. But above all, he remembered the unrelenting ache, the feeling of too much energy and too much power building inside him. Khthonios had been more than willing to provide him with the release he needed—on her terms—but memories of those agonizing and humiliating weeks had no place here, not when he was determined to be everything his own sire wasn't.

Though he suspected, when it came to Lexie Grace, that pendulum was going to swing dangerously close to indulgence.

He eased two fingers inside her and held her body tight to the wall with his own while she ground her hips and rode his hand. Her fangs sliced her plump bottom lip and he tracked the bead of blood as it formed and slid slowly down her chin.

"More," she gasped, grasping at his shoulders. "Boy, I *need* you."

Her words only echoed the jumbled thoughts and intense desire pulsing in his head and he obliged, lifting her up and slamming inside her in one hard thrust. She wrapped her legs around him with a primal moan and he pounded into her without the restraint required when she was human and far more fragile. Her fingers clawed at his chest and scratched down his back as her orgasm hit and he arched his head back, encouraging her to feed, and shuddering through his own release when she did.

Their lips met with a clash of tongues and fangs as he slowed his movements as her hunger for blood and sex temporarily ebbed.

"Boy?" she whispered while she disentangled herself from him and straightened her clothes.

Tossing his torn shirt aside, he lifted a brow and waited, wondering if this would be the start of the questions and accusations he knew would eventually come.

Instead, she trailed her hand down his bicep and looked up at him, her blue eyes blackening moments before her smile turned feral. "Run."

****

Lexie Grace blinked a few times before realizing her bedroom was nowhere near as dark as it usually was at night. Even in the absence of light, she could clearly see every imperfection in the ceiling, every roller mark in the paint on the walls. Tiny dust particles glowed like stars in the air and she sat up, reaching out tentatively to see if they would spark against her fingers and jumping when she realized she wasn't alone.

Boy lay stretched out on his stomach beside her on the small bed, his feet hanging over the edge and his arms tucked under the pillow beneath his head. His blond hair hid his face and his entire position looked like he'd collapsed onto the mattress exhausted and fallen asleep instantly.

And naked.

Her gaze traveled the length of his broad shoulders down to his tapered waist and perfect ass and she licked her lips, wincing when her tongue sliced and she tasted blood.

Boy woke with a start. He sat up and shoved his hair out of his eyes as he checked her over, his brows knotted in concern.

She touched her fingers to her mouth and felt the sharp tips of fangs graze her skin as memories of the last few weeks pummeled her.

Boy.

Nichol.

The hideouts and the walking and the heat.

Khthonios.

Fear.

Gunfire.

Jumping to her feet, she ran to the bathroom, flicked on the light, and stared at her reflection. She splayed her hands across her abdomen, checking herself for wounds she remembered feeling as her body was broken apart by round after round of bullets.

"I'm dead," she murmured, touching her teeth again as she met Boy's worried gaze in the mirror. "I *was* dead. You came back for me."

He nodded. *I'll always come back for you.*

Jaw dropping, she spun around as he wrapped a blanket around her naked body. "Oh my God. You talked."

Technically I thought. But given our situation, let's not get hung up on semantics.

"Are you—" She replayed the deep baritone voice in her mind and blinked once. Twice. "Are you being a smartass?"

His lips quirked up a fraction before his expression turned serious again and he led her back to the bedroom. *How much of the past three weeks do you remember?*

A haze of images flitted through her mind, coming into sharp focus one by one as she sat beside him. "I remember you bleeding in the light," she said slowly, her gaze drifting to his wrists. "I remember the black blood on the sand, the way it bubbled and moved, like it was trying to, I don't know, crawl back to you."

Khthonios, he stated with a hard edge. *I exorcised her at dawn knowing she didn't possess my ability to walk in the sun.*

"So she's gone?" she asked, scooting closer to him and feeling instantly more content. Safer. "For good?"

He nodded and reached over to tuck her hair

behind her ear. *For good and forever.*

She took a deep breath and frowned when she realized the intake of air didn't feel necessary. "I remember your eyes. They were so black but for a second I saw blue and I knew you were still in there. But—"

But?

"But then they went even blacker than before. Ultrablack. And there was this pressure building in my head." She focused on the memory which felt detached from her, as though it happened to another person in another life. "It was like a scream and all I knew was I needed to get away from it. I...I shot you. Boy, I *shot* you!"

'Twas just a scratch, he replied with a smirk as he stretched out on the mattress and tucked his arm behind his head. *What else do you remember?*

"The gunfire. How much it burned. The sand in my mouth." Exhaling the unneeded air, she curled up against him, sighing when one strong arm wrapped around her and she felt him kiss the top of her head. "And I remember you picking me up. After that—"

More visions flashed through her mind and her eyes widened, her cheeks pinking with embarrassment as snippets of the last few weeks came to life in her mind. She heard herself commanding him to run. Tasted his blood on her tongue. Felt him thrusting inside her while she demanded more, harder and faster. Saw the mixture of amusement and exhaustion on his face as she stalked him, fed from him, and fucked him.

Burying her face into his side, she groaned. "I'm sorry. I told you I could be too much to deal with sometimes."

His fingers raked gently through her hair. *You will never be too much for me. If anything, you're just right. The only apology should be coming from me.*

She looked up to see him studying her, his expression a combination of uncertainty and regret. "What for?"

For turning you without permission. For refusing to allow you a peaceful death. For being too selfish to allow Khthonios to take you from me. For being too weak to let you go.

Tossing her legs over his hips, she pushed herself up and straddled him as she gave him her sternest glare even though she knew he would hear the sappy thoughts running through her mind. "I'm gonna basically live forever now, right?" When he nodded and she heard him start to qualify his response in his head, she swatted his chest. "And I'm never gonna get sick or old, right?" Another nod. "And you're essentially stuck with me for eternity, right? Even when I get stronger and more powerful than you, you're still gonna be my Big Guy, right?"

He outright rolled his eyes with her last proclamation but conceded. *Right.*

"And you love me, right?"

Right.

"So you're apologizing for what exactly? Saving me? Coming back for me?"

I took the sun from you.

"Oh freaking well. And we don't even know that, do we? I mean, look at you." Holding her wrist to her lips, she scored it with her fang and watched as his pupils dilated. "If I can read your mind, I can probably read others. And maybe I'll be a sun-walker like you.

You're the biggest, baddest vamp ever so it would make sense I'm gonna be the biggest, baddest vamp-chick someday too."

Maybe the baddest and definitely the prettiest, but I doubt you'll ever be the biggest.

Ducking her head down, she grazed her lips over his, smiling when his hips shifted between her thighs. "I'm the only, Boy. That makes me number one in every category. Now stop being a wiseass and kiss me."

Chapter Thirty

Boy passed a bag of blood over to Lexie Grace and watched her face while she sampled it, grinning when her nose wrinkled and she handed it back to him without a word. Polishing it off without a second thought, he reached over, dragged her rocking chair closer to his, and opened his wrist for her.

You spoil me.

He did. He did, he loved it, and he wasn't going to stop anytime soon. At some point in the future he would need to train her, test her, and push her, but not yet. She was a mere three nights past her completed transition time and still adapting to her new reality. There would be plenty of time for him to piss her off later.

Unlike Kaius's re-turning months ago, Lexie Grace had no humans tempting her senses, no warm veins screaming to her core, and no timeline hanging over her head. Her only prey was him and he was more than capable of handling himself—and her—whenever her hungers overpowered her restraint.

If he was being honest with himself, he rather enjoyed when she lost control and gave into those primal instincts which blackened her eyes and made her possessive and ravenous for his blood and his body. He reveled in the shift in her thoughts from clear and calculating to a tangled pulse of need, the simple word *mine* playing on a loop while she stripped him, grasped at him, and sank her fangs into his veins.

You're thinking about what we did on the motorbike, aren't you? she purred in his mind while she fed.

His new favorite personal porn movie danced in the forefront of his thoughts and he licked his lips, deciding then and there he wanted a repeat. *I don't think I'll never not be thinking about it.*

A quiet hum from above broke the silence of the night and he narrowed his eyes at the approaching drone.

"This is a treat," Rhys called through the speaker. "Boy is fully clothed. It's been weeks since I manned this video feed and wasn't subjected to his naked ass."

Flipping his hauntmate off, he kept his attention on Lexie Grace while she unhooked her fangs and kissed his healed wrist before she sat up and lounged back in her rocker. Her long legs were accented by her lime green shorts, her pink and black sweatshirt hanging off her shoulder and putting her cleavage on display for him.

And Rhys, given the drone's position.

In a move too fast for Lexie Grace or Rhys to track, he used the porch railing to launch himself high enough to smack the drone, satisfaction rippling through him when he heard both Nichol and Rhys's voices cursing from a good three hundred feet away.

Seriously? his pretty little vamp huffed, her feigned exasperation making him grin. *Boy, what if they had something important to tell us?*

They could do it without ogling you.

He sat back in his rocker and glanced over to find

her smirking and running her tongue along one tiny fang. *Jealous, Big Guy?*

Vigilant.

She laughed and shimmied playfully, the movement drawing his eye and getting him back on his feet as his need to stake his claim over her rose. *Guarding my virtue?*

Towering over her, he reached down and tipped her chin up. *Exactly. Lexie Grace?*

Yes?

Run.

****

Lexie Grace stood inside her doorway a week later, her arms crossed and eyes narrowed as she glared at the stubborn vamp blocking her way. "Move."

A single brow lifted, but it was the only movement he allowed.

Her lips pursed and she winced as the sharp tip of her fangs pierced the delicate skin. "Boy."

He wasn't even thinking. Not anything she could hear, at least. It infuriated her to no end, knowing he had the ability to block her from listening in on his thoughts while she wasn't able to do the same.

Yet.

Their silent standoff continued, her with a temper growing by leaps and bounds and him, a vault of stoic, gorgeous annoyance.

"I'll wait until you're sleeping," she finally countered, shifting her weight and placing her hands on her hips in a pathetic attempt to appear more threatening. "You can't watch me all the time."

Try me.

There was a delicate change happening in the sky

behind him, one which vampires sensed deep in their bones. The stars which blinked in the deep navy sky dimmed and the moon no longer looked as bright. A shiver went through her body and she doubled down, knowing the sun would rise soon.

And she was damn well going to be out there when it did, even if her best arguments had done nothing to sway her captor.

"You're stunting my growth."

Your growth was stunted long before I arrived on site, Short Stuff.

"I'll never know unless I try."

Plenty of time to try when you're older and stronger and when your recovery will take hours instead of weeks.

Groaning in exasperation, she threw up her hands. "I want to, okay? I want to know if I can stand out there and not burn. I want to know if—no, when—we have trouble, I can run without frying." Sensing he was wavering, she took a step closer. "Please? You'll know if I can't handle it and I know you'll get me inside before I get too hurt."

His blue eyes narrowed but he nodded once and she fought back the urge to skip as she slipped past him and stood on the porch. He was at her side immediately, his hands on her hips and his chin on the top of her head as they waited for the first rays to stretch across the basin.

I hate this, he murmured in her mind. *I love you, but I'm furious with you right now.*

"I know, Big Guy." She sighed as she leaned her weight against him and he accepted it, his arms wrapping around her while he kissed her hair. "I love

269

you too. Even if you are kind of overbearing and a tad hyper-reactive."

The sun breached the horizon and she retreated instinctively from the beams creeping toward her, her resolve strengthened by Boy's unwavering power behind her.

"Could you always do this?"

Not always. I was closing in on my third millennium when I discovered I could be in the light, but the change started long before that. At first, I was capable of moving short distances in the sun without debilitating injury and eventually I could survive the full cycle.

Snuggling tighter to him, she watched the changing colors of the sky. "How did you hide it all this time?"

Blood manipulation, he replied quietly as he nuzzled the top of her head with his cheek. *I forced my body to react and burn to avoid detection. It was unpleasant but necessary.*

"What will it feel like?" she whispered as she stared at the retreating shadows at her feet.

Warm at first. Then hot. Except the hot goes too deep, like it's passing through your skin and heating you from the inside.

She shuddered but held position when the rays caressed her toes. His hold on her tightened but he made no move to haul her inside so she waited and tracked the light as it touched her legs and continued its path to her face. Seconds felt like hours as she monitored the warmth on her skin, expecting the fire to ignite her veins at any moment.

I think it's safe to say you're a sunwalker, Boy chuckled in her mind, his low voice husky.

"So you got yourself all worked up for nothing?" she teased, the tension and worry she'd been carrying since she decided to tempt fate evaporating.

I got myself worked up over the thought of my mate taking a risk which could damage her and disappoint her. I have it on good authority this is typical of the males in my bloodline. Bianca can give you pointers on how to handle it.

Turning in place, she looked up at him and tucked his hair behind his ear, loving the way the white-blond highlights were so much more pronounced in the sun. "Thank you for letting me try this."

He studied her, his expression solemn. *You're more powerful than I was when I was turned, and growing stronger every day.*

Does it scare you?

It scared her. She felt the power in her body night and day. There was a buzzing in her veins and a thrum in her core fighting to be released, and she knew she had neither the strength nor the ability to control it should it be left to fester for long. Boundaries didn't exist anymore. She could do anything she wanted and the urge to push out and put her budding power to the test was rising.

Boy continued to examine her while she sank deeper into her thoughts, his voice finally piercing through louder than usual. *I don't fear you. I fear for you.*

She scoffed and rolled her eyes. "I'm invincible."

You're bold. Powerful. Someday, you'll be stronger than me in every way and while I cannot wait to see that day, I also know you will spend the rest of your existence with a target on your back. Right now, it will be because of me. But eventually it will be because of you.

His words hung in her mind as Nichol's drone drew close and a loud, exasperated sigh came from the speaker.

"Oh lovely. Another sunwalker," the cranky vamp grunted. "Get inside and power up your laptop, Boy. I have a few questions for you and this little tidbit of intel only makes our discussion more urgent."

With a nod, Boy led her inside and closed the door. His thoughts were focused on the improved security system he wanted Nichol to order while she turned on her computer and waited for the video call to load.

Kaius and Nichol's faces filled her screen and Boy sat beside her on the sofa, draping his arm across her shoulders and ignoring Kaius's slight lift of a brow as he cleared his throat. "Good morning to both of you. We won't keep you long, but Nichol and I have a few updates and issues to address."

Before she could greet them, Nichol's hazel eyes narrowed. "Where are they, Boy?"

Boy shrugged and turned his attention to the ceiling while she frowned in both confusion and annoyance over Boy's mental block rising instantly. "Where is what?"

"The Deviants," Nichol growled. "I've scoured every piece of footage we have from that night and there are seven thousand Deviants unaccounted for who didn't ignite. And those figures aren't including the hundred or so stragglers who keep filtering into the Basin and magically disappearing."

Turning to Boy, she glared. *Boy? What the hell is going on?*

My hauntmates have their survival strategies. I have mine.

Her eyes widened. *Tell me those things aren't wandering around wherever out there.*

Boy continued to study the ceiling with an infuriating indifference. *They are neither wandering nor wherever. They've returned to dormancy deep beneath the sand where they will remain until we need them.*

We will never need them, she hissed in her mind. *Those things are dangerous.*

Those things are our army, tied to me and eventually to you. He met her gaze and stared her down without apology. *Had Nichol not interrupted us on the porch, I would have told you because you need to know the lengths I will go to for your protection. I'm the most powerful vampire in existence. Someday, you will be. And with power comes enemies. I've merely taken steps to protect us should the safeguards the Kaius haunt are putting into place fail. I will not lose the woman who stands at my side.*

With her lips pursing, she shook her head. *Boy—*

He leaned back against the armrest of the sofa and drummed his fingers on his thighs, his thoughts once again going silent for a moment before he spoke to her. *If you were not here now, if I'd been too late or failed in your turning, I would have annihilated every soldier in that platoon and then moved on to the closest town. One by one, I would eliminate every human and vampire in my path until the world paid for taking you from me. Knowing I have the tendency to react poorly to threats to you and your safety, a small army of Deviants to act as both a warning and a defense is a small concession to make in exchange for me not going off the deep end.*

Swallowing, she considered his words over and over until she truly heard him. *That is strangely, disturbingly romantic.*

I have my moments.

Grinning, she bumped his arm lightly with her forehead. *I love you, Big Guy.*

She turned to the screen and gave Kaius and Nichol the same shrug Boy had. "Looks like he doesn't know anything about that. Moving on."

Epilogue

Eight Months Later

Lexie Grace tightened her jacket around her waist and stepped into the war zone formally known as the living room. She threw up her hands in surrender and backed up immediately when Boy growled at her from behind the pile of debris. "Fine, fine. I'm nowhere near the deadly two-by-fours. Happy?"

His blue eyes narrowed but he nodded.

One wooden sliver two weeks into their renovation of the old farmhouse was all it took for Boy to ban her from the construction zone. Not that she was complaining. Relegated to any space not deemed a demolition room meant she was tasked with ordering supplies and furniture and selecting paint colors through Nichol's private server. It was a job she rather enjoyed because it gave her time to chat and gossip with the Kaius Haunt women while Boy worked to modernize the tiny place they called home.

Making a show of ensuring her toes were behind the invisible line, she crossed her arms and leaned against the wall. "Our ride is arriving in an hour, so you're going to need to wrap up here and shower because I don't want you shaking drywall dust all over my new dress."

New dress?

"Go shower and I'll let you see it."

He stepped around the mess, unhooked the tool belt hanging low on his hips, and yanked his dirty shirt off, balling it up as he stalked toward her and reached out to tug her jacket open.

"Nope," she sang, snapping her fangs at his fingers when they passed within biting distance. "Shower first."

With the roll of his eyes, he swatted her ass and disappeared into the newly renovated bathroom.

She loved that bathroom.

Boy's plan of attack included raising the ceiling and installing a state-of-the-art shower with a dozen sprays and even more settings. Expanding it into an old linen closet, he added a gorgeous clawfoot tub custom-built to accommodate his size—with enough room for her to slip in. It was bright and clean and beautiful and she felt like a queen every time she stepped inside.

The rush of shower water started and she took a few minutes to double-check their suitcases and set them by the door before heading into the bedroom to wait for Boy. Sitting at her vanity, she examined her hair and makeup in the mirror, a wave of nervousness washing over her when Boy exited the bathroom with a towel wrapped low around his hips.

"Boy?" she murmured as she leaned in closer to check the evenness of her eyeliner. "Is my outfit okay?"

Boy hiked his cargos up and lifted a single brow. *Show me.*

Standing, she shrugged her jacket off and did a slow spin so he could see her new dress. "I bought it because I know you like this color, but I wasn't really thinking about how short it is or the whole cleavage thing when I decided to wear it tonight," she rambled as she second-guessed the pink sundress she bought online on a whim. The fabric of the bell sleeves was so delicate and pretty and she knew Boy would love the sweetheart neckline and flirty kick of the skirt, but now she wasn't so sure it was the best choice to wear when she met his family because despite the soft color, it was a bit too bouncy, a bit too bright, and a bit too revealing.

You bought it for me?

"Well yeah," she stated with a frustrated huff when he took his time tugging his black shirt on. "So? What do you think? Should I change? Maybe wear something a little less...loud."

His expression darkened. *No.*

With a nervous laugh, she checked her reflection over again. "That's easy for you to say. You don't have to impress anyone because you're already Mr. King Supervamp."

He spun her around and caged her against her vanity mirror, his eyes hard. *You. Aren't. Changing. You want to know what I think? I'm giving you a ten second head start before I show you exactly what I think about the way you look in this dress.* He straightened up and stared down at her with a desire so intense she stopped worrying about the appropriateness of her dress and started worrying it wouldn't survive the next two minutes.

Lexie Grace?

"Yeah?" she responded, inching toward the door.

Ten. Nine. Eight.

****

Boy kept Lexie Grace's hand wrapped firmly in his

while the helicopter landed in a clearing adjacent to the Kaius haunt. Her excitement and anticipation were palpable in the small space, but her self-doubt was long gone, having been fucked out of her system until the chopper arrived and interrupted their third round.

Boy?

Lifting a brow, he followed her gaze to the crowd assembling in the distance and waited for her question to fully form in her mind.

Her knee was bouncing, making the ruffle trimming her skirt dance across her thighs. *Are you nervous?*

The only thing making me nervous is the knowledge you'll be joining forces with the other women and I have it on good authority that this union could result in my being sent to the dog house, he replied honestly, pleased when she smiled. *Other than that—and the likelihood Rhys will say something I'll have to stake him for—no.*

Her knee stilled. *I just realized I can't hear the thoughts of the guy flying this thing. Or the group over there.*

Relief unknotted some of the tension he'd been carrying in his shoulders since takeoff. While Lexie Grace could hear his thoughts, he worried about whether she would pick up those of others. The Deviants lying dormant in the basin were silent to her, but they made for a poor test case. The fact she couldn't hear the pilot or his hauntmates in close proximity was a bonus right now when her abilities were still fresh, but he suspected that would change in time.

The blades of the helicopter slowed to a stop and he hopped off before escorting Lexie Grace down with extra attention to the hem of her skirt when he heard his hauntmates approaching from the south.

Lexie Grace clasped his hand, her body turning into his and sending his protective instincts into overdrive.

I know I forgot to tell you earlier, but you're really pretty, he murmured into her mind while he kissed the top of her head.

She squeezed his fingers with her small ones and bumped his bicep with her forehead before squaring her shoulders to greet his hauntmates. *That right there might save you from the dog house tonight, Big Guy.*

****

Kaius surveyed the chaos barely contained in the common room where his hauntmates, their partners, Louis, Jonathan, and all seven of their foundlings were amping the conversation decibel level to nuclear levels.

"I blame Dominic," Nichol stated as he took Harper's vacated seat on the sofa. "If that kid hadn't gone and gotten himself connected to Molly and set the events of the past seven years into motion, I'd be sitting in my room listening to a nice science podcast right about now."

Chuckling, he glanced around the room and spotted his youngest canoodling with Molly while she argued with two of the Minks-Forbes vamps about who made her top ten drummers list. "Do you remember what you told me the night I dragged his carcass home?"

"*That looks like an issue,*" Nichol reminisced with a grunt, shaking his head. "I wasn't wrong."

"No, you weren't." Smirking, he glanced around the room. "You said something similar about every one of them."

"Again," his eldest stated with a chuckle, "I wasn't wrong."

Jagger nodded over at them, his arm slung over Bianca's shoulders while she, Harper, and Audra explained attachment parenting to Louis and Jonathan. Mickey hovered nearby, sneaking light gropes of Audra's backside and feigning innocence every time she chastised him. Rhys and Lis were off to the side with Boy and Lexie Grace, Ms. Kelly holding her own against Rhys's ingrained lecherous comments and Boy keeping a watchful eye over the five orphan vamps crowded around the gaming system.

Nichol sat back and crossed his arms, surveying the crowd. "So, Great Leader, did you offer Boy the crown?"

Amid the mayhem of Lexie Grace's transition, ongoing negotiations in the establishment of a secure perimeter around the Nevada basin, and the media nightmare stemming from the livestream of Boy's Deviant army, one issue quietly rose to the forefront.

Kaius was no longer the rightful leader of the haunt. That honor belonged to the silent vamp who was leading his lady into the corner of the room.

"I did," he replied, a warm feeling washing over him when he caught Harper's eye and she smiled at him. "He stared at me for precisely ten minutes then walked away."

His eldest scoffed, observing the vampire couple with studious interest. "They talk, don't they?"

"They do." Kaius watched as Boy offered Lexie Grace his wrist to stave off her hunger. Something passed between them and Boy grinned as she eagerly sunk her small fangs into his vein. "Go ahead and say it."

Nichol's nose wrinkled. "That's going to be an issue."

"Yes, it is. Which is why the women are helping me recruit Ms. Kelly to convince Boy to take this damn group of misfits over at some point in the next few centuries and give you and me a break."

A word about the author...

Katja Desjarlais is a music teacher by day and a romance writer by moonlight. She is an unapologetic music addict and has an obsession for bad Bach puns despite her irrational aversion to Baroque. Her favorite words include 'plethora' and 'dapper', and she is physically repulsed by the word 'moist'. Katja's interest in the paranormal can be traced to her early childhood film choices and to the revolving book collection on her phone.

Desjarlais lives in the Okanagan Valley with her husband, three children, and two black cats. Her ideal summer vacation is spent traipsing through the United States with her family and attending heavy metal concerts.

katjadesjarlais.wordpress.com